kitty's
BIG TROUBLE

D0300896

kitty's
BIG TROUBLE
Carrie Vaughn

First published in Great Britain in 2011
by Gollancz
An imprint of the Orion Publishing Group
Orion House, 5 Upper St Martin's Lane, London WC2H 9EA
An Hachette UK Company

1 3 5 7 9 10 8 6 4 2

A CIP catalogue record for this book is available
from the British Library

ISBN 978 0 575 09868 8

Printed in Great Britain by CPI Mackays,
Chatham, Kent

The Orion Publishing Group's policy is to use papers
that are natural, renewable and recyclable products and
made from wood grown in sustainable forests. The logging
and manufacturing processes are expected to conform to the
to environmental regulations of the country of origin.

www.carrievaughn.com
www.orionbooks.co.uk

For my family

The Playlist

NORMAN GREENBAUM, "Spirit in the Sky"

SOCIAL DISTORTION, "Making Believe"

WARREN ZEVON, "Lawyers, Guns, and Money"

THEY MIGHT BE GIANTS, "Wicked Little Critta"

P.K. 14, "The Other Side"

BLONDIE, "Atomic"

VERNIAN PROCESS, "The Maple Leaf Rag"

SQUIRREL NUT ZIPPERS, "Le Grippe"

PJ HARVEY, "Down by the Water"

CARSICK CARS, "You Can Listen, You Can Talk"

THE B-52'S, "Mesopotamia"

BILLY PRESTON, "Will It Go Round in Circles"

LISSIE, "Little Lovin'"

Chapter 1

I KNOW," I said into my phone. "This isn't exactly standard—"

"It's impossible," said the poor, long-suffering office
receptionist at the Calvary Cemetery in St. Louis. He was
too polite to just hang up on me. "It's absolutely impossible."

"Maybe you can give me the name and number of
someone who might be able to authorize this kind of request? Is there any representative of the Sherman family
on record?"

His responses were starting to sound desperate. "That
information is confidential. In fact, I don't think you'll be
able to get any further on this without some kind of a
warrant or a court order."

I was afraid of that. I'd been hoping there'd be a
friendly way to accomplish this. That I could find a sympathetic historian who would back up my request or explain the situation to one of the descendants and get

permission that way. Surely they would want to know the truth as much as I did. Also, I didn't think I'd be able to convince a judge to issue said court order. The request was based on little more than rabid curiosity.

I soldiered on, as it were. "There has to be some kind of standard procedure for an exhumation. Can you tell me what that is?"

"Ms. . . . Norville, is it?"

"Yes, Kitty Norville," I said, thinking *calm*. I could wear him down with patience.

"Ms. Norville—can I ask why you want to have General Sherman's body exhumed?"

General William T. Sherman, hero of the Civil War on the Union side, war criminal on the Confederate side, considered one of the greatest soldiers and strategists in American history, and all-around icon. And yeah, I wanted to dig him up. It was a little hard to explain, and I hesitated, trying to figure out what to say. Last week I'd received a package from the Library of Congress containing a copy of an interview transcript from the 1930s. It had been made as part of the Federal Writers' Project, a New Deal program that employed journalists and other writers to record local histories around the country. Many valuable stories were collected and preserved as part of the program. The one I'd been sent was an interview with a Civil War veteran—one of the last to survive, no doubt. He'd been sixteen when he joined the Confederate army in the middle of the war and was close to ninety when he'd been interviewed, and he claimed that he'd witnessed General Sherman transform into a wolf during the Battle of Vicksburg. A librarian who was also a listener and fan of my radio show discovered it and sent it to me. I had always had my suspicions about Sherman—he looked so rough and tumble in his photos, with his unbuttoned collar, his unkempt beard, and a "screw you" expression. If any Civil War general had been a werewolf, it would be Sherman. But was my hunch and a single interview proof? No. Which was why I wanted to exhume the body, to test any remaining tissue for the presence of lycanthropy.

Maybe it was best to lay it out there. "I think General Sherman may have been a werewolf and I want to run tests on his remains to find out."

Of course, a long pause followed. I kept waiting for the click of a phone hanging up, which would have been fine; I'd have just called one of the other numbers on my list. I hadn't expected this to be easy.

"Seriously?" he said finally. The same way he might have said, You're eating *bugs*?

"Yeah. Seriously. So how about it? Don't you want to help me rewrite American history?"

"I'm sorry, could I get your name one more time?" he said. "Could you spell it for me? And tell me where you're calling from?"

I felt a restraining order coming on. So in the end, I was the one who hung up.

Oh well. You can't win them all.

* * *

AT HOME that evening I sat on the sofa, library books lying open on the coffee table next to me and my laptop screen showing a half dozen Web sites open. I was supposed to be researching Sherman. Instead, I was reading through the transcript for what must have been the twentieth time.

Tom Hanson had enlisted in the Confederate army at the age of sixteen. At several points during the interview he mentioned how young he'd been. How innocent, and how foolish. The interviewer kept having to prompt him to return to the focus of the story, his encounter with General Sherman under the light of the full moon.

One night while his squad was on patrol outside of Vicksburg, Hanson had gotten separated from the others and lost his way in the swampy forest some distance from where the Confederates were camped. Trying to find his way back, he'd stumbled across a pair of Union soldiers—an enlisted man arguing with an officer. The enlisted soldier kept calling the other man "General," and Hanson swore the officer was General William Sherman himself. He couldn't explain the argument because it hadn't made any sense to him—the enlisted man was telling the general that he'd overstepped his bounds, and that he wanted to challenge him. Hanson had heard that Sherman was crazy—he could understand anyone on the Union side wanting him out of command. But that wasn't up to an enlisted man, and they certainly wouldn't have been discussing it in the middle of a swamp.

Hanson didn't understand it, but he described what happened next. "The general, he took his clothes off. I couldn't move or he'd've heard me, so I didn't dare. I just sat there and watched. So there he was, naked in the moonlight. And then he changed. Like his body just melted, and I heard his bones snapping. I can't say that I ever saw a wolf before, but that's what he turned into— big, shaggy, with yellow eyes. That other soldier, well—he just ran. Didn't do him any good. That big ol' wolf chased him down."

The door to the condo opened and closed—my husband, Ben, lawyer and fellow werewolf—arriving home. He set his briefcase near the desk of his home office, a corner of the living room, and regarded me where I sat on the sofa, papers on my lap, my head bent in concentration.

"Still on that transcript?" he said, his smile amused.

I sighed. Ben had seen me reading it every night this week, searching for some insight. "It's fascinating, isn't it? What if it isn't just a story? What if he's right?" I pulled one of the books over, referring to a timeline of Sherman's life. "Did you know that early on in the war Sherman had a nervous breakdown? He was relieved of duty, and the newspapers and everyone said he was crazy, that he couldn't take the pressure. But he recovered and when he came back he was this badass general. He and Grant started kicking ass and eventually Sherman marched the Union army through Georgia and won the war. What if that's when it happened? Somehow he got attacked and infected around the Battle of Bull Run, it knocked him for a loop, he took time off to deal with it, and when he came back he was a super soldier. A werewolf general."

"I suppose it's possible," he said. "But if you're right, he kept it really well hidden."

"Lots of people keep it really well hidden," I said. "I'm betting it was easier to keep it hidden then than it is now."

He sat on the sofa beside me, which was too tempting an invitation. I leaned toward him, pulling his arm over my shoulder and snuggling against him. As I hoped, he hugged me close and bent his head to my hair, breathing in my scent as I took in his. Our wolf sides, claiming each other.

I said, "I just keep thinking—who else is out there? What secret histories slipped through the cracks because people kept it hidden or no one believed it? I'm not talking about Vlad Tepes being Dracula. What if Sherman really was a werewolf? Who else might have been werewolves? Maybe there was a reason Rasputin was so hard to kill, and Jack the Ripper was so bloodthirsty—"

He stopped me with a kiss, which was okay with me. I touched his cheeks and smiled.

"What would it change?" he said. "If Sherman really was a werewolf, would it really change anything?"

"We'd know the truth."

He looked skeptical. It was a fair question. Did this mean any more than slapping labels on people? In Sherman's case, it meant a reinterpretation of his history— his nervous breakdown looked a whole lot different if he was a werewolf. But even that was speculation. He might have been infected with lycanthropy years before.

It wasn't just the labels. It meant history had a whole other layer to it, and that supernatural beings might have played an active role in guiding human events for centuries. I could almost get conspiracy minded about it.

"How can you even confirm something like this for sure? In a way that would hold up in court?" he added. Always legal-minded.

"I've been trying to find out how to get his body exhumed—"

He looked at me. "You *haven't*."

"Um, yeah. It's a lot harder than I thought it would be."

"Of course it is. You can't just go around digging up graves. Especially famous ones."

"Yeah," I said, wincing. "I know."

"You need to find a vampire who knew him," he said. "Get a corroborating eyewitness account from someone who wasn't a scared teenager confronting a guy like Sherman."

He probably meant it as a joke, but I turned thoughtful. "You know," I said, "I could probably do that."

"Honey, if anyone can do it, you can."

Damn straight.

* * *

"GOOD EVENING, it's Friday night which means it's time once again for *The Midnight Hour,* the show that isn't afraid of the dark or the creatures who live there. I'm your ever-eager host, Kitty Norville, and I hope you're ready for another illuminating evening of supernatural shenanigans."

Sitting at my table in the studio, in front of the microphone, headphones on, just a few lights glowing in the darkened space, I could imagine myself in the cockpit of an airplane or at the controls of a spaceship, commanding great power. Through the glass, I watched Matt, my sound engineer, at his board. Above the door, the on-air sign glowed red. Epic.

"I've been thinking a lot lately about history and what to do with it. Vampires and werewolves and the like have only been public for a few years. Some of us are milking that publicity for all it's worth, I'm not ashamed to say. But we've been around for a lot longer than that. We must have been. What impact have vampires, werewolves, and magicians had on history? Were any historical figures—let's say General William Sherman, just as an example—supernatural creatures themselves? Those histories have been deeply buried, either because people didn't believe or because the stories were written off as folklore and fantasy. Let me tell you, when you start digging there are a lot of stories out there. What I'm looking for now isn't stories, but proof. That's where things get tricky, because traditionally, the supernatural doesn't leave a whole lot of proof lying around.

"That's my question for you tonight: what kind of proof should I be looking for, and what kind of proof would you need to be convinced that a beloved historical figure had a toe dipped in the supernatural world?"

Shows like this, where I threw open the line for calls right from the start in a freeform brainstorm, were often a crapshoot. I could get a lot of thoughtful discussion and gain some new insight. Or I'd end up yelling at people. NPR to Jerry Springer, my show ran the whole spectrum. Brace for impact . . .

"For my first call tonight I have Dave from Rochester. Hello, Dave."

"Hi, Kitty, thanks for taking my call, it's so great to get through." He sounded suitably enthusiastic—a good opener.

"Thanks for being persistent. What have you got for me?"

"Well. It seems to me you're just assuming that supernatural beings have been around for a long time. This stuff has only been making news for a few years now, and maybe that's because it hasn't been around that long. What if vampires and werewolves are actually the result of some government experiment that got loose and is totally out of control?"

"I can assure you that I'm not the result of some government experiment," I said flatly.

"Well, no, not directly, but maybe it's some virus that escaped and spread, and *that's* where vampires and werewolves came from. *That's* why we don't have any historical evidence."

"On the other hand we have five thousand years of folklore suggesting that these beings have been around for a long time. What about that?"

"Planted. It's all a hoax."

I blinked at the microphone. That was bold, even for this show. "You're saying *The Epic of Gilgamesh* is a hoax? That the story of King Lycaon isn't really an ancient Greek myth?"

"That's right. It's all been made up in order to convince people that supernatural beings have been around for thousands of years when they've really only been around since World War II."

"World War II?" I said. "Like some supernatural Manhattan Project?"

"Yes, exactly! In fact—"

Oh, yes, please say it, sink my show to this level in the first ten minutes . . .

"—it was the Nazis," Dave from Rochester said.

I clicked the line to a different call. "And that's enough of that. Moving on now, next call please. Hello, you're on the air."

"Hi, Kitty, I'm a big fan of the show," said a female voice, cheerful and outgoing. Suze from L.A. "I just wanted to say, isn't most of history based on eyewitness accounts? People reporting what they saw? We should have evidence somewhere of people talking about this. But I'm not sure how you'd go about proving something that no one ever talks about."

I was right on the edge of whipping out that FWP transcript—a report that had lain buried and forgotten because no one believed it. I wanted my proof before I brought it into the light.

Instead I said, "Or maybe people have been talking about it, writing about it, whatever, but those accounts were buried because no one believed them. Which leads me to a big question: How trustworthy are eyewitness testimonies? We depend on them for historical accounts, memoirs, battlefield reports, so of course this is going to be high on the list. But is one eyewitness's story enough? How about two, for corroboration?"

"The more the better, I guess," she said. "But you still have the problem of separating truth from fiction."

"Exactly. Part of the reason I'm always trying to get vampires on the show is I figure they've got to be some of the best eyewitnesses out there. They've been around for decades, for centuries. Not only have they seen a lot, they often seem to be in the front row, watching events play out. But I gotta tell you, they don't seem particularly interested in sharing what they've learned. I think they really like keeping secrets from the rest of us. That's why we haven't had any vampire celebrity tell-all books yet. Oh, and if there are any vampires out there writing a celebrity tell-all book, please let me know. Thanks for your call, Suze."

Matt flagged a call on the monitor—from a vampire. Ooh, was I going to have my wish granted? I liked nothing better than to feature an exclusive. What were the odds?

"Hello, you're on the air."

"Kitty, if we keep secrets, perhaps it's for your own good." The woman had a faint accent, probably European, topped with a touch of finely aged arrogance.

"So you're a vampire," I said. "May I ask how old you are?"

"You may, but I won't answer."

The usual response; it didn't surprise me. "Oh, well, I always have to try. Thank you for calling. My second question for you: Why do you get to decide what should be kept secret? Don't you think everyone has a right to the truth? Even a dangerous truth?"

"Your attitude about the truth is a bit naïve, don't you think? The truth isn't an artifact you can put in a box and study."

"But I don't want to be lied to outright," I said. "I especially don't want to be told I'm being lied to for my own good."

"Tell me this: What if you did find the definitive proof you were looking for—a DNA test for lycanthropy for example, or a photograph of someone shape-shifting, or proof that someone was killed with a stake or a silver bullet. What would change? Why would it matter? The events surrounding that person's life wouldn't change. Their identity wouldn't really change—just your knowledge of it."

Ben's question again. I kept saying I just wanted to be treated like a human being—that vampires and lycanthropes of any stripe should be allowed to live normal, law-abiding lives. Would exposing any supernatural secret identities damage that? Make them freaks instead of the historical figures they were?

"I guess I'm looking for a connection," I said. "I've been floundering, wondering where I fit in the world. Would having a role model be too much to ask for?"

"I thought being a role model was *your* job," she said, with that haughty amusement that only vampires could manage.

"Oh, heaven help us all," I replied. "But I have to say that yes, it is important. Being a werewolf is an important enough part of my identity that I've been basing a show on it and writing about it for the last five years. If I'm going to be an authority on the subject I really want to be an authority. And that means speculating like this."

"As long as you're aware that you may never find the answers you're looking for," the vampire said.

"Yeah, I'm used to that. Maybe the important thing is to keep asking the questions anyway."

And get other people asking them, too. Keep knocking

on the door until someone answered. Or until they hauled me away and locked me up.

AFTER THE show I invited Rick, Master of the local vampire Family, to meet me at New Moon, the bar and grill that Ben and I owned. I was careful not to say anything like, "Let's go for a drink," or "How about we grab a bite." Not that Rick would have taken me literally, but I didn't want to open myself up for the kind of teasing I'd get. Rick was a vampire, feeding on the blood of the living, although I was pretty sure he only drank from volunteers and just enough to stay functional. Still, you had to be careful about what kind of invitations you offered to vampires.

Rick was a friend, and I trusted him. That didn't mean he told me everything.

He was handsome, with a hint of old-world aristocracy to his fine features and straight bearing. From what I could gather, he came by it honestly—he'd been the younger son of a Spanish noble family who traveled to the New World seeking his fortune in the first wave of immigration in the sixteenth century. I didn't know if he ever considered his fortune found. He wore an expensive trenchcoat even in summer, a button-up silk shirt, and well-tailored trousers. Perfect, elegant. You couldn't help but respect him.

"Hi," I said, letting him through the glass front door. "I'm not even going to ask if I can get you anything to drink."

"I'm fine, thanks," he said, glancing around. "Business seems to be doing well."

The place wasn't crowded—not surprising at this late hour—but enough people sat here and there to create a friendly buzz.

"Lack of pretension," I said, guiding him to a table in the back, where my beer was waiting for me. We took seats across from each other. "I think that may be the secret."

"I think you may be right," he said. "Now, what's the problem?"

"Everyone always assumes there's a problem."

"This is you we're talking about," he said, perfectly good-natured.

"I just wanted to have a nice, friendly chat," I said. "How's life—er, unlife—been treating you? What's new in your neck of the woods?"

"Is that a pun?"

I had to think about it a minute, my brow furrowed. "Ah. Not intentionally."

If Rick wasn't laughing at me, he was at least chuckling, and I scowled.

"Nothing to report," he said. Gaze narrowed, I studied him. "Kitty, I don't ask about every detail of the workings of your werewolf pack, I'm not going to tell you every detail about my Family."

"You can't blame me—I've built a career out of gossip."

"All the more reason for me to keep my mouth shut."

That wasn't what I wanted to hear. I blundered on. "I'd like to ask you about a story I'm tracking down. Did you know Sherman?"

"As in General William T.?"

"Yeah."

"I'm afraid not, though I'm sure he was fascinating."

I must have looked deflated.

"It's not like I knew every public figure who lived for the last five hundred years," he said.

"But you knew Coronado. And Doc Holliday. That's a pretty amazing roster right there. Five hundred years is a lot longer than most of us get. Do you know anyone who might have known Sherman?"

"Any vampires, you mean?"

"Anyone who might be able to tell me if Sherman was a werewolf."

He pursed his lips, considering, making him the first person who hadn't looked at the claim with outright skepticism. "What's your information?"

I told him about the interview with the Confederate soldier, and my own hunch, which couldn't exactly be called information. You couldn't tell a werewolf in human form just by looking. Unless maybe you were psychic, which was something to consider. Maybe I could call my friend Tina, a psychic with the TV show *Paradox PI,* and see if she could channel Sherman.

"That would be amazing if you could prove it," he said. "We'd have a whole new perspective on his career."

"But the only way I can *really* prove it is to test a tissue sample, assuming a testable sample still exists, or talk to someone trustworthy who might have known him."

"And no one's very excited about exhuming the general's body, I'm guessing."

"Exactly."

"Alette's the only one I can think of who would know. She has her fingers in everything, even going back to that period. If Sherman spent any time in D.C., she would know."

"Sherman spent a ton of time in D.C. She'd have to know," I said, excited. Alette was the Master vampire of Washington, D.C., and had been in the 1860s. She was already on my list of people to call after talking to Rick. If she didn't know, I'd probably never find out.

"Something to consider," Rick continued. "Even if she does know, she might not tell you. You're not the only one who's been asking these sorts of questions since lycanthropy and vampirism went public. Alette could have leaked the information herself if she wanted people to know."

That vampire sense of superiority again. I shook my head. "She shouldn't be the one to get to decide what people know."

Rick made a calming gesture, forestalling the rest of my rant. "Consider this: if Alette knew Sherman, knew that he was a werewolf, but hasn't told anyone, it may be because *Sherman* didn't want anyone to know. The secret may be his, and Alette—or anyone else who has the information—may be keeping a promise with him."

Sherman was dead and gone, he shouldn't get a say in it. Historical public figures were fair game for all kinds of digging, as far as I was concerned. But a vampire's promise went on forever, didn't it? I had a thing about exposing people who didn't want to be exposed. My own lycanthropy had been made public against my will. Afterward, I took the publicity and ran with it as a survival mechanism, but I could understand why Sherman wouldn't want something like this made public. It would overshadow his entire record and all that he'd accomplished. His autobiography—considered one of military history's great memoirs—would become next to meaningless because it doesn't say a word about it. Which meant that maybe he didn't want anyone to know. If Sherman's ghost appeared and asked me to drop the question, what would I do?

Thoughtful, I rested my chin on my hand and said to Rick, "How many promises like that are you keeping?"

Smiling, he glanced away.

"Oh my God, you are," I said, straightening. "You know. You've got something juicy on somebody famous. What is it? Who?"

"You've gone this long without knowing, why should I say anything now?"

"I just want to know," I said. "It's important to know that people like me have existed for thousands of years, living their lives, surviving. Roman's been recruiting vampires and lycanthropes for his secret supervillain club for two thousand years. I have to assume that vampires and lycanthropes have been opposing him as well, like us. To know who they were, to have some kind of history—who knows what it could tell us about his methods? You *know* Roman would have tried to recruit Sherman. I'd love to imagine that Sherman told him to shove it."

Rick sat back. He seemed amused, thoughtful, studying me through a narrowed gaze. As if he was considering.

"What?" I said. I got the feeling I'd said something funny or strange.

"It's a cliché, you know," he said. "Eternal life being boring. Maybe for some of us it is, the ones who lock themselves away in mansions or castles, cut themselves off from the world and the people in it. For the rest of us, there's always something new coming along, if we know where to look. We stay interested by having a stake in the game."

"The Long Game?" I said. The Long Game, a conspiracy among vampires. The few people who knew about it spoke of it in whispers, in hints, if at all. Near as I could figure, it really was a game, but one that dealt in lives and power. And the one who dies with the most toys wins.

Rick shrugged. "Not always. After all, Kitty, you're one of the people who keeps life interesting."

He gazed over the dining room and bar, waiting for me to respond. I'd already finished my beer or I would have taken a long drink. "I'm flattered, I think."

"If you want my advice, you're narrowing your focus too much," Rick said. "Don't just look for the secret vampires and lycanthropes. Look for people who might have hunted them. People like your friend Cormac."

Now there was an idea. "You're not going to give me any hints about where to start, are you?"

"Think about it for a minute. If I met Doc Holliday, who else do you think I might have known?"

Western history wasn't my strong suit, but my knowledge was better than average. I remembered the stories of the Wild West and the O.K. Corral, and a few choice Hollywood treatments of the same, and my eyes grew wide.

"Wyatt Earp?"

Rick just smiled.

Chapter 2

AFTER MY TALK with Rick, I called Alette, vampire Mistress of Washington, D.C. Because that was how little sense of decorum I had.

"Whatever you want to know, I probably can't tell you," she said, an amused lilt to her matriarchal tone.

"So does that mean you don't know, or you know but won't tell me?"

"Ask your question, and we'll see."

"Was General Sherman a werewolf?"

She paused a moment, and I imagined her sitting in the refined Victorian parlor of her Georgetown home, phone to her ear, smiling an indulgent smile. I was asking a favor; I couldn't force her to tell me. I depended on her kindness. Her tolerance.

"I can't say," she said finally, which made me think she knew, and that the answer was yes. Not that I would ever get her to admit that. I let out a growl, and she chuckled. "Did you expect me to say anything else?"

"I had to try," I said. "I always have to try."

"Yes, you certainly do. Have you asked Rick?"

"Asked him first. He didn't know anything about Sherman, but he did bring up Wyatt Earp. I don't suppose you have any good dirt on him, do you?"

"Well, I don't know about dirt . . ."

She told me a story.

In the early 1870s, a group of vampires had traveled west and settled near Dodge City, Kansas, hoping to take advantage of the lawlessness, of people traveling anonymously across the plains—cowboys on cattle drives, prospectors, traders, settlers. They could feed without consequence, kill as they liked, with no one the wiser. But someone noticed, and their den was burned to the ground and all of them killed. The established East Coast vampire Families heard of the slaughter but never discovered who was responsible—though truth be told they were relieved that the anarchic vampires had been disposed of. Shortly after, Families began sending their own representatives west to establish enclaves in the burgeoning cities, to prevent such lawlessness from happening again. Alette let drop the information that Rick had already been in the region for decades and that the eastern vampires were startled to find one of their kind of his age in the lawless West. I'd have to ask him about that.

The timing of the fire that destroyed the anarchic vampires coincided with the time that Wyatt Earp spent as deputy marshal of Dodge City, and rumor had it that his law-enforcement activities extended to the supernatural. I thanked Alette for the tidbit and promised to keep in touch.

Research into ghost towns and fires in 1870s Kansas followed, and I marked likely spots on a map. Not that burned vampires left any hard evidence behind. I was never going to find solid proof, a diary or letter in Wyatt Earp's handwriting stating, "Yes, I killed vampires while I lived in Dodge City." But I hoped to get . . . something. That was how, a month later, Ben, Cormac, and I ended up standing in the middle of a stretch of prairie about fifteen miles northeast of Dodge City.

Getting Cormac out here had been a challenge in itself. He was on parole after serving time for a manslaughter conviction and officially wasn't allowed to leave the Denver area for the time being. But we were family—Ben was Cormac's cousin, and I was Ben's wife. So that made us cousins-in-law. Or something. We explained to Cormac's parole officer that we were going to visit a dying relative. The story must have been convincing, because Cormac got permission to leave, but we had to make a lot of promises about getting him back to Denver to check in and sign a lot of papers taking responsibility if anything happened while Cormac was with us.

We'd jumped through all the hoops because I'd wanted his perspective out here. And, if I had to admit it, the perspective of the ghost he'd picked up in prison—a nineteenth-century wizard named Amelia Parker. She was either haunting him, had possessed him, or was just along for the ride. It was a long story.

I asked, but Cormac said she hadn't known Wyatt Earp herself.

"It's not like the movies," he said. "Not everybody knew each other."

"I know that. I figured it was worth asking." I was getting frustrated with everyone treating me like this quest was naïve and silly. It was easy to get frustrated, standing on a stretch of grass that went on for miles with only 140-year-old rumors as a guide.

While he might be an American hero, Earp hadn't been the nicest guy in the world. His name came up in a lot of court cases involving things like running prostitution rings. Much like Sherman and his nervous breakdown, Earp had some missing time in his history, a couple of years when historians couldn't quite track down where he'd been or what he'd been doing. One account had him hunting buffalo across the Great Plains.

I had a feeling he'd been hunting *something*. Not that I had any hard evidence.

Late afternoon, the summer sun was setting, casting a warm golden haze over a landscape of rolling hills, rippling grasses, and a copse of trees leaning over a trickling stream. Birds fluttered, and a swarm of gnats hovered nearby. I could almost smell the sunshine—ripe grass, rich soil, life thriving just out of sight.

Sweating in the sticky air, we'd hiked a couple of

miles off the end of the dirt road where we'd had to leave the car. I had a GPS navigator, and according to the coordinates, there used to be a farmstead around here. We fanned out to search for evidence.

"What are we looking for again?" Ben said.

"I don't know," I said. "Timbers, foundations, scraps."

"Fire," Cormac said. His expression was unreadable behind his sunglasses. He wasn't carrying guns, but he looked like he should have been. He wore a leather jacket over a T-shirt, worn jeans, scuffed biker boots, determined scowl—ready for action. In the pockets of the jacket he was probably carrying something that he—that Amelia—could use as weapons. Amulets, charms, potions, spells. I didn't know what all she could do, through Cormac's body. Cormac would appear to be the wizard to anyone who knew what to look for. You had to really know Cormac to recognize that he wasn't always the one in charge. I tried not to think too hard about it.

"This is like looking for a needle in a haystack without even knowing if the needle is there," Ben said.

"Everyone needs a hobby," I said.

"We don't have a whole lot of daylight for this," Cormac said, glancing west. A bright orange sun had touched the horizon and was sinking fast.

I turned on him, arms out. "I'm sorry. Next time I'll make sure someone puts out neon lights so we know exactly where to go."

"Kitty, calm down," Ben said.

"I'm calm." I frowned.

We hunted. I kicked the grass as I walked through it, hoping to uncover something odd, and took in slow, easy breaths, searching for incongruous scents. This was silly—what evidence could possibly have lasted after 140 years?

My toe knocked up against a blackened length of wood. I knelt beside it. Half of it was buried, but it looked like a board, planed smooth and square at one time, but now it was charcoal, burned through and cracked. It could have been a year old or a hundred, protected from the elements by remaining buried all these years. A recent storm might have uncovered it.

It could have been anything, but my imagination spun the tale I wanted to see. Had this been part of the building that sheltered the rogue vampire family? Had Wyatt Earp really destroyed them by burning it down?

"Hey," I called to the others. "You want to come look at this?"

They joined me, kneeling on the hard ground, looking to where I pointed—a straight, artificial line under matted prairie grasses.

Cormac moved a couple of steps out, then a couple more, pulling away vegetation, uncovering more of the blackened timber. In a few minutes, he'd traced out a rectangle, maybe ten by twelve. A tiny little house, reduced to a charred foundation.

There was history here. I could feel it. The place had probably belonged to some pioneer family scraping by. Nothing here would speak to the mystery I wanted to solve.

Standing back, hands on hips, Cormac regarded the remains of the building. "Vampires would have dug down. Built themselves a cellar, out of the sun. The structure would have just been there to protect the entrance. Anything else was most likely buried. We won't find anything unless we dig."

Digging would involve a lot more time and equipment, not to mention permits from the regional park service that owned the land and the involvement of any archaeology departments interested in mid-nineteenth-century settlements. I hadn't really expected to find more than this. But the answers felt close, as if I could read them in a book if I could only find the right page.

"Look at this," Ben said. He'd parted a section of grass and scraped away a layer of dirt just outside the burned foundation to reveal a slender length of wood, blackened but not burned through like the rest. Giving a yank, he pulled it free of the dirt. About a foot long and a couple of inches in diameter, it tapered to a dull point.

"Let me see that," Cormac said, reaching. Ben handed it to him.

Cormac ran his hand along the length of the aged wood, then hefted it as if testing its weight.

"It's a killing stake." He gripped the end of it and made a quick stabbing motion. Kind of like you'd do to stab a vampire.

"How do you know?" Ben said. "It may have marked out a garden or held down a tarp."

Cormac tossed Ben the stake, giving him a chance to heft its weight and test its peculiar suitability for stabbing. "It's a nonnative hardwood. Somebody carved it and brought it here for a reason."

"I think we're letting our imaginations get away from us," Ben said.

"You could say that about this whole trip," Cormac answered.

I scowled. "I wish we had a metal detector."

"Maybe see if we can find some silver bullets?" Ben said.

Wouldn't that be comforting?

We walked over the immediate area, studying the ground for whatever else we might happen to stumble over. We found a few more burned timbers. Everything was old, weathered smooth, and I didn't know enough to be able to guess the age of the buildings that had once stood here.

We wouldn't be able to stay out here much longer; the sun was below the horizon now, and the sky had turned a deep twilight blue. The first stars were flickering. We'd only stayed out this late because Ben and my werewolf eyes hardly noticed the change in light. Cormac had pulled a penlight out of a pocket.

I was about to call off the hunt when Ben stopped, head cocked as if listening.

"Assuming this was a vampire lair," he said, "and that it really was burned down by Wyatt Earp, or whoever, a century ago—should I be able to still smell vampire here?"

I took in a slow breath, nostrils flaring to scent what he'd noticed. Because no—smells on the landscape faded, washed away, scoured by wind in a matter of weeks. But he was right, a touch of cold lingered on the earth here. It wasn't ice, it wasn't rot, but a distinctive, living cold.

"It's recent," I whispered.

The three of us were statues, waiting for a sign.

A scraping noise pattered against the earth about ten yards away. It might have been a nocturnal rodent emerging from its den. It didn't matter—Ben and I moved next to each other, backs together in a defensive posture.

The undead smell of vampire grew stronger.

"I don't believe it," Ben muttered. I shushed him and looked for Cormac, who stood calmly, hands at his sides.

The earth before us erupted, a fountain of dirt spraying as something forced its way up from underground. A trapdoor, covered with earth, had hidden a cellar. A gray-skinned being emerged, hissing, lips pulled back to show long fangs.

It had been human. It had the shape—torso, thin legs meant to walk upright, slender arms, a hairless head and face with all the right details. But it had shriveled, mutated—drying flesh pulled taut over bones, every knobby joint visible. Under a hanging, threadbare shirt that had rotted away to clinging fibers, the shape of a rib cage stood out, and the concave belly couldn't possibly have held organs. The teeth were yellow, and the eyes that stared at us were clouded, milky. Shredded trousers were even worse off than the shirt.

It moved like a sprinter, straight toward us.

I braced and shouted, hoping to startle it into stopping its charge. Ben was beside me, hands clenched into the shape of claws, teeth bared.

A light flared, like a camera flash that didn't fade, searing into my eyes. Ducking, I put up my arms to block the light, and Ben hunched over with me for protection. The creature stopped, cowering on the ground before us, sheltering under its raised arms, pale eyes squinting against the onslaught.

Cormac held the source of light in his hand, raised above his head. It wasn't the penlight—no penlight was this strong, this pervasive. Instead, he held some kind of stone—something magical. My vision adjusted to the glaring white light. The creature's didn't. It continued writhing, mewling, cowering away from an enemy that was everywhere. This gave us a chance to study it.

"That's not a vampire," Ben said. "It can't be."

The pair of slender fangs, visible when the being bared its teeth at us, said that it was. But I'd never seen anything like this. All the elegance, the arrogance I associated with long-lived vampires was gone. All the humanity was gone, stripped down to pure, undying hunger. A dry, graying tongue worked behind its teeth; the column of its throat trembled under its skin.

It—He? She? I couldn't tell—had to be one of the old group of vampires that had settled here. It had survived the destruction of the lair and remained here, buried, feeding on whatever chanced by. Starving, rather. For a hundred-plus years. How sad. I reached out for it.

"Stay back." Ben gripped my shoulder, and I lowered my arm. The vampire only *looked* weak, after all.

"Who are you?" I asked. "How long have you been out here?"

It hissed, its limbs reaching blindly. It kept trying to open its eyes, then ducking away from the light.

"Cormac, you ever see anything like this?" Ben asked.

"No," Cormac answered.

I said, "We—we can help you."

"Kitty—" Ben said warningly. Surely the vampire was beyond help.

"We can try to help you," I revised. "I know people who can help." I had to call Rick; there had to be something we could do. "Please, what's your name?"

It—he, I thought, based on the square line of his jaw—closed his mouth. The flesh moved as he ran his tongue along his teeth. Then he inhaled, inflating his lungs—a preparation for speaking. The skin around the rib cage creaked and cracked. How long had it been since he had drawn breath?

"Werewolves," he said in a rasping whisper. "Filthy animals."

So that was how it was going to be. The creature's vampiric elegance may have vanished. The arrogance was still healthy.

"Excuse me, but you're the one living in a hole in the ground," I said.

He hissed again, flailing under the light, but it seemed to be held at bay for the moment.

"Why are you here?" I asked, crouching, moving as close as I dared. "Why not leave? Can you at least tell me your name?"

He leaned toward my voice, blinking, mouth working. I wondered if he saw us as food. As if he was trying to figure out how to get at us. If I could just get him to talk . . .

I tried again. "I want to find out about Wyatt Earp—"

The ravaged vampire screeched the howl of a cat and held his hands over his ears as if the sound of the words pained him. Startled, I fell back—even Ben took a step back. Cormac didn't move.

Drawing a rattling breath, the vampire said, "Did he send you?"

Victory. Earp had been here. He'd killed them. My secret history of the world gained another paragraph. Now if only I could get this guy into a studio to record an interview.

"No," I said. "Wyatt Earp died eighty years ago."

"Who killed him?" the vampire breathed.

"No one. He died at home of old age." The vampire had lost all sense of time—did he realize how long he'd been here, stuck? Maybe thinking Earp would return for a final showdown? Was that what he was waiting for? "It all happened a long time ago," I said.

The vampire shook his head, spreading his mouth wide to show his fangs, tipping back his head to bellow at the sky. Then he jumped at me.

Arms reaching, he launched himself and grasped clawed hands around my neck. I fell back, and he knelt on me, pinning me. He surged toward me with an open mouth, teeth pressing against the skin of my face.

I yelled and kicked. The vampire fell—he hardly weighed anything, but he was fast, and sprang back before I could sit up. This time I grabbed him, managing to hold him away from me, but it was like trying to hang onto an angry badger. An angry, skeletal badger. He clawed, kicked, snarled, and thrashed.

Ben shouted, seemingly right in my ear. The vampire seized, back arcing, ribs straining, face frozen in an agonized grimace. And he disintegrated, ash falling around me like soft snow. So little had been holding him together, he was just gone. A hard, metallic object fell onto my chest.

Ben crouched above me, still stabbing the old stake through the space that used to be the vampire's heart. The point of it was centimeters from my own chest. We looked at each other and tried to catch our breath.

"You okay?" he said finally.

A fine powder of former vampire covered me. I coughed—it smelled like dirt and death. The thought of sucking that ash into my lungs made me cough harder. I wanted to howl. Ben threw away the stake and gripped my shoulders. "Kitty—"

"Yeah. I'm okay." I leaned against him and tried not to think about it. My breathing steadied, and my Wolf settled. "That was crazy."

"I think we're a couple of steps past crazy on this one." He was right, as usual. I tried brushing myself off. The stuff just smeared. I grimaced. My hand knocked off an object—the piece of metal that had dropped onto me. Holding it up, I studied it: round, blackened with age and strung on a length of braided leather, it held the worn lines of a design etched into it. It looked like a coin, heavily tarnished, the size of a nickel. The vampire must have been wearing it.

In the meantime, the light that had flared over the twenty feet around us for the last few minutes faded.

"What did you do?" Ben asked.

Cormac showed us a clear quartz crystal the size of his thumb. Its luminescence was fading. Another trick of Cormac the wizard. I'd never get used to it.

"You get what you needed here?" Cormac said.

I chuckled, shaking my head. "I guess I did. I knew it. Wyatt Earp, vampire hunter. I just *knew*."

"You still can't prove it," Ben said.

"Yeah, I know. But still." I'd take what little victories I

could get. "So what do you guys make of this?" I said, offering the ancient pendant.

Ben took it, ran a thumb over it. "What is that, bronze? Was that thing wearing it? What's it say?"

Cormac took his turn with it, squinting at it. "I don't know. But I'm thinking we should get moving."

Ben held his hand out to me and pulled me to my feet. I brushed myself off, then searched the ground—I had to get back on my knees and feel around for the stake that Ben had tossed aside. It took a few minutes, with Ben and Cormac standing on, impatient.

Ben said, "Kitty—"

"Just a sec." Then I found it, and held it out to study it. A killing stake, Cormac had called it. Over a century old, belonging to Wyatt Earp once. I didn't know that for sure, all the evidence was circumstantial, but this was all the proof I had that vampires had been here. I'd take what I could get.

"Okay, let's go," I said.

"Good," Cormac said.

"If you didn't want to come along you could have just said so," I said.

"Somebody's got to look after you two."

"We were doing fine," I said.

"Then why did you even drag me out here?"

Ben said, "Everybody shut up."

The three of us trekked back to the car. The sun had set; the sky was dark. Every rustle in the breeze made me jump. I needed a shower. I kept scratching my hair and having ash fall out.

We were in sight of the car when I smelled werewolf. Ben stopped me, his hand on my arm, the same time I muttered, "Oh, not now."

"What is it?" Cormac said.

My shoulders tensed in place of hackles rising. Ben and I stood arm to arm, both of us looking outward, tracking the intrusive scent—skin and fur, that distinctive mix of human and wild, neither one nor the other, and something more. Like us, but strangers. Enemies, even. Werewolves were territorial, and this wasn't our territory. I had in fact considered that we'd be invading someone else's territory on this trip. I also figured the chances of doing so in the middle of Kansas were pretty low. So much for that.

A nondescript SUV was parked near Ben's sedan. There were two of them waiting at the car, one leaning on the hood, his arms crossed, the other standing a few feet away, watching our approach. Both were male, mid-twenties, wearing T-shirts and jeans. The one by the car was average height, on the stout side, with a shaggy beard. The other was taller, a square-jawed frat-boy type, straight out of a beer commercial.

"What's the plan?" Ben whispered.

"We talk. What else?" I said.

"There's only two. We can take 'em," he said. Cormac had stepped a little ways to the side, to flank them. I shook my head at him.

"Hi," I said when we reached spitting distance.

"You mind telling us what you're doing here?" said the tall one. He curled his lip and bared his teeth. Not a happy camper.

I pointed over my shoulder. "You know you had a starving vampire living in a hole back there? Took care of that for you."

"Wait a minute," said his companion. "That voice— I know you. You're Kitty Norville."

I straightened and beamed at him. "Yeah, that's me. You listen to the show?"

Bearded guy glanced at tall guy and looked chagrined, ducking his gaze. "Oh, you know. Once in a while."

Tall guy frowned even harder. "It's a dumb show. And it doesn't explain what you're doing here."

"C'mon, Dan. Give her a break."

The tall guy—Dan—just glared at me. I glared right back. Ben and Cormac had taken up tough-guy poses, like bodyguards. I almost yelled at them to just chill out, I could handle it.

"I'm doing some research," I said. "I didn't expect to be here long enough to ruffle any fur."

"What's this about a vampire?"

This wasn't going to make any more sense when I explained it to him. "Is there a restaurant or diner or something where we can maybe grab a cup of coffee and talk about this like human beings?"

Dan squinted, apparently confused. "What?"

His buddy tapped his arm. "I told you, it's Kitty

Norville. That's her thing. You'd know if you listened to her show." Dan glared at him, and his compatriot's shoulders slouched, cowering.

I crossed my arms and regarded them. Bearded guy was a fan, which was cool. But Dan was the more dominant werewolf and had decided I sucked. If I appealed to the weaker wolf, that would piss off Dan even more. But Dan didn't seem inclined to be sympathetic.

"I really don't want to step on toes," I said. "We can just get out of here—"

"Tell me about the vampire," he said, stepping in front of the driver's-side door.

Ben tensed up and approached the guy—about as aggressive a move as he could make. Cormac looked relaxed, but he held his hands in the pockets of his jacket, probably holding onto something weaponish.

I went to stand in front of Ben, holding his arm, willing him to relax. I didn't want a fight to start—not because I thought we'd lose, but because I was pretty sure we *wouldn't,* and I didn't want to leave any messes.

"Short version," I said. "I got some information that a den of vampires settled here about a hundred and fifty years ago, and that Wyatt Earp might have been the vampire hunter to finish them off. Cool, huh? So I came out here looking for evidence. And, well, it turns out Deputy Marshal Earp didn't get them all, you know?" I held up the stake, as if that explained it all, as if it looked like something other than a stray twig we'd found. "I'd

have called to ask for permission first, but werewolf alphas aren't exactly listed in the phone book." But maybe
they should be. There was an idea . . .

Dan's stare had changed from a werewolf's stare of
challenge to a purely human stare of bafflement. "Huh?"

"Oh my gosh, *really*?" said his friend. "Wyatt Earp
hunted vampires?"

"Mike, shut up, let me handle this," Dan said.

"Yeah," I said, talking around Dan to Mike. "I want to
do a whole show on it if I can get enough information."

"Both of you, shut up!" Dan said.

"She's telling the truth. You can smell the damn thing
all over her," Ben said. Their noses wrinkled. Clearly,
they could.

"So," I went on. "Are you guys part of a big pack
around here or is it just the two of you?" I tried to look
innocent.

Dan put his hands to his temples and made a noise like
a growl.

"Dan—hey Dan," Mike said, reaching for his friend,
tentative. "You okay?"

Taking a deep breath, getting ahold of himself, Dan
straightened. "One more time. What are you doing here?"

"I already told you," I said, quiet and straightforward
this time. I didn't want to push him any further.

"You're not here to take over?" Dan said.

"Why the hell would we want to take over Dodge City,
Kansas?" Ben said.

Mike and Dan didn't answer, because Ben had a point. Instead, Dan nodded at Cormac. "And who are you? You're not a werewolf."

"Nope," Cormac said. "I'm just along for the ride."

Dan looked at us, disbelieving. We must have made a strange picture.

"Look, seriously, I'm really sorry if we freaked you out," I said. "We have rooms in a hotel on the other side of town, but if you don't want us here, say so, and we'll just . . . we'll just . . ." Oh God. I couldn't bring myself to say it.

"Get the hell out of Dodge?" Dan said, raising his eyebrows.

I shrugged. Ben was holding his forehead like he had a headache.

"No offense," Dan said. "But I'd feel better if you weren't anywhere within a hundred miles of here."

There wasn't much of anything within a hundred miles of here. Leaving would mean driving all night. But staying meant picking on these guys, which didn't feel particularly productive or necessary.

"All right. We'll leave. Thanks for understanding," I said. I waved at the guys, and we headed for the car. Dan and Mike stepped out of the way.

Then the pair had a brief, whispered conference. Dan still looked sullen, but Mike was bouncing. Dan gave a frustrated shrug, throwing his arms up and stalking away, and Mike turned to me. He really was bouncing, his eyes alight. Confused, I regarded him until he slunk toward me.

"I'm sorry," he said. "I really don't mean to bother you. But—could I get your autograph?"

MIKE GOT his autograph on a piece of scratch paper, and then we were driving west, looking for a hotel that wasn't within a hundred miles of Dodge City. I'd been looking forward to a hot, cleansing shower at the hotel. I itched, and every time I scratched, a fine powder of ash rose up from me. I pulled out my ponytail, shook my hair, and created a cloud of dust. Ben, who was driving, sneezed.

"Sorry," I muttered.

"Don't apologize," he said. "The whole thing's pretty funny when you think about it." He was smirking. I couldn't tell if he was laughing at the situation or at me.

"I'm trying not to think too hard about it," I said.

From the backseat Cormac said, "We probably could have just checked into the hotel and those guys never would have known."

"It doesn't matter," I said. "I told them we'd leave so we left."

"I'm just saying," he said.

"It's too late to bitch about it now." My phone rang, and I dug it out of my pocket and flipped it open. Someone calling at this hour of night could only have bad news. "Hello?"

"Kitty. It's Anastasia."

Bad news. Right. The hair on the back of my neck rose, tingling. I didn't need this now.

"Hi," I said. Ben glanced at me, concerned at the sudden change in my tone of voice.

"I need help."

"Is it Roman?"

"Yes, it is," Anastasia said. Her voice was hushed but not panicked, as if she was in hiding but not in immediate danger. Not that she'd stop to call if she was facing down Roman *right now*. At least, I hoped not.

"What's happening? Where is he? Where are *you*?"

"San Francisco. When can you get here?"

I blew out a breath. "Not for a while—I'm in a car in the middle of Kansas right now."

"Kansas?"

"Never mind. Are you in trouble? What's going on?"

She took a deep breath, gathering air for a speech. "I'm safe for the moment. I've kept ahead of him. Roman is here looking for an artifact of immense power. I know where it is—I can get to it first. But he's brought allies with him."

"You need foot soldiers, then," I said, frowning. I wanted a chance to stop Roman, certainly. I didn't really want to be cannon fodder.

"I wouldn't have called you if I didn't think you could handle it," she said, and maybe she believed that, and maybe she just wanted to use me as a decoy while she got the goods, this artifact. Which, I had to admit, made me curious. Immense power, huh?

Cormac had shifted forward to lean in between the front seats, and Ben was glancing at me from the driver's seat.

"It'll be a few days before I can get there," I said.

"He hasn't moved yet," Anastasia said. "If I have to do this on my own, I will, but I could use help. Should I wait for you?"

Glancing at Ben and Cormac I said, "Let me call you back." I clicked off the phone and put it away.

"Well?" Ben said. "I heard 'Roman' and 'help.'"

"A terrible combination, isn't it? So—do you want to go to San Francisco?"

"And do what? Stand between two ancient, all-powerful vampires? Not particularly."

"You know how I feel about vampire politics," Cormac said, grimacing.

"This isn't exactly vampire politics," I said. "It's bigger than that. I think."

Ben chuckled, but the sound was bitter. "So we run off on the next quest before the last one is even done. You keep getting us wrapped up in this shit, and you want to have kids? How would that work?"

I sank back in the seat and glared out the window. "It's a moot point anyway so why bring it up?"

"There's adoption. We've talked about this."

I didn't want to talk about it. Not right now. Ben was

making me face the question, yet again—did I have any business being a mother? How did someone be a mother and a crusader at the same time?

If I had kids, would Roman come after them?

"If I don't go, who will? What happens the next time Roman decides to take us out?"

Cormac shrugged. "This Roman character can't be as badass as all that."

"Oh, I think he can," Ben said.

The hunter's lip curled; he liked a challenge.

"I'm just not sure I can actually help. What does Anastasia expect me to do, talk Roman into submission?"

"You stood up to him once," Ben said.

That didn't mean I wanted to stand up to him again. Once was enough. On the other hand, if Anastasia and I had a chance to stop him, I'd rush to San Francisco.

"Amelia's game," Cormac said.

"Does she get a vote?" I said.

Cormac glared at me, but maybe it wasn't Cormac doing the glaring. Yes, then.

"This isn't your fight, you don't have to go," I said.

"Will Porter even let you go?" Ben said. "I know we got you a few days off for this, but San Francisco?" Porter was Cormac's parole officer.

"I'm a model student," Cormac said. "He'll let me."

I wondered sometimes if wizard Amelia had some kind of spell to put the whammy on Porter—he let Cormac get away with so much. But I wasn't going to complain; I'd feel better with Cormac watching our backs. Not that I would necessarily say that out loud.

Ben said, "We go to San Francisco, then. Check things out. But we get out of there the minute things go south."

"Too bad I don't usually notice things have gone south until it's too late to run," I said.

The silence I got in reply to that was a little too pointed.

Chapter 3

I CALLED ANASTASIA back and told her we'd be in San Francisco in a couple of days. She said she would manage until then—Roman hadn't made his move yet, and she would keep out of sight until he did. We had enough time back in Denver to wrap up some details: Cormac checked in with his parole officer, Ben cleared some work with his law practice, I dropped in at the radio station and New Moon to remind them I was still alive. And I went to see Rick.

Tonight, Rick was at Obsidian, the art and antique gallery he owned, where he made his headquarters. He and the dozen or so vampires in his Family slept out their days in the basement. I didn't know if they actually used coffins, but I had it on good authority that coffins were optional and most vampires didn't bother with the affectation.

After parking the car behind the building, I went down the stairs and knocked on the unmarked steel door. I put on a surly attitude because I expected to have to argue with a flunky—one of Rick's vampire underlings who acted as gatekeeper. Most of them had a thing against werewolves and didn't understand why Rick was so friendly with me. The more stubborn they got, the more I had to bait them. We'd stand there calling each other names until Rick came along.

There I stood, hands on hips, glaring at the door—which Rick himself opened. I blinked at him, my attitude blowing away like dandelion fluff.

"I got your message," he said. "Come in."

A minute later, we were sitting in Rick's office, a large, comfortable, parlorlike room, with a desk, computer, and shelves cluttered with books and trinkets on one end, sofas and padded chairs on the other. Throw rugs on the worn hardwood floor and soft lighting made the place seem shockingly normal, unlike what I thought of when I thought of vampires. No pretension, no arrogance or attempts to intimidate, no showing off the collected wealth of centuries. Which was Rick all over, really.

"Can I get you anything?" he asked.

"No, I'm fine. I just have a couple of things I want to ask you about. First off, we found something in Kansas." I pulled the old coin on its cord out of my jeans pocket and set it on his desk.

He leaned forward and moved his hand toward it. "May I?"

I gestured a yes. He held the object up to the light, studying it.

"You ever see anything like it?" I asked.

"Maybe. It looks a little like an old Roman coin."

I might have choked out a gasp, and Rick looked at me over the coin. I straightened, regaining some semblance of composure. "We found the burned-out homestead outside Dodge City. There was still one vampire left. He was wearing that."

"Really?" he said wonderingly. "The vampire—what kind of shape was he in?"

"Terrible. I hardly recognized him as a vampire," I said. "He's gone, now."

Rick shook his head, making a small tsking noise. "Amazing."

I pointed at the artifact. "If that's a Roman coin, you don't think it has anything to do with Roman the vampire, do you?"

He tilted his head, smiled. "The Roman empire was much bigger than Roman the vampire, Kitty. It might have just been a souvenir."

I didn't want to admit that he was probably right. We found the vampire, the old stake, and this relic. It had to have some significance because the vampire had been wearing it all this time. "So it doesn't mean anything? It's just flotsam?"

"If it means something, I'm not sure what," he said.

I sighed, disappointed. Maybe I thought I had another puzzle piece. Another clue in the mystery of the vampires' tangle of allegiances. I put the coin back into my pocket. Maybe Anastasia would know something about it.

"And now for the second thing?" Rick said, drawing me out of my thoughtfulness.

I nodded. "Anastasia called me. She's in San Francisco, facing down Roman and needs help."

"Ah, hence the flinch."

"I didn't flinch."

He suppressed a smile. "And you're going?"

"Yeah. I want to check it out. She says Roman's looking for this artifact—she actually used the phrase 'immense power' to describe it. We have to keep him from getting it."

I tried to read some emotion off him—was he shocked, wary, confident? What did he think? He seemed calm, mildly curious.

"What do you need from me, then?" he said.

"An opinion. I can't help but wonder what she isn't telling me," I said. The last time I'd seen Anastasia, we'd been on the same side battling some particularly destructive enemies. We'd trusted each other because we didn't have a choice. I trusted her now because I'd trusted her then. So what was I missing?

Rick leaned back, lacing his fingers. "Here's what I know about Anastasia. She's older than I am. She came to this country sometime in the nineteenth century with the first wave of Chinese immigration, I imagine dodging some trouble in China but I don't know exactly what.

She rose through the ranks and became a trusted advisor of the then-Mistress of San Francisco. She controlled Chinatown for her, as I understand it. Then the situation completely unraveled." He shrugged. "Vampire Families can remain stable for centuries. London's had the same Master since the seventeenth century. But when they go, they can go quickly, spectacularly, and without any warning. San Francisco was like that."

"You were there for it?" I asked.

"I saw bits and pieces. I tried not to get involved." He winced a little—he'd spent centuries trying not to get involved, until a few years ago when he personally destroyed Denver's previous Master and took over. Everyone had been surprised. It was one of those spectacular changeovers he was talking about.

"Anastasia got out, of course. There was a lot of speculation—did she get out because she was afraid of the new management, or because she'd betrayed the old? Some people said she orchestrated the whole thing."

"But why? Wouldn't she have stuck around, then?"

"Her whole reason for going to San Francisco in the first place might have been to topple that Mistress and her Family. When her work was done, she packed up and moved on to her next project. The fact that she's back now and in need of help suggests to me that she isn't any more friendly with the current Family—she could just go to them for help."

"What can you tell me about them?"

Rick said, "They're a laid-back bunch, but don't underestimate them. Behave yourself and they won't give you any trouble. To tell you the truth, most of us were happy with the change in management."

I thought a moment, lips pursed, leaning my chin on my hand. "Roman must have brought werewolves with him. That's why she needs me." If he'd brought vampire minions, Anastasia could have depended on the local Family to oppose them.

"Is there a local pack in San Francisco? What are they like?" he said.

"Word has it the pack there is centered in Oakland and tends to stay out of San Francisco proper. Roman probably knows that."

Rick glanced away, chuckling.

"What is it?" I asked.

"It's the same old story. Both Roman and Anastasia bringing werewolves as hired muscle. Vampires as nobility and werewolves as peasant foot soldiers. The patterns are ingrained among the oldest of us and we keep falling into them."

That kind of thing made me angry. Made me mouth off when I ought to stay quiet. It almost made me look forward to the upcoming conflict.

"That just means I have to stand up for myself, don't I?"

"I don't see you having any trouble with that."

"Thanks," I said. "Any other advice?"

"If you see Roman, get out," he said.

"That's already on the agenda." I figured if I actually saw Roman, it would already be too late.

"Keep in mind that Anastasia is not the most powerful thing you might meet out there. If she and Roman are both after this artifact, that means it's more powerful than both of them. Be careful."

"I'm not really all that interested in power," I said.

"That's why those in power find you so interesting. They really don't like rogue elements getting in the way of their plans."

"You sound like you're speaking from experience."

"Do you know I was probably the only vampire in North America for about a century?"

"Alette might have mentioned something along those lines. How the hell did that happen?"

"It . . ." He paused, looking off to some distant time—some very distant time. "It's a long story. But when the second wave of vampire immigrants arrived, they were a little surprised to find me."

To be a fly on that wall. I could see it now, some kind of crazy Monty Python–like sketch with vampires going back and forth: "What are you doing here?" "I live here." "But how can you? *We're* the first vampires here." "If *you're* the first vampires here, then what am I?" And so on, until the skit ended with some kind of pratfall involving stakes.

"Maybe I'll tell you the whole story sometime."

"Rick, you have *never* told me the whole story. You just drop maddening hints."

"How about this: We'll trade stories when you get back from San Francisco. Deal?"

"Deal."

I just had to be sure I came back with a lot of stories.

Chapter 4

TWO DAYS OF driving later, we checked into a lower-rent, unassuming motel in the middle of the city, off the tourist tracks. That was Cormac's idea. He said we could come and go without drawing as much attention. I thought maybe he was just self-conscious about staying someplace with room service.

I stood at the window of our room. It didn't have much of a view, which was frustrating, because less than a mile away was water, San Francisco Bay, its famous bridges, and so on. All I saw were buildings and a busy street. The sky was bright but hazy. The temperature was surprisingly cool. So much for a California summer.

We'd been sure to arrive during daylight hours so we could get our bearings before we had to face Anastasia after nightfall.

"You ever been to San Francisco?" Ben asked. He drew close behind me, resting a hand on my hip, his cheek against my hair.

"Nope," I said. "I'm fighting an urge to run off and take the boat tour to Alcatraz."

"Let's do that after we've figured out that Roman isn't really here and we're not in trouble."

"Roman can't come out in daylight," I argued, but the sense of foreboding lingered.

"Yeah, but Roman has minions. I thought that's why we're here."

I drew his arms around me and hugged him close. "We'll be careful."

A knock came at the door. We were expecting it, but Ben checked the peephole anyway before undoing the dead bolt, then the chain, and opening the door for Cormac, who was staying in the room next door.

He stepped inside. "Ready to go hunting?" He had his leather jacket and sunglasses in place, ready for action. He'd taken possession of the stake we'd found back in Kansas and had that hidden somewhere, and probably a few more stakes besides.

Ben carried the semiautomatic pistol that normally lived in the glove box of the car in a shoulder holster under his blazer. It was loaded with silver bullets. Guns made me nervous, and I wasn't sure if that was because I didn't like guns, or I didn't like how often we seemed to need them. I reassured myself that he probably wouldn't have to use it.

In addition, Cormac gave us all crosses on chains to wear. Just in case.

I'd guessed that Roman had werewolf minions in town; we were going to try to flush them out. Not necessarily confront them—just see how many there were and what they were up to. Maybe follow them to Roman. If we found them first, they couldn't jump us.

The chances of finding anything in this huge, packed city were slim. So I kept telling myself.

We planned to meet Anastasia a couple of hours after sunset at an address in Chinatown. That gave us some time to drive into the heart of the city, check out the area, watch for anything that seemed wrong. We decided to start in Fisherman's Wharf and work our way south. After parking, Ben and I would go together; Cormac would follow separately. I didn't like splitting up the pack. We needed to look out for each other. Safety in numbers.

As we left the parking lot, I looked all around, taking in the sights and sounds of one of the most touristy locations in the country, squinting against a wind blowing off the water, watching gulls dive and soar. We'd already discussed the plan. I still tried to argue. "I'd feel better if we stuck together."

"Too obvious," Cormac answered. "You two look fine as a couple. I don't look like I belong with you."

"But—"

"He's right," Ben said.

I wore jeans and a light blue blouse; Ben wore khaki slacks and a button-up shirt and blazer. Give us sunglasses and a couple of cameras and we'd look like yuppie tourists. On the other hand, Cormac looked like he ought to be riding a Harley on some dusty back road.

"I'll keep you in sight, but don't go looking for me. Got it?" Cormac patted a couple of pockets, as if checking for something. He nodded, apparently satisfied, and walked off in the opposite direction from us.

In ten minutes, Ben and I reached the waterfront around Fisherman's Wharf. The place was crowded, chaotic, lots of traffic, cars crammed together in makeshift parking lots, a mix of buildings from every decade for the last century, restaurants and junk shops, hotels and offices. Piers crammed with boats: sailboats, fishing boats, tour boats. And people. This late in the day, there seemed to be a ton of screaming children who were too tired and hungry to be interested in cotton candy anymore. I stuck close to Ben, our arms touching as we walked.

"No werewolf in his right mind is going to be stalking us here," Ben said. "This place is a zoo."

"Well, we know that *now*," I said. In fact, this area might be a good place to hide if we wanted to avoid werewolves.

I had a vague sense of Cormac walking about a block behind us. I had to resist an urge to glance over my shoulder, to check my hunch. My senses were going haywire with all the sensory input. Cars, trucks, buses all made different sounds, had slightly different-smelling exhausts. Music from distant radios clashed. Streetlights, traffic lights, signal lights. Dozens of buildings, and every one had a different set of signs, and rows of windows looked down on us. And the people. Hundreds of people, who all looked and smelled different, who spoke a half dozen different languages. It felt like getting trapped in the middle of a herd of cows.

All big cities shared certain characteristics—lots of buildings, lots of cars, a myriad of scents, from gas fumes to pigeon droppings. It was what made them big cities. So I was amazed at how different San Francisco smelled from Denver. I probably would have noticed it even if I hadn't been a werewolf, but having a werewolf's sensitive nose made the odors obvious. In Denver, I could always catch hints of mountains and prairie around the smog and steel of the city. The wind brought tastes of the surrounding countryside. Here, I could hardly even smell the concrete and asphalt smells of the city. Mostly, I smelled the ocean, saltwater and fish, a slightly rotten smell of decay in the water, pollution from all the shipping and traffic. The smell was strange, alien; my nose constantly twitched, trying to define and recognize its various textures. I walked with my shoulders bunched up, tense.

"I can't smell anything but fish," I said. Anything upwind of us would be invisible under the breeze from the water.

"Yeah. It's going to be tough spotting anything sneaking up on us from the wrong direction." He scanned the streets ahead of us, noting the people and storefronts we passed. He wasn't hiding his nerves any better than I was.

"I'm not even sure what we're looking for."

"Anything that doesn't smell right," he said.

"That's everything here. Makes me want to go home."

He squeezed my hand. "It's kind of making me hungry. We're going for seafood for dinner, right?"

"It would be a crime not to, I think."

We ducked down a side street—a length of boardwalk along a pier, really—to get away from the crowd for a moment, catch our breath, and take stock. The air seemed a little fresher away from all the people, but the ocean wind still wouldn't tell us anything about what was lurking in the city.

Across the water, toward the west, I spotted the towers of the Golden Gate Bridge silhouetted against the setting sun. There was a sight to mark off the bucket list.

Further on, I was drawn by a guttural, animal noise. I wouldn't have noticed it, or I'd have written it off as a weird dog barking, except that it was so *strange*.

Ben and I turned a corner, looked over a wooden railing, and saw a blanket of brownish, rubbery sea lions splayed out on a series of anchored platforms floating on the water. They were all gurgling and bellowing, craning their necks back and wriggling whiskered snouts.

"Huh," Ben observed. Both of us were native Coloradoans. The scene before us—the massive marine creatures lounging and stretching, shaking their whiskers and blinking up at the pier full of gawking tourists—was completely alien.

"I wonder if any of them are lycanthropes?" I said.

"Excuse me?" Ben said.

I was studying the smaller ones that seemed as if they only weighed as much as an average person as opposed to the massive ones that weighed hundreds of pounds—and trying to catch the right smell to indicate that there was something supernatural going on.

"You know, were–sea lions." I'd met a were-seal once, and was open to endless possibilities.

"Why would a were–sea lion hang out with a bunch of the real thing?"

"Hiding out? Maybe Roman has were–sea lion minions."

"I think you're stretching," he said.

We continued on, leaving the waterfront and sea lions behind to enter the grid of streets and buildings with kitschy souvenir shops, crowded restaurants, and tourist traps. Telegraph Hill and its ornamental Coit Tower lay to the south. If we kept walking, we'd enter the hills and warrens of the next neighborhood. So far, no werewolves. This wasn't exactly werewolf territory. I wasn't disappointed. We had plenty of other neighborhoods to check.

After a couple of blocks, Ben's phone rang. He answered, and Cormac's voice responded.

I waited while Ben made yes and no noises and suggested getting back to the car and heading to Chinatown. We'd left the crowds behind on the Wharf. The sun was setting; dusk fell faster among the buildings, away from the water. Lots of corners, shadows, and hiding places here. It made me think of a forest, with wide trees and deep ravines. We were strangers here, outside our territory. My shoulders stiffened, like hackles rising. All I could smell was city and ocean. I paced a few steps up the street and back, as if that would make me see into the shadows more clearly.

"You okay?" Ben said, shutting off his phone and slipping it into his pocket.

"Just nervous."

Picking up on my cues, he lifted his chin, gazing around, searching as I had. "Let's keep moving, then."

Hand in hand, we walked down the street and back toward the waterfront parking lot where we'd left the car. "Did he spot anything?"

"It didn't sound like it," Ben said. "He didn't say much."

Cormac never did.

Another characteristic all big cities seemed to share was a visible homeless population, and San Francisco was no different. The street people here looked the same as they did everywhere, bundled in ill-fitting clothing, hunched over, tired-seeming. Identifiable not just by the way they looked but by the way they moved, at a different pace and with a different purpose than the people around them. My inner Wolf perked her ears when we passed them, because they didn't quite fit. They were eddies in the flow of life on the street.

A man with a matted beard, knit gloves, hat, and a green coat of heavy canvas was slowly making his way up the other side of the street. I glanced at him, started to look away, then paused. Wolf didn't just perk her ears; my shoulders stiffened, hackles going up. Something was definitely wrong. Ben's hand tightened on mine.

"Are we being followed?" I murmured.

"Look," he murmured back.

A second figure, this one with a stubbled face, wearing jeans and a flannel shirt, had joined the first, who had changed direction. They were now walking shoulder to shoulder—moving with purpose and direction. They didn't look like street people anymore, and that put Wolf on alert. Under their loose clothes they were broad-chested, powerful.

At this distance, and with all the interference, I couldn't smell them. But with their steady pacing and bunched shoulders, they walked like werewolves. We were being stalked.

We didn't change our pace or direction, giving no indication we'd spotted them. At the moment we were on a side street, little traveled and currently empty. In a few minutes we'd be near the water again, where there was more traffic and more people. Not to mention we'd be heading toward Cormac. Get our pack together, then turn on them. Ben reached for the gun.

But these were wolves on the hunt, which meant some of them had the job of getting us to run and chasing us down. And somewhere, another wolf had the job of flanking us.

That one stepped around the next corner and into our path.

Chapter 5

TALL AND FULL of muscles, he was a white guy with a dark crew cut, square jaw, and a wry smile. His T-shirt was tight, his jeans faded. Bully. Enforcer.

We stopped, squaring ourselves before him. Somehow we managed to stay calm. Tilting my head as if curious, I regarded the stranger. Ben smirked as if bored. We were posturing, showing dominance—but we couldn't hide our emotions. He would hear our heart rates speeding up, smell the sweat of tension breaking out. See our shoulders tightening, stiff as hackles. But we stood our ground. Running would only encourage him. Ben held the gun at his side, finger on the trigger.

"Is there a problem?" I said.

Ben glanced over his shoulder—the other two werewolves were crossing the street, moving in behind us.

"I have a message from Roman," the guy said.

When Ben started to raise the gun, I touched his arm, forestalling him. "What message?"

The guy bared his teeth and sprang, hands outstretched, fingers clenched like claws. I ruined Ben's first shot with my arm in the way, and the second missed because the guy was fast and already on top of us, knocking the weapon out of Ben's hand. I went sideways, dodging—Ben dived in the opposite direction as the two others grabbed at him. I couldn't see where the gun had gone.

The big guy snagged me as I swerved, taking hold of my arm, swinging me around the corner and into the side street he'd come out of. I slammed into the wall, banging my head and seeing stars. Falling, I dropped into a crouch and growled, glaring up at my attacker.

Ben tackled him.

Caught off guard, the big guy fell, and the two rolled onto the pavement. The other two jumped on top of him. Letting out a guttural shout, I lunged into the fray, slashing with inadequate fingernails instead of claws. My only thought: to get them away from Ben, to drive them off. Taking hold of a handful of hair, I yanked back—the first henchman's face came up, his teeth bared to show the start of fangs, which snapped at me, millimeters from my arm. I let him go and raked claws across his cheek. The second henchman kicked me, and I fell against the wall again.

We all looked human, but we fought like wolves, with lupine strength and speed. Instead of throwing punches, we slashed, snapped, wrestled. Instead of grunting and shouting, we growled and snarled. I could feel Ben's anger lashing out at them; my own rage narrowed my vision to the three enemy wolves and my need to rip into them.

Ben managed to wrestle out from under the pile of bodies. Lips drawn back to show teeth, face contorted in fury, he grabbed the head of the one who had his hands on me and wrenched. With a yelp, the guy fell over, scrambling to regain his balance.

A shadow and the scent of a newcomer—human— appeared at the end of the street. The intrusion was shocking to all of us; we broke apart, separating into our packs. Ben and I stood shoulder to shoulder, facing the three men fanned out before us.

The figure at the end of the street was Cormac. The smell of him boosted me, giving me the confidence to turn on our attackers.

"Message from Roman, huh?" I shouted at them. "Screw that!"

They were wary of Cormac, glancing at him when they weren't staring at me. Backing away from us both, they finally broke and ran around the next corner.

I would have chased them, but Ben fell to his knees, groaning. He smelled of blood, seeping out of cuts across his face and the chest of his torn shirt. And he smelled of fur. Agitated, he struggled out of his blazer—also torn—and yanked at the strap of the gun holster, trying to pull it off. His hands showed wolf's claws, and tawny fur brushed his arms.

Cormac did chase them, to the corner at the next block, but he stopped and looked back when Ben fell.

"Ben, no," I said, crouching before him and clutching his arms. His muscles were taut, bracing against the need to shape-shift.

He clamped shut his eyes, grit his teeth, and doubled over, hugging himself, as if he could hold it inside. Trying to hold the wolf in when the Change was so far along hurt—so much easier to let it go. We were in the middle of San Francisco—he had no place to run. We weren't safe. I folded myself over him, holding him as much as I could, helping him. Resting my face on his shoulder, I murmured at him, letting my breath caress him so he could smell me trying to give comfort, to anchor him.

"Keep it together," I said. "Hold it in, please Ben, hold tight."

His body trembled. I couldn't tell if he was shaking from shock, or if that was his wolf breaking free of his human skin. I thought he was going to burst. His breaths came in rapid, heavy gasps.

Cormac approached.

"No!" I shouted at him. "Stay back!" I might have snarled, baring my teeth at him, threatening.

Ben threw his head back and screamed. I held tight, my arms wrapped around his body; no matter what happened I'd keep holding. He clung back, and the scream faded to a moan.

"Please stay with me," I breathed against his ear.

We stayed like that for such a long time. My legs cramped, the pavement bruised my knees, but I didn't dare move in case it pushed him over the edge. I had to wait, hoping he trusted me, felt safe with me, and pulled himself home.

Then, Ben's hands closed over my arms. And they were hands, with human fingers and no claws. His breathing slowed. Inch by inch, muscles released, softening. He leaned against me instead of holding himself rigid.

Kneeling in front of him, I put my hands against his cheeks. He was chilled and sweaty. I tried to press warmth into him, to make his face relax along with the rest of him. Sweat soaked his hair.

"Look at me," I whispered. He showed me hazel eyes, catching what little light still reached us to glow gold. Exhaustion, sadness pulled at his features. "Shh, you're fine, you came back to me. It's okay." I kept murmuring until he could do more than stare at me.

He collapsed into my arms. "Kitty," he moaned, his arms squeezed tight around me, hands clenched against me. I hugged back, my eyes stinging with tears. This had been so close, but we were both human now, solid and human, body against body.

"It's okay," I said, my face against his neck, skin to skin. I licked his chin, a wolfish gesture. He tipped his head to catch my lips with his and we kissed, needy and relieved.

Maybe he believed me, maybe he was all right. But he didn't let go.

I glanced up; Cormac waited patiently at the end of the

alley, keeping his distance. That prompted Ben to turn, to follow my gaze. He quickly looked away again, leaning his head against my shoulder.

"How is he?" Cormac called.

"How are you?" I whispered to Ben. He shook his head, but heaved a sigh, and the last of the rage and terror left him. When he pulled away from me, I felt cold.

He met my gaze. "That was too close." His voice scratched, rough from growling.

"Yeah," I said, rubbing my arms, returning to warmth.

"They wanted to hurt you."

"They didn't. I'm fine." He rubbed a spot on my jaw, and the skin stung. A scratch or cut. So they'd gotten me. "I'm sorry—I should have let you shoot him."

He shook his head. "He was faster than me—they all were. I'd have missed."

"Let's get out of here," I said, pushing to my feet, holding my hand to him. We helped each other up.

We faced Cormac, who just stared. I couldn't guess what he thought of this.

"I had you in sight," the hunter said, breaking the silence. "Spotted them just as they moved on you."

"You weren't planning on trying to stop them, were you?" I said. Cormac used to hunt rogue werewolves. He had a whole arsenal of weapons and silver bullets, but since serving a prison term for a manslaughter conviction, the guns were off limits. Him getting into a hand-to-hand fight with a werewolf was unthinkable.

"I think I may have distracted them. Scared them off. Ben—you okay?"

Ben looked away.

Any chance we'd had to follow our attackers was gone. Maybe we could track their scent, but it would be easy to disappear in the city. Staying with Ben was my priority. I wrapped my arm around his, keeping him close.

"Did you get a look at them?" I asked Cormac.

"They had a van waiting," Cormac said. "I got the plate, but I don't know how much good it'll do us. They looked like professional heavies to me."

I shook my head. "Well, we got what we wanted and flushed them out."

Cormac asked, "Do you think they were trying to kill you or just hurt you badly?"

"There are easier ways to kill a couple of werewolves." My breathing had steadied, but my senses were still on trip wires. I took a moment to look myself over, and Ben. We were scratched and bruised, clothing torn, blood flecking our arms and faces. Our skin had gravel embedded in it from where we scraped along the pavement. We needed to wash up. We needed to get out of town— and maybe that was the point. Send a message, scare us off. "Let's find someplace to sit down," I said.

Ben retrieved his gun, which was lying hidden in the gutter, and we moved out.

We were in no shape for the nice sit-down seafood dinner I'd envisioned for us. My shirt would clean up with a little scrubbing in a restroom sink, but Ben's jacket and shirt were ruined, torn and streaked with blood. We didn't look anything like yuppie tourists now.

While we waited, Cormac ducked into a souvenir shop to find a cheap replacement. He returned with a black shirt with words in a white typewriter font printed on it: I ESCAPED ALCATRAZ.

"I suppose you think this is funny?" Ben said.

"I could have got the one with the big heart on it," he replied.

"As in, 'I left my heart in San Francisco'?" I asked.

"It was pink," Cormac said.

Shaking his head, Ben tore off what was left of his old shirt and slipped on the new one. It looked obnoxious on him. I kind of liked it. He tucked the gun into his waistband, under the shirt, and left the holster in the car.

Back at the waterfront, we picked up clam chowder, sourdough, and sodas to go and ate them at a shabby bench off the sidewalk. Restless, wary, we kept looking over our shoulders. None of us were very hungry and ended up picking at our food, but Ben and I drained the sodas and went back for more. The fight had sucked us dry.

Cormac kept glancing at us, surreptitiously studying us. Making sure we really were calm and collected.

Ben stared at his uneaten food and smiled wryly. "I guess you're used to shooting werewolves like me who can't keep it together."

"I'm not going to shoot you, Ben," Cormac said, sounding tired.

"You kept it together." I brushed my leg against his, hoping to transmit calm and reassurance. In turn, he shifted his leg to rest a little more firmly against mine. He'd be okay. "Now, what are we going to do about those freaks? Wait until they hit again or go after them?"

"They won't hit again, not like that," Cormac said. "Their cover is blown. If they just wanted to send a message, they already did that."

"I have to say," Ben said, pulling apart a chunk of bread, "this meeting with Anastasia is looking a whole lot more sinister than it did an hour ago."

I pulled out my phone and dialed her number. Roman knew that we were in town, and I had to warn her. The phone rang, and rang, and rang, and the voice mail came on. I hung up.

"She's not answering," I said.

"So something's happened to her?" Ben said.

The sun was only just setting. She may not have been awake yet. Maybe she turned her phone off. I put my phone back into my pocket. "I guess we'll find out when she shows up for the meeting."

Or, when she didn't show up.

Chapter 6

WE DROVE SOUTH a couple of miles, parked the car, and wandered into Chinatown. The neighborhood was identifiable, self-contained—the high-rises stopped at its borders. The streets narrowed. The buildings were mostly brick, three or four stories, crammed together, some of them topped with painted pagoda rooftops that would have been cheesy anywhere else. Signage in both Chinese characters and English announced restaurants, tea shops, souvenir shops, herb shops, import shops, and so on. Narrow alleys showed a forest of steel balconies and fire escapes. A couple of blocks had round, red paper lanterns strung over the street; I couldn't tell if they were there for the tourists or if they meant something. After dark now, the crowds were thinning, and many shops were closing up, steel grates pulled over their storefronts. We kept a lookout for Roman's werewolves, but no one was tracking us. I could humor myself that we'd scared them off, but I thought it more likely that they'd be back once they gathered reinforcements.

In true classic vampire fashion, Anastasia had given a complex set of instructions to find her in an obscure meeting place. The address was on Grant, in the heart of the touristy section of Chinatown, and led us to a storefront. The shop—a discount import place that was part souvenir shop, part dollar store—was an island of bright light on the street.

Inside, shelves were crammed with Chinese-style embroidered silk shirts, baskets of slippers, fancy lacquered chopsticks and tea sets, bags of candy labeled in Chinese, open jars of fresh ginseng, bamboo trays, porcelain rice bowls, paper lanterns, and so on. The smells here were rich and varied, both familiar and odd: cardboard, dust, old linoleum tile, too many people; and also strange teas, incense, scented tissue paper, and silk. I had an urge to touch everything, to stop and explore.

The Chinese woman—thin, short, her hair graying—behind the counter and cash register only glanced at us. All tourists coming into the shop must have looked this awestruck. Well, I was awestruck. Ben and Cormac stayed alert, gazing around, searching for trouble.

Stairs led down to even more shelves, boxes, and baskets filled with stuff. I wanted to look for tea sets to buy and bring back as presents. My mother and sister could use a Chinese tea set, right? Cute little pot and tiny matching cups, painted with stylized bamboo. Or maybe some silk jackets. Ooh, sake sets. Wait a minute, weren't those Japanese? I pulled my attention back. We were on a quest. Shopping later.

Anastasia told us to come to the far end of the base-ment, that she would be waiting for us there. The place was cluttered, floor-to-ceiling shelves preventing a clear view, making it impossible to judge the room's size or layout. The only exit seemed to be the stairs. Which meant it would be far too easy to stage an ambush here.

"Wait here," I said to Ben and Cormac. "I'll check it out."

Instead, Ben followed me. "Cormac can watch the stairs," he said. "I'm keeping an eye on you."

He brushed against my shoulder. Together, we moved forward into the maze of shelves and boxes.

Even with fluorescent lights on the ceilings, the stacks of goods cast shadows, making the room seem dim. My nose worked hard, taking in the air, searching for a chill, the scent of living cold, incongruous against the com-mon background.

We turned the last corner, reaching the back wall, which had a plain door, maybe to a storage closet or an-other room. When we appeared, so did Anastasia, open-ing the door and emerging from behind it.

Her black hair was twisted into a bun at the back of her head. She had Chinese features, skin as smooth as ivory. Her clothing was expensive without being ostentatious— a perfectly draped burgundy silk blouse over tailored black slacks, high heels, diamond stud earrings, and a simple beaded choker. She wasn't tall. Slender, elegant, and wary, she gazed at us with dark eyes and a thin frown.

"You came," she said.

"I said I would. Ben, this is Anastasia. This is Ben O'Farrell, my husband."

She studied him; he tensed.

"Hi," he said flatly.

"It's good to finally meet you. Kitty speaks well of you."

He gave me a wry glance, and I managed to look innocent. "We need to talk," I said. "Roman's wolves attacked us."

"Yes, I know. You're covered in dried blood." She brushed the collar of my shirt, and I managed not to flinch away from her. I wouldn't meet her gaze—that hypnotic vampire gaze. "We should talk in private. Would you like to call your friend over?"

I'd been about to gloat that Anastasia hadn't known Cormac was there, standing watch. But of course she'd known about him—she could sense his beating heart and warm blood.

Without being called, Cormac appeared from around the last row of shelves. He was tall, lean, a stereotypical tough guy in jeans. I couldn't guess what Anastasia saw when she looked at him. After all our history together, I just saw Cormac.

He held his left hand at his side, closed around some small object. An amulet, probably. Maybe even a cross—defense against vampires. He hadn't done that sort of thing before going to prison. He'd depended on brute force and firearms, before. Whatever amulet he held belonged to Amelia, really.

"And who is this?" Anastasia asked.

"Cormac Bennett. He's a friend." She must have noticed that he held something, maybe even suspected that he was a hunter with experience killing vampires. If she didn't, I wasn't going to volunteer the information.

Anastasia waited a moment, but Cormac didn't say anything. I didn't expect him to. He'd staked more vampires than he'd conversed with.

Finally, Anastasia nodded. "You have your own entourage, I see. The tables are turned this time."

When I first met Anastasia, she was flanked by a young vampire protégé and her very handsome human servant. They were both dead now. I certainly hoped the tables weren't turned. Not like that.

I masked my discomfort with a smile and an offhand shrug. "Yup. My own little wolf pack. I guess I expected you to have a friend or two along for this."

"No," she said. "Not anymore. From now on I think it's best if I have only myself to look after. Why don't we step inside?" She gestured through the doorway to what looked like an adjoining warehouse.

"Is there another way out of there?" Ben asked.

"Of course," she said, arcing an offended brow as she led us inside.

Cormac took one last glance behind him before closing the door.

This was a good-size room, obviously storage for the import shop, but lots of cardboard boxes and wooden crates made the place feel cramped. Dim lighting didn't help. Ben and Cormac were looking around, marking the lay of the land, the exit marked by a red light across the room.

"Do you own this place?" I said, gesturing around. The stuff showed a clash of cultures—rolls of an American brand of toilet paper stacked on top of cardboard boxes labeled in Chinese holding who-knew-what, exotic paper lanterns resting on shelves that also held mundane cleaning supplies, with mops and brooms propped in the corner. "Is that why we're meeting here?"

"I'm calling in favors," she said. "I used to have a lot of contacts here. Turns out I still have a few. We'll be safe. Now, tell me what happened."

"Ben and I were attacked. Werewolves. I tried to call you after it happened, but you didn't answer."

"You appear to have handled them without any trouble," she said. Her expression didn't change—I was looking for a show of surprise, of fear. That I didn't see any reaction didn't mean anything. I realized I'd have felt better if she'd found a new protégé or human servant. Anastasia by herself wasn't worried about protecting anyone.

"That, or we got lucky." I glanced at Cormac, then looked away. Anastasia caught the gesture.

She considered a moment, then said, "We can assume that Roman knows you're here now."

"Does that change anything?"

"No. We're still ahead of him. Let him think we're stronger than we are."

I looked around. "Even though it's just the four of us?" The four of us were pretty badass, but still.

"No. There's one more." Her twitch of a smile chilled me. "Kitty, what I'd really like for you and your pack to do is stay on the streets and serve as a distraction. Roman knows you're here—we can use that. It will give me more time to find the pearl."

Next to me, Ben bristled. I stared. "Cannon fodder. That's why you called me here, so you could throw me in Roman's path while you get away."

"I wouldn't have suggested it if I didn't think you were capable," she said.

I huffed. "There's a saying: you don't have to run faster than the bear, you just have to run faster than the other guy."

She crossed her arms and glared, her dark eyes shining. "If you want to help me—"

"I can't help you if you send me away."

Vampires didn't breathe—they no longer needed oxygen to survive. So when Anastasia sighed, it was on purpose, and a mark of her frustration. "As much as I would like to end Roman's existence, and will if I ever have the opportunity, the pearl is more important. Keeping it away from him is my priority."

"A pearl?" Ben said. "This is all about a piece of jewelry?"

Anastasia surveyed and disregarded him with a glance, which made me want to get in her face even more. How dare she diss my guy. An older vampire, Anastasia wasn't used to werewolves talking back. I'd seen her get pissed off, and I wondered how far I'd have to push her before she got pissed off at me. Wasn't going to find out this time. I eased Wolf back and stayed civil. "Anastasia, I want to know what we're fighting for here. Tell me about this pearl."

"The Dragon's Pearl," she said. "It's an artifact of great age and power."

I wrinkled my nose. "What's it do?"

Cormac, who'd been lurking and nigh unto invisible, stepped forward and said, "It's a bottomless container. The stories say you put it in a jar full of rice, the jar will produce an endless amount of rice. Or gold. The artifact itself was said to be a gem or a pearl, carried by divine dragons. But more likely it was a charm created by a human magician, probably as an imperial gift or status symbol." On second thought, it was Amelia who said all that, but Anastasia didn't have to know that.

"How do you know that?" Anastasia asked. Her gaze was narrowed, suspicious.

"I've been around," he said. "Picked up a few things." There. That was Cormac talking.

"Yes," she said, skeptical. "Clearly."

"Was it made by dragons or magicians? Is that important?" I said.

"It was created by a magician," Anastasia said. "There's no such thing as dragons."

I raised an eyebrow at her. I never knew anymore what was going to turn out to be real and what wasn't. Being a werewolf tended to give one an open mind. Or made one totally confused. "So dragons aren't real but this thing that could possibly grant someone untold riches is?"

"Roman doesn't need the money, though I'm sure he'll take it," she said. "He's going to use it to try and replicate a spell—a magical copy machine, if you like."

I looked at Cormac. "Would that even work?"

"Don't know," he said, studying Anastasia with interest.

Anastasia's tone was serious, her expression grave. Even more grave, rather. "Roman's followers wear a talisman. A coin that marks them—to Roman, and to each other. There's a binding spell attached to the coins."

The walls suddenly felt very close, and the room suddenly got very hot. "A coin from ancient Rome?" I asked. "On a leather cord?"

"Yes," she said, surprised, suspicious. Cormac and Ben were looking at me with startled expressions.

To think I'd wanted to write it off as coincidence.

I'd put the coin I took from the vampire in Kansas into my pocket because I'd wanted to show it to her, which turned out to be a pretty good call. I drew it out and offered it to her.

Her jaw tightened as she stared at it. "Where did you get this?" she said, with as much shock and emotion as she'd yet displayed.

"From a starving vampire in Dodge City."

"Dodge City? Don't tell me you found the vampire den that Wyatt Earp burned?"

"Oh my God, you know about that? Should I have called you first?"

"I wasn't there, I only heard rumors." Wearing a faint, twisted smile, she shook her head. "He uses those to mark his followers. He can make more himself, but the spell is time consuming and Roman coins in good condition aren't as plentiful as they used to be. He's going to try to use the Dragon's Pearl to replicate not just the coin, but the spell attached to them."

"He's expanding his army," I said. "Exponentially."

Cormac said, "Kitty, if that thing is bound to him, that means Roman knew you were here before that wolf pack found us. He tracked you with that."

I said, "We have to get rid of this."

"Will defacing the coin work?" Cormac asked.

"The vampire who wore it is destroyed?" Anastasia asked.

"Yeah," I said.

"Then it should."

"I'll need a hammer," Cormac said.

Anastasia went up the stairs and called in Chinese to the woman at the counter. After a moment, she returned, carrying a hefty sledgehammer, which she gave to Cormac. He lay the coin on the concrete floor, raised the hammer over his head, and brought it down with a heavy crack, then a second, and a third. The thing sparked under the blows, bouncing. When Cormac moved aside, I picked up the coin—flattened, now. All the markings had been mashed, erased. It almost seemed a shame. I held it up for Anastasia to see, and she nodded.

"That should do it," Cormac said.

I held it away from me, looking at it askance. It probably belonged in the nearest trash can, but I shoved it into my pocket. I'd deal with it later.

Anastasia started for the exit in the back of the room. "We have to meet the one who will take us to the pearl."

Ben, Cormac, and I regarded each other in a silent conference. Was it too crazy? Too dangerous? Or fascinating enough to make it all worthwhile? Cormac gave a curt nod—he was game. I imagined that Amelia's curiosity played a part in his willingness to continue. Ben's lips were pursed. He wasn't happy, but he wasn't going to argue. His back was straight, his stance confident—he'd follow whatever decision I made.

I wanted to see this Dragon's Pearl. With the two men following, I joined Anastasia, who waited by the open door. We went through it to another set of stairs.

Chapter 7

WE FOLLOWED THE stairs up to a doorway, wood with rusted hinges, that opened into a narrow alley between tall brick buildings. Lights shone through shaded windows, the sound of a TV carried. This should have been a mundane scene, evening in a city neighborhood, but the voices were in Chinese and I felt a sense of incongruity, as if I had entered another country, another world. Pagoda rooftops across the street gave the skyline a foreign air.

Leaving the alley, we walked for a time, rounding a couple of corners. The streets were arranged on a grid; even so, I didn't know whether I'd be able to find my way back. The place seemed narrow and mazelike. I stayed close to Anastasia. Ben and Cormac trailed, keeping watch behind us. My nose worked overtime, taking in scents. At one point, we must have passed a restaurant—the air became warm, heavy with the odors of spices, vegetables, and cooking meat. It tickled my nose, then my stomach. We continued on and the smell faded.

Finally, we turned down a small, quiet street and stopped before a door—the back of a shop, maybe. A handwritten sign, laminated and taped to the door, announced the name of a shop and its hours in both English and Chinese: Great Wall Video. This wasn't what I was expecting of Anastasia's secret contact. We should have been meeting someplace truly clandestine and mysterious. Gambling parlor, opium den . . .

Anastasia knocked, and a moment later a young woman opened the door. She was in her midtwenties, Asian features, dark eyes, pink plastic-rimmed glasses. Her short dark hair was dyed in magenta streaks. She wore a black baby-doll T-shirt, faded jeans, and big black shit-kicking boots. Techno music played in the shop behind her. The back room walls were covered with movie posters.

Her arms were braced across the doorway, and she wore a serious frown. "Yeah?"

"May we come in?" Anastasia said in her most suave, amenable voice.

"Why? Who are you?" She glanced over Anastasia's shoulder to the rest of us, who were watchful and bristling.

"My name is Anastasia. I need to speak with you."

"Why not come to the front like everyone else?"

"Because I need to speak with you quietly, Grace Chen."

The woman's eyes widened. Her lips pressed together, as if determined not to ask the next obvious question—she clearly didn't know Anastasia, so how did the vampire know her?

"I can't let you in. Tell me what you want right here," Grace Chen said, nodding at the threshold.

Anastasia said something in a language I presumed was Chinese and handed over a rolled slip of heavy paper that she'd drawn from her trouser pocket. Still glaring, the woman unrolled it and studied the text written on it for a long moment.

In the alley, I fidgeted, feeling cornered. I kept looking one direction and the other, but the far corners of the street were hidden in shadows. Ben was right there with me, and brushing his arm only comforted me a little. Cormac didn't seem bothered.

Chen rolled up the slip of paper and pointed it at Anastasia. "Where did you get this?"

"From the man who wrote it."

"This is five hundred years old," she said, and I gaped.

"Yes."

With a sigh, the woman stepped aside. "Fine. Come in."

We followed Anastasia inside as Chen looked us over. The back room was tiny, barely managing to hold a workroom sink and cleaning supplies in one corner, and a few rows of shelves stuffed with cardboard boxes and dusty merchandise. Visible through the back doorway, the front of the store—a video rental place specializing in imports—wasn't much bigger than the back room. Narrow, dim, closetlike, the place was crammed as if it had been collecting items for decades. Shelves, racks, and piles of DVDs and CDs pressed together. You could analyze the accumulation; discover the layers of Bruce Lee under the Chow Yun-Fat movies. On the dark walls were more posters for Chinese movies—some of them recognizable, films like *Titanic* and *Spider-Man* with the titles and credits listed in Chinese. Something epic, full of costumes and kung-fu moves, played on a tiny, twelve-inch TV screen shelved in the corner behind the counter.

Since Anastasia didn't seem to be paying any attention to us, I introduced myself. "Hi, I'm Kitty. These are my friends, Ben and Cormac." Ben smiled thinly; Cormac didn't seem to be paying attention, studying his surroundings instead.

"Grace," she said. "What's your deal?"

I glanced at Anastasia. "I'm not sure I exactly know."

"Kitty, you and the others can keep a lookout," Anastasia said.

"I guess we're the hired muscle," I said, donning a wry grin. "I'd actually rather stay and watch. Five hundred years old you said?"

Anastasia set her jaw and refused to be baited, but Grace seemed intrigued, as if annoying the vampire gave me a point in my favor. Grace offered me the scroll.

It didn't seem like five-hundred-year-old paper. It should have been dusty, crumbling at the least touch, but it had been very well preserved and felt smooth and strong. Which meant, if it really was that old, it had to be magic. A column of Chinese characters was inked on it. Cormac stepped over, and I offered it to him. He ran a finger over the surface, then shook his head.

"I don't know," he said, handing it back to Grace.

"What would you expect to know about this?" Anastasia said.

He hitched his thumbs on the pockets of his jacket and looked away, smiling wryly. I knew what people saw when they looked at Cormac: tough guy, man of few words, maybe not too bright. He cultivated the image.

Anastasia said to Grace, "You have the Dragon's Pearl, yes?"

"If you get the Dragon's Pearl, what are you going to do with it?" Grace answered.

"*If* I get it? Does that promise mean nothing to you?"

"I have to ask, it's part of the deal," she said.

Combat sound effects echoed from the TV at the front of the store.

"I don't want it for myself," Anastasia said. "I want to protect it. A very dark power is looking for it."

"I thought I was protecting it."

"This is bigger than you are."

Grace laughed. "That's what you say to someone you want to help you?"

I stepped in. "It's a vampire thing. They have this innate sense of superiority. Just ignore it."

"Vampire?" Grace said, skeptical. "You don't look dead."

"I'm not *jiang shi*," Anastasia said with forced patience. "I'm much more than an animated corpse."

I had to admire Grace for seeming confused rather than frightened. As if five-hundred-year-old messages showed up on her doorstep all the time. "So we're talking *Dracula* here?"

"You've been watching too many movies," Anastasia said. "But yes. And I'll get what I came for."

Looking tough with her punk hair and punk glasses, Grace stood with her arms crossed. She was solid as a wall, and not afraid of the vampire.

"Anastasia," I said. "You need to stop acting like everyone's a bad guy. We're all on the same side here."

"I thought hired muscle wasn't supposed to talk much," Grace said.

"They aren't," Anastasia said stiffly.

"Hey, you knew what you were getting when you asked me for help," I said. Love me, love my big fat mouth.

Anastasia took a settling breath. "Grace Chen, I need to know that the pearl is safe. I need your help."

She gave a curt nod. "The pearl's not here. I'll have to take you to it. Wait here while I close up the store."

Anastasia's lips pressed together as if she held back a retort. But all she said was, "Thank you."

Grace went to the front. I followed, after glancing at Ben and catching his eye. Nodding, he stayed behind, pacing a couple of steps back and forth.

I could have browsed in the store for an hour, picking through the crowded bargain CD bin, ogling DVD

packages stacked two deep along the wall. My gaze
skimmed the posters and signs—it was sensory over-
load, especially not being able to read the language that
three quarters of everything was written in. Grace was at
the front door, locking up. I was about to say something
friendly and ice-breaking, but she beat me to it.

Glancing at me over her shoulder, she said, "Your
friend there, the quiet one." She nodded toward the back
room. "You know he's got two spirits?"

"Really?" I blinked, not entirely surprised but fascinated all the same. "What does that even look like?"

"It's weird. Everybody's got their energy and it usually
tells me something about the person. Like you and
him"—she pointed at Ben—"are wild, lots of animal in
you. So you're what, werewolves? Her—she's dark. Stuck,
in a way. She's got energy, but it's frozen. Strange to look
at. But him—he's like yin and yang, but there's no har-
mony to it."

"Yin and yang, that's like male and female, right?"

"There's a lot more to it than that. You know what's
going on with him?"

"It's not really my story to tell," I said.

"I'm not sure I have the nerve to ask him myself," she
said, moving to the counter where she locked the drawer
on an old-fashioned cash register. There was a safe under
the counter, and she locked that, too.

"He has that effect on people," I said. "What's your
story?"

"What's there to tell? One of my ancestors made that chick a promise and I have to make good on it."

"But you're, what: Magician? Psychic?"

"I don't even know what you'd call it. But yeah, something like that. So what about you? You really working for her? Is that how it usually happens, werewolves working for vampires?"

"I don't know how it normally works," I said. "I thought I was doing her a favor, but she doesn't much act like that's how it's working. I think you threw her off her stride as well. She's used to people being a little more intimidated."

"Vampires aren't the scariest thing out there." She pulled a green canvas courier bag over her shoulder, across her chest, and went to the back room, turning off the lights as she reached the doorway. I didn't have a chance to ask her what *was* the scariest thing out there.

"Ready?" Grace said to the others.

"As long as it doesn't take all night," Anastasia said, a wry arc to her brow.

We set off down the alley in the opposite direction we'd come from. Full night now, the city seemed strange, foreboding. Skyscrapers beyond the edges of Chinatown suggested forest outside this island of a neighborhood. The sky was overcast, stars and moon invisible, but city lights gave the air a yellowish glow. The narrow streets, the fire escapes, the dark brick buildings made me claustrophobic. This was not our territory, and those enemy wolves were still out there. We had to keep moving.

"How far is it?" Anastasia asked after we'd rounded our fifth corner.

"It's a ways yet," Grace said.

"We could drive," Ben said.

She shook her head. "No, we have to go on foot."

That sounded ominous.

Ben, Cormac, and I walked like soldiers in a hostile jungle, pacing softly, hyper aware, looking everywhere. My back tingled, as if my Wolf's fur was standing on end. If Anastasia had any qualms, she masked them, walking with her usual poise. She would hear the heartbeat of anyone approaching. Anyone mortal, anyway. Heck, why should she worry? If we were attacked she'd just throw us in the way while she continued on her quest.

Finally we turned into another narrow alley. This one had clothes left drying on one of the fire escapes, and further on a doorway was framed by a dozen red paper lanterns. The ordinary and exotic bumping up against each other again. The door Grace stopped at felt particularly old, made of wood, planed smooth. The handle had an old-fashioned keyhole below it, the kind with a circle on top of a tall triangle. Grace had the key for it.

She turned the key, the lock clunked over, and the door slipped open. Dust puffed into the gap. I smelled age—old wood, damp earth, and cold stone. The back of my neck prickled.

From her bag, Grace pulled a small, brass candle lantern—square, with scratched glass windows—and a lighter to light the candle inside. The soft, yellow glow it cast seemed weak against the darkness around us.

"Why not just bring a flashlight?" Ben said.

"For the same reason we didn't drive," Grace answered. She pushed the door wide.

I wasn't psychic, but an ominous sense of wrongness pressed at me. I touched Ben; his hand reached for mine and grabbed hold.

"It's in here?" Anastasia said and walked through the door, undaunted by the lack of light.

Squinting against the candlelight, my own vision was adjusting—the door opened into a long, brick-lined hallway. The vampire's dark form was already invisible.

Grace sighed, as if she dreaded following. We all hesitated. This felt like walking into the maw of some leviathan.

"What kind of magic is this?" Cormac asked.

"Which one of your souls is asking?" she said.

Ben looked sharply at her, then me. "How does she know about that?" I squeezed his hand, quieting him.

Cormac pursed his lips. "It's not important. I was just curious."

"We've all got our crazy, huh?" she said, smirking at him. "Me, I don't know where the magic comes from. My grandma taught me. She came over from China right after World War II. I've got a brother and sister, but she picked me to teach, and it didn't matter how much I argued, I knew she was right. Just like she was right about leaving China, because I'm not sure she or the pearl or anything she knew would have survived the Cultural Revolution. When the vampire handed me that slip of paper, I just knew. I don't know what kinds of magic you're used to. This is just my family's magic and it's been around for a long time."

"The Chinese practice ancestor worship," Cormac said. But I was pretty sure it was Amelia this time. Her words, her phrasing.

"No—we honor our ancestors. That's different. Just who the hell are you?"

Cormac nodded into the darkness. "What's in there?"

Glaring at him, Grace said, "This thing she wants, you can't just put it in a safe or a bank deposit box. So you make a door to someplace else. That's what this is."

"That's not encouraging," I said.

"At least we probably won't get attacked by mercenary werewolves here," Ben said.

Grace looked at us. "She wasn't kidding. There really is someone after the pearl."

"Yeah," I said.

"Night's not getting any younger," Cormac said, and walked through the doorway.

The rest of us finally followed, and Grace closed the

door behind us. On the back side of the door hung a length of paper showing several Chinese characters painted in broad ink strokes.

"What's it say?" I asked.

"It's a blessing," Grace said. "To protect whoever passes through the doorway."

"'Abandon every hope, ye that enter . . .'" Ben murmured. I elbowed him.

I couldn't see much, even with a werewolf's eyes, so I tried to scent danger. But I didn't know what I was smelling for. The air here didn't smell exactly wrong. But it didn't smell quite right. Decades of incense saturated the brick walls. The place was still, but it didn't seem empty.

A set of wooden stairs, worn shiny by years of traffic, led down. Anastasia waited about ten steps along.

"You decided to join me?" she said. Her face emerged, illuminated by Grace's candle, pale and shadowed.

"We have to keep moving," Grace said. "Come on."

"How far is it?" Anastasia said, letting the young woman into the lead.

"It's still a ways." Grace went on, holding up her lantern, a sphere of light.

Ben, Cormac, and I, the pack of three, stuck together behind the others. About twenty steps further, the stairs finally reached a packed dirt floor.

Ben said to Cormac in a low voice, "When she said 'a door to someplace else,' what exactly did she mean?"

"Like Odysseus Grant's box," I said. Odysseus Grant

was a Las Vegas stage magician. Except that he was also really a magician, and he had a box of vanishing that was actually a doorway. I'd caught a glimpse of where it led to—a dank, musty swamp full of strange smells and things that slithered. I had no interest in exploring that place further.

"That's what I was afraid of," Ben muttered.

This wasn't that place, but the principle seemed the same, which was enough to make me nervous. I felt eyes staring at me, but couldn't guess from where.

I had to fill the silence. "Grace, these tunnels— I thought they were just an urban legend."

Ahead, her voice muffled by the brick walls surrounding us, she said, "It's just that not many people know how to find them."

We came to an intersection. Grace turned left, and we followed. Then came another set of stairs down, only four steps this time, and another intersection. We turned right. I wondered if I ought to be leaving bread crumbs.

Grace stopped at another wooden doorway, gray and weathered even though by all appearances it had always been indoors. This door had another scroll nailed to it, a yellowed length of paper with more Chinese characters painted in a column. Another blessing for protection? Or a warning? Grace set the lantern on the floor, took another key out of her courier bag, and unlocked the lock.

Pushing the door open, she held the lantern up and looked inside. This room was mostly a closet, too small for us all to crowd in after her. Looking over her shoulder,

I saw an old-fashioned iron safe, two feet on each side, with a combination lock and a big steel handle, sitting against the far wall. It seemed awfully mundane after all the talk of magic.

Anastasia was looking over her other shoulder, tapping her hand against her thigh.

Grace put the lantern on the safe and worked the combination. The air was still—nobody even breathed for several heartbeats.

I spun to face a noise—I'd heard something pattering in the darkness, I'd have sworn it. "What was that?"

"Nothing," Grace said, not looking away from the safe.

"Nothing? Nothing what?"

"Stray spirits. Nothing."

The safe's door creaked open.

"Crap," Grace said, peering into the safe over her glasses.

"What?" Anastasia said. "What is it?"

"It's not here."

"What do you mean it's not here?"

"I mean it's supposed to be here, and it's not here." Grace turned on Anastasia and glared.

"Then where is it?" The vampire's voice was quiet, cold, and her arms hung loose at her sides, her hands open and ready.

"I don't know," Grace said, shrugging wide.

Anastasia closed her eyes and looked up, as if beseeching a higher power. "Then it's too late," she whispered.

"Now wait a minute," I said. "It doesn't look like the

safe was broken into. Can we figure out what happened? Track it somehow? Did anyone else know this was here and know the combination?"

"I didn't think so," Grace said. "But I don't know that for sure. If someone knew what to look for they might have been able to find it."

"But you know what this is—you ought to be able to track it, right?"

She winced. "I don't know."

"Cormac?" I asked.

"I have some tracking spells, but I'm not the one who knows what to look for," he said, looking down the hallway. He and Ben were keeping watch in both directions.

Ben had been pacing, a few steps in each direction. Then he stopped, his head cocked to listen, his nose flaring to take in scent. He smelled wolfish. I focused on what had caught his attention. A sound echoed ahead, at the end of the corridor and around the next corner. Trying to make the noise out, I crept forward. The sound was uneven, high pitched, alive and upset—

It was a crying baby, sounding neglected at the very least, but more likely it was hurt.

I ran.

"Kitty, wait!" Anastasia and Grace both called. They took off after me.

I charged around the corner. A faint light came through an open doorway. Another small room, lit by an old-fashioned oil lamp sitting on a box in the corner. This might have been a storage closet for yet another shop, this one cluttered with more boxes and shelves, buckets and brooms. I paused at the doorway, letting my nose take in a picture of what lay before me. A spicy, musty scent filled the space; I'd never smelled anything like it. It didn't smell at all like a baby.

There, on the floor in the corner, was a bamboo cage as tall as my hip. Inside was a foxlike creature with thick ruddy fur, a narrow snout, and a mouth open to reveal needle-sharp teeth. I would have called it a fox, except it had a thick bouquet of tails flickering off its backside. Disconcertingly, it was making the crying noise, as if it had swallowed a baby whole and alive.

I approached cautiously, trying to reconcile the contradictions of sight, sound, and scent before me. The creature was trapped, anxious, circling in the cage, pressing against the bars. The cage was sturdy; the bars didn't budge. The creature looked as if it barked, a lost puppy drawing attention to itself. But the sounds that emerged were those all-too-human cries. The tails, thick and covered with fur, slapped against the bamboo bars.

When the creature saw me, it stopped moving to stare up at me with amber eyes, large and shining. Wrinkling its nose, it let out a couple of warning yips.

"What is that thing?" Ben said. The others had stopped at the doorway.

"I've heard of this," I said. It was the multiple tails—I

couldn't count them all, because the creature kept flicking them, agitated. But there were a lot. "In Japanese folklore, there are these fox spirits, *kitsune*. The more tails they have the more powerful—"

"Kitty, get away from it!" Anastasia said. The vampire lunged for me, grabbing my arm with both hands and shoving me back until we were both pressed against the far wall. Her speed and force knocked the wind from me. She was so easy to underestimate physically, with her slim, small frame, designer clothes, and fragile features. My arm hurt where she held me.

With a short growl, I yanked away. "What is your problem?"

Ben and Cormac braced in the middle of defensive actions, pausing in the moment of a breath between realizing that something was wrong and moving to attack. She had moved too quickly for them, and they seemed stunned to realize it. Cormac held a long, narrow length of sharpened wood in one hand, tucked away.

Grace had slipped into the room and stood, lantern raised, staring at the creature in the cage. "The *kitsune* is Japanese," Grace said. "You're in Chinatown. This is completely different."

Anastasia pressed herself against the wall, arms spread, as if she could fall through it. All elegance vanished, her eyes wide, she stared at the thing in the cage with a slack-faced intensity.

"What is it?" I said, backing away from her. If she had

an all-out panic attack I didn't want to be anywhere near her.

"The *huli jing*. Nine-tailed fox," she said.

Well, that answered that question.

The creature, the nine-tailed fox, sat on its haunches, tails fanned behind it, looked us over, and yawned, showing off its mouthful of teeth.

"And?" I said.

"It lures people in with the sound of crying, then devours them."

Ben was scratching his head, skeptical. "That's actually pretty clever."

I said, "However scary it is, it's in a cage. What's the problem?"

"It's also a companion of the gods," Anastasia said, with the devoted certainty of a true believer. "So who caged it?"

The answer, of course: something even scarier than the carnivorous nine-tailed fox. And the gods.

"What, whoa. Gods? What?" I said.

"The gods are under assault," she said, still staring at the thing, her eyes wide and glassy.

"I thought this was about Roman."

"It is!" she said.

I couldn't come up with a snappy comeback to that.

"I think we should get out of here," Grace said.

The nine-tailed fox opened its mouth and wailed like a baby who'd been dropped. Then the wild, angry scent

of human sweat and animal fur washed into the room—
werewolves.

"Kitty—" Ben said, warning.

"Everybody get back," I ordered. The room didn't have
any other doors. No escape route. I lunged back to the
corridor with Ben and saw them. The three werewolves
who'd attacked us earlier, and this time two of them had
shifted to wolf form, flanking their leader—the one in the
T-shirt, tall and muscular, toned rather than bulked, suggesting powerful agility. But I already knew that about him.

They approached us down the corridor, blocking our
only way out.

Chapter 8

I GOT OUT in front with Ben, who held his gun in hand, ready to fire. He could take out one, maybe two of them before they attacked. I'd be ready to follow up. Not taking a chance this time, he pulled the trigger—and nothing happened. He squeezed it again, and again. "Jammed," he muttered, and threw the thing away, growling.

It wasn't the gun, I thought. It was the tunnels. No flashlights, no gun, probably no cell phones. At least I couldn't mess up his aim this time.

The lead werewolf smiled.

"You have a plan?" Ben said. His hands flexed, his shoulders bunched. He met the man's stare across the few paces separating us. Way too few paces. I glared at the wolves, challenging, not backing down. They were big, two hundred pounds—bulky, lupine versions of their human forms and even more threatening. Their teeth were bared, their ears pinned back.

"Keep them away from Cormac and Grace," I said. Anastasia could damn well take care of herself.

"Generic. Flexible. I like it," he said, with a little more snark than the situation called for.

"Okay then."

Anastasia shouldered past me, upsetting my balance so I rocked into Ben. "Hey!"

"They must have the pearl," Anastasia said. "They know where Roman is."

I tried to growl at her while not taking my stare off the wolves. "Anastasia—protect them." I pointed at the two humans behind us.

Intent on staring down our enemy, she didn't seem concerned with them at all. If we had an escape route, I'd be happy letting her take care of the wolves all by herself. But we were cornered and someone had to look after the most vulnerable in the group. The three of us formed a wall across the passageway. On the plus side, the space was defensible—as long as we could keep the werewolves out of the room, Cormac and Grace would be safe. On the other hand, we had no space. No room to pace, to circle, to flank, to attack. They must have felt the same way, because they didn't attack, either. We were sizing each other up. I must have seemed insignificant to them. Ben wouldn't look like much more of a threat. But our experience counted for a lot.

The pack of werewolves had halted their approach. The human thug said, "All right. Where is it?"

I blinked and cocked my head. "Where is what?"

"You know what I'm talking about. The safe is empty— what did you do with it?"

"We thought you had it," I said.

Ben glanced at me. "You don't have to tell them that."

"Well, I'm confused," I said. I pointed at them. "You guys don't have it?"

"We're not stupid. Hand it over and you can leave," the leader said. The two wolves stepped forward, their lips drawing back and noses wrinkling as they snarled.

Anastasia donned a regal pose, chin up, staring down at the peons around her. "Your Master must know he can't win," she said to our opponents.

The wolves' hackles were getting stiffer, the fur down their back standing straight up, and they weren't going to back off. "We just want what was in the safe."

"Yes, and we leave here alive, you said that," she said. "Or, if you'd rather, you can deliver a message to Roman for me—and I will allow you to leave here alive."

The guy actually took a step back, uncertainty tightening his features—a show of weakness that made my own Wolf perk up. *We can take him . . .*

But he shook himself and pulled back his lips, showing teeth. "Then you really don't have it. So there's no reason to keep you alive at all."

The wolves launched.

Ben and I sprang forward to meet them. Inside me, my Wolf snarled, her teeth bared and claws outstretched, ready to slash. My crooked fingers matched the impulse. I would keep myself together as long as I could, but I would shift if I had to, to win this fight. I was cornered, and that might be my only option.

Ben slammed into the wolf on the right, and they both tumbled to the floor. The wolf on the left, the one I was about to tackle, squealed and writhed in a sudden pain. I stumbled as I pulled up—I hadn't touched him yet.

Cormac yelled, "Kitty, the knife, it's silver! Use it!"

Sure enough, the wolf had four inches of slim wooden handle protruding from his shoulder. If the blade was silver, the wolf was finished. Cormac must have thrown it from behind me. I didn't want to think about what would have happened if he'd missed and gotten me instead. Despite all we'd been through and all the times he hadn't killed me, I still worried.

Whining with each breath, the wolf was twisted back on himself, trying to bite and claw out the knife. I rushed forward to pull it out and finish the job, and move onto the next one—but the leader beat me to it. He yanked the knife out and stayed crouched over his henchwolf, holding the weapon with a sure grip and a braced arm, defensive. I backed away.

The guy and the knife were still way too close to Ben and the other werewolf. Ben had blood on him, streaking from cuts on his arms. He was doing a good job keeping the wolf away from vital bits—the wolf attacked, and Ben kicked his belly, sending him tumbling away. The creature sprang right back, biting and slashing. Ben blocked with his arms, which took the brunt of the attack, but he couldn't keep this up forever.

The leader of the trio stayed by the fallen wolf, a hand

resting on his fur, trying to comfort the animal even as he held the knife ready. The wolf lay flat now, panting for breath, whining as the silver did its work, poisoning his blood. They might have been mercenaries, but they were still a pack.

The damned fox thing wailed again. A second later, a ball of ruddy fur rocketed over my head and slammed into the werewolf leader, using those needlelike teeth on his face. I looked over my shoulder—Grace stood by the now-open cage, a penknife in hand. She'd opened one side of it, cutting the twine that held the bamboo poles together. Lips pursed, she looked scared but determined.

The nine-tailed fox thrashed and yipped, biting at the werewolf leader's face. Blood spattered as the man screamed and batted at it, slashing with the knife, trying to shove it away. The fox wasn't interested in us or our fight. As soon as it had cleared the blockade of people in the corridor, it raced ahead and away, around the corner and out of sight.

Pain and anger pushed the leader over the edge—jagged flaps of skin hung loose from a bloody cheek where the fox had ripped into him. His eyes had turned golden, and he bared his teeth in a snarl. I could jump him while he was shifting—maybe distract him long enough for the rest of us to get away, or at least draw the other wolf away from Ben. But he still held that silver knife.

Anastasia stepped between us. Growling, the werewolf slashed at her—and she moved. I assumed she moved; it happened too quickly for me to see clearly. She was in front of me, took a step, and then she stood next to the werewolf, holding the knife while she twisted his wrist and wrenched his arm behind him hard enough to make the joints pop. Crying out, he fell against her, bending back to relieve the pressure. Calmly, she placed the knife across his throat.

At his leader's cry, the other wolf fell back, leaving Ben alone. In the pause that followed as we assessed, all of our breathing was audible as panicked, nervous gasps. All except Anastasia.

"Nobody move," she said softly, which seemed redundant.

I glanced at Ben, who had slumped against the wall, catching his breath, keeping us all in view. He was cut and bruised, but gave me a quick nod—he'd survive. The still-functioning wolf faced us, stiff-legged, as if not knowing whether to attack or run. He was watching his leader, who twitched like he wanted to move, but every time he did, Anastasia squeezed his arm or pressed the knife to his skin. I could feel Cormac behind me, looking over my shoulder. Grace was still far back in the room.

On the floor in the middle of our gathering, the wolf Cormac had injured had started to shift back to human. Bones melted and resolidified in their original forms; gray and tawny fur faded, thinned, and once again became skin, now marred with black streaks along the veins, radiating from the wound in his shoulder. The silver poisoning had killed him.

Anastasia leaned close to the ear of her captive. "I very much suggest you answer my questions now."

He managed to snarl without moving.

"Where is Roman?"

"I don't know," he said around growls huffing with every breath. His hands flexed, his body braced, tense. He was on the edge, ready to shift in panic despite the vampire's threats.

Behind me, Cormac watched. He had a second knife in hand, a slender, aerodynamic piece designed for throwing. Where did he get these things? His felony conviction kept him from carrying guns. Were knives okay then?

Grace peered out from around the doorway. The knife she'd used on the cage was a mini Leatherman-type tool on a keychain. It wouldn't do any good against werewolves, but at least it was something. Her other hand held the candle lantern, the light of which wavered as her hand shook.

I went to her, taking her hand. "You have to get out of here."

Anastasia watched as I led Grace to the wall and edged around the group. Nobody said anything, but they didn't look happy, either. Like I was disturbing the delicate, temporary peace by moving, introducing variables. I just wanted one less vulnerable party trapped in the room. I kept her behind me, until we were past the vampire and werewolves, until she had a way to escape.

Once we'd reached open corridor, I pushed her. "Get out of here, go!"

"But you can't—"

"I don't want you to get bitten. We can find you later."

Frowning, she studied me a moment. Then she turned and ran, the light of her candle bobbing along with her. The remaining wolf twitched, as if to chase her, but I planted myself in front of him and showed teeth. *Just try it,* my Wolf said to his. He drew back his lips but didn't move. The sound of Grace's footsteps retreated, then disappeared, and I felt better. Not a lot better, but better.

Now, the only light we had came from the lantern in the room. That, and a dim, phosphorescent glow seeping from the walls around us, as if it was growing there. My vision adjusted—the figures before me were still shadows, monsters writhing in the darkness. Behind me, Cormac snapped on a penlight, which flickered before burning out in a flash. He shook the device, but it stayed off.

The impasse with the werewolves still remained.

Anastasia purred at her victim, "Moving on, then. Can you tell me, does Roman know that I'm here?"

"Obviously he does, he sent these clowns," Ben said. The vampire glared at him, and he glared right back, wiping blood from his chin with the back of his hand and wincing.

I wanted to rush over, snuggle against him, and lick his face—an action that was perfectly natural to my Wolf, but felt odd in human skin. One of those things that made my divided self seem even more divided than usual. If we'd been alone I might have given into the impulse. But I had to stay here and keep the hallway blocked to make sure the wolf didn't decide to chase after Grace. I wished Ben knew what I was thinking.

Anastasia returned to her interrogation. "How much does Roman know?"

"I don't know."

"You must know something."

"Keep them busy. Get the thing from them if they have it. That's all." He rolled his eyes at me.

"Keep them busy because they're helping me?"

I glared at her. "Geez, this isn't all about you!"

"Stay out of this, Kitty."

"God, your name really is Kitty," the captive said, stifling a chuckle.

"Quiet," Anastasia breathed.

"You're already too late." He grimaced, lips drawn back, jaw rigid—a vicious snarl. He'd given up. All he had left was anger and rebellion. Lunging forward, he pressed himself toward the knife at his throat; she pulled it away before he could cut himself on it. No matter how much he thrashed, she was too strong. He couldn't break free. It was so incongruous—she looked so small, so elegant. Yet she could overpower a werewolf.

"Quiet!"

"You wanted me to talk! I'm talking." He snapped his teeth, saliva spattering from his mouth. His chin tipped up, and his face was breaking, jaws growing, eyes turning gold, ears narrowing—he was shifting to wolf, and he was laughing.

She dropped the knife and held onto him with both hands. Wrenching his arm back even more, she bared her own teeth, showing fangs, which she planted into the side of his neck, the softest part, where the artery pulsed. Her victim jerked once, but was helpless.

The wolf in front of me barked out a growl and leapt to save his leader. I dived to intercept him, and Ben lunged with me. Together, we tackled him.

We didn't even have to talk about it, and it seemed so natural, as if we stood side by side in the kitchen chopping vegetables for dinner. Throwing myself onto the animal's back, I wrapped my fingers in the fur, forcing him to the ground, while Ben grabbed the head and wrenched in the opposite direction. The wolf squealed and flinched, but with weight holding him in two different directions, he couldn't get the leverage to free himself. My Wolf thrilled, because we were hunting with our mate, as it should be.

The human body didn't have the right tools to kill with bare hands. Human hands could strangle and break, but they couldn't rip and tear like teeth and claws, which was the only way to kill properly, decisively. Spill the prey's blood, let it soak the ground around you. I willed my claws to grow, to gain the power to break skin, and the power surged through me. Skin split under my touch as Wolf's claws dug into my enemy's gut, and blood and warmth spilled out.

A crack sounded—the wolf's neck breaking, as Ben yanked his head even farther back. The animal fell still, but its heart still beat, its blood still flowed. My mate's sharp claws slashed across its neck, and more blood spilled. Next our teeth would become fangs and we would bury our faces in our enemy's corpse to feast.

Gasping for breath, I shoved away from the twitching body. We couldn't afford this, we didn't need this. We didn't dare turn Wolf, so far from home and with no safe place to run or sleep when we were done. With silver knives lying on the floor. Keep it together, keep it together—

Inside me, Wolf howled. Blood filled her nose and she wanted to *run*. No, no, no, I murmured over and over, hugging my knees to my chest, squeezing my eyes shut, focusing on my human body. Fingers, not claws. I needed my fingers.

"Ben!" I called.

He looked up from the open wound he was digging in the wolf's throat. His gaze was wild, his hazel eyes flecked with gold and amber. Blood streaked across his face.

"Stop, Ben," I said. He stared a challenge at me, and his lip curled, showing teeth.

Cormac's silver-inlaid knife lay on the floor where Anastasia had tossed it, within my reach. I grabbed it and stabbed it into the wolf's belly, then scrambled away. Just touching the handle made my hand itch.

Ben also shoved himself away from the knife, backing on all fours, until he crumpled, folding over and hugging himself. The groan he let out was human.

"Ben?" I crept toward him, hesitant, waiting for the groan to turn to a growl, for his arms to take on a sheen of fur and start to melt into a wolf's limbs. "Stay with me, Ben," I murmured.

Blood covered our hands. I wanted to hang onto him, but slipped. He hunched over, his back heaving as he tried to catch his breath, as he tried to hold onto himself. I took hold of his face. He was injured from his fight with the wolf, claw slashes crossing his cheek, and a dark bruise colored his left eye.

He clenched his arms, trying to hold on. And his body didn't break. He stayed human. I brushed my hand along his arm, smearing blood as I went. Human hands. I watched my own hands, making sure they stayed human. Finally, he turned his face to me, appearing exhausted but in control. I smiled weakly. If we'd been any closer to the full moon, we might not have been able to pull ourselves back.

I licked blood off his chin, moved up his cheek, bringing him back to himself, and back to me. Wolf to wolf, I spoke to him. He turned his face, and for a moment we shared breaths, which slowed as we calmed, and his arms closed around me—human arms with hands and fingers that clenched my shirt. I kissed him, and he sighed.

"Doing this twice in a day is too much," he said, his voice rough. "Are we okay?"

"I don't know."

I didn't want to look, but I did, in time to see Anastasia drop the bloodless corpse of the last werewolf. She stood and brushed off her clothing, arranging herself and regaining her poise. She hadn't spilled a drop of blood. Unlike Ben and me, who were swimming in it.

Cormac stood behind her, stake in hand, raised and ready to strike.

He could take care of himself. He knew to stay out of the way—but now he saw a threat. His whole life had been about taking care of threats.

She ducked and swung, planting an elbow in Cormac's gut and pivoting into the clear. Cormac's swing went over her shoulder and missed. Grabbing his arm and using it for leverage, she slammed him into the floor. The stake skittered away from him. She stepped her nice sharp heel on his chest—and he punched her knee, wrenching the joint the wrong way. Grunting, she fell, and Cormac scrambled to his feet.

"Stop it!" I shouted. "Get away from each other and just . . . just stop it!" My voice had dropped—it sounded like a growl, a lupine snarl.

They stopped. Anastasia looked at me, eyebrows arced,

lips pursed, as if she was amused that I would be giving orders. As usual, Cormac didn't reveal anything in his expression—a cold gaze and a calm bearing hid any emotion. I could never guess what he was thinking.

The hallway smelled like blood. I couldn't smell anything else. Not sweat, anxiety, incense, or anything. I paced, fast, back and forth across the hallway as if I could plunge through the walls to get some fresh air, to break free and run. I clenched my hands into fists, a growl stuck in my throat.

Ben put his hand around my ankle, and I stopped. He didn't grab, didn't force, didn't squeeze. Just held me with a firm grip, and the touch warmed me, anchored me. Reminded me that I wasn't alone. That we had to stay calm.

We had three dead bodies on the floor. Ben and I were covered with blood. It was congealing on my clothing and skin, getting sticky, itchy. I shivered inside my clothes, trying to better fit into my human skin. Sick of this place, I wanted to get my pack out of here. Ben stood and put his hand on my back, and I sighed, my muscles unclenching.

"Well," I said finally. "Are we finished here? Now that we've built the set for our own B-grade horror flick?" I glanced at Cormac, hoping for some clue about what he thought of all this. Of me and Ben almost losing it and digging into a dying wolf with our bare hands.

His gaze was downturned as he went to the body of the werewolf Anastasia had killed. With his second knife, he cut off a big scrap of the man's shirt and used it to retrieve the silver dagger from the now-human corpse that Ben and I had ravaged, with gaping wounds in its neck and belly. It was the man with the matted beard we'd seen earlier. The now frail-seeming body looked like an animal had been at it. He cleaned the knife, careful to scrape out all the cracks and seams where the blade joined the handle. Then he tossed the bloody cloth away. He didn't say a word. Didn't look at Ben and me.

It wasn't like he'd never seen us covered in blood before.

Anastasia's skin had taken on the warm, almost healthy sheen of the newly fed vampire. Quickly she crouched by her victim and searched, patting down his few pockets, feeling under his shirt for anything hidden. Nothing. Standing again, she hugged herself as if cold. "They must have already delivered it to him. It's lost, it's all lost. Roman's won."

It sure felt like it, but I couldn't believe it. We were alive, which was a point in our favor. Grace was safe, I assumed, which was another point. This wasn't over by a long shot.

I shook my head. "No. Something else is going on here. Maybe they locked up the nine-tails, but they don't have the pearl—they were still looking for it. Which means Roman doesn't have it. Someone else took it. There's a third party."

Ben chuckled. "That's the good news, isn't it?" He

hunted around the floor for the gun he'd tossed aside, found it shored up against the wall, and covered in blood. Picking it up with two fingers by the very end of the grip, he said, "I'm really getting tired of this. Why'd I bring this again?" Cormac tossed him another scrap of shirt, and he started wiping it down. The scene was looking increasingly ghoulish. We needed to get out of here.

"Do we need to clean up the bodies?" Cormac asked.

"No," Anastasia said. "The tunnels take care of themselves."

Now I really wanted to get out of here. "Who else wants this pearl?" I said to the vampire.

"Anyone who knows about it would want it. Any magician, wizard, any other vampires. The gods."

"Gods? Seriously? Let's not make this more complicated than it has to be. What's our next step then? Go looking for the pearl?"

"Take a shower?" Ben said. "Go home?"

"That gets my vote," Cormac said. "This isn't our fight."

Anastasia didn't say anything to that. I expected her to argue. She didn't, maybe because Cormac was right. But that wasn't how I felt. Roman was my enemy, too. Here or somewhere else, he'd come after me and mine again.

I tried to acquire some veneer of dignity despite the fact that I was still too close to turning Wolf for comfort. And that I was spattered with blood. Rounding my shoulders, I went the few steps down the hall to the closet with the safe. Both the room and the safe were still open.

I held myself still and began breathing softly, taking air through my nose, smelling the space and what had been here.

Mostly, I sensed what I expected: old stone and grime, a century's worth of salt air lingering, the cold steel of the safe, smoke and wax from Grace's candle. Werewolves, humans, and vampires. We'd been walking around on top of each other's scents, which blurred together. I heard a distant pattering, like raindrops or the footsteps of mice, always at the edge of hearing. Mysterious gazes, always at the edge of seeing. I listened for the sound of a crying baby, and didn't hear it. I hoped Grace was safe.

I knelt closer to the safe, putting my nose right up to the steel. A trace of Grace's human scent lingered on the handle and combination dial. I even stuck my head inside the safe and took a few deep breaths, hoping to catch a trace of the artifact itself. I only smelled more steel, more dust. If I'd had to guess what had been here, I'd have said it had always been empty. Scary magical items should smell like something, shouldn't they?

"Find anything?" Ben said.

I shook my head. "You want to try?"

I stepped aside and let him go through the same routine. After a moment of searching he muttered, "I don't even know what I'm looking for."

"Let me," Cormac said, moving toward us around the bodies. He carried the hurricane lamp and its golden halo of light from the storage room with him. We got out of the way and watched.

He took some kind of stone from his pocket, keeping it partially hidden in his hand. It had something magical to it, no doubt. Since his release from prison, he'd replaced his collection of guns with amulets and talismans.

If he was using magic, it meant Amelia was probably in charge now, which made me bristle. It didn't matter if Cormac seemed all right with the arrangement. I didn't like the idea of him being used.

He passed the amulet over the safe as if it were some kind of Geiger counter.

"What's he doing?" Anastasia asked, moving next to me.

"He's kind of a wizard, I guess," I said.

"Kind of?"

"It's hard to explain."

She glared unhappily.

Straightening, Cormac pocketed the stone amulet. "Something magical was there but it's gone now."

"I don't suppose it left a trail?" I asked. He shook his head.

"It's a trap," Anastasia said. "This has all been a trick, and I fell for it—"

"I'd just like to point out that we're not the ones lying dead on the floor," I said. "If this is a trap we're not the only ones who got stuck."

The silence drew on as we contemplated that unpleasant thought. Once again I started pacing, as if that would make the corridor larger, as if a way out would appear before my eyes. My shoes, coated with blood, started sticking to the floor. The stench of blood was making it hard for me to think.

"We need to get out of here," I said. "Find Grace and start over."

We moved forward, back the way we'd come until we reached the intersection.

"Left," Cormac said, before I could ask if anyone remembered which way we'd come.

"I knew that," I muttered.

We turned and went on, strung out in single file in the narrow hallway, which my imagination was making narrower, and darker. This section seemed to go on a lot longer than I remembered.

"Aren't there supposed to be stairs here?" I said. "I remember there being stairs."

"Did we take a wrong turn back there?" Ben said.

"It wasn't wrong," Cormac said.

"But there were definitely stairs."

Finally, we came to the next intersection. But this one didn't branch off at right angles as the others had. Instead, the hallway split in a Y. It may have been my imagination, but the stone seemed to give way to dank earth, as if the passage left the city and continued on in wild, underground tunnels. I smelled dirt and mulch coming from the way ahead.

I stated the obvious. "We haven't been here before."

"So we took a wrong turn," Ben said.

"This is much, much more than a wrong turn," Anastasia said, her voice muted and anxious. She stood outside our small circle of light and her features were shadowed.

I faced her. "Do you know something or is that just more doom and gloom?"

Cormac said, "It's that we can't get out of here without Grace leading us. She's got the key to the place. Until we find her, we're stuck."

Chapter 9

I BACKTRACKED, LETTING the others follow me as they would, until I came to that first intersection. Or what should have been that first intersection, the one that led to the closet and the storeroom where we found the nine-tailed fox. The light was almost nonexistent now, and I was seeing the place through wolfish eyes. Maybe that was why I didn't recognize it. I couldn't have taken another wrong turn. I heard the others come up behind me, stepping softly, breaths echoing against the stone. The light from Cormac's lantern pressed forward like a wall.

Crouching, I took in the smells. I caught the other werewolf pack, their maleness and foreignness; their ill intent in hunting us, all musky and sour, full of adrenaline. I took in our own smells: the chill of the vampire, Cormac's human warmth, the familiar scent of Ben. I thought I even caught a hint of Grace—a trace of what her store smelled like, retail scents of cardboard packaging and money overlaid with the smoke from her candle.

But when I tried to follow it, her trail vanished, as if she had simply taken off from the spot and flown away.

There should have been pools of freshly spilled blood, its odor wafting through the tunnels. I only smelled the drying blood smeared all over Ben and me.

I pressed my hands against the rough brick. It was hard not to feel as if the walls were closing in on me, or imagine unseen gazes of otherworldly spirits drawing closer, the skittering of movement growing louder. It was beginning to sound like laughter.

"What have you gotten us into?" I said to Anastasia. Growled, rather.

"You knew the risks," she said.

The risks being that *something* completely unexpected and bizarre would happen? Okay, then. " 'It's Roman, he's taking over the world,' you said. 'Okay, I'm on the way,' like I'm some kind of superhero. When am I going to learn?" I started marching, following the wall. It couldn't go on forever. "There's got to be a way out of here."

"Kitty," Ben called, and I stopped. That was all he had to say. Taking a breath, I calmed myself.

Anastasia sounded tired when she said, "I called you because I don't have anyone else to turn to. Not anymore." She was supposed to have her protégé and her servant, Gemma and Dorian. But she'd led them into a trap and gotten them killed.

She'd done the smart thing, bringing a guide here to make sure we had a way into and out of whatever magical cubbyhole this was. *I* was the one who'd chased Grace off—for her own good, of course. From a certain point of view this was my fault.

Pointing fingers wasn't going to get us out of here.

A few paces behind us, Cormac had set down the lantern and by its light was drawing on the floor with a piece of chalk. Along with the amulets and charms, he evidently carried chalk in his pockets now, too.

I crept closer for a better look; the white lines of the chalk drawing stood out in the semidarkness, almost as if they glowed.

"Stay back," he said, and I stopped. He had drawn a quick design, arrows and arcs, a couple of letters. It looked like scribbling.

"Will that help us find Grace?" I said.

"I don't much care about Grace. I'm just trying to find a way out of here."

"How long is this going to take?"

He ignored me and kept working. I started pacing because what else could I do? I looked back and forth down the corridor, wondering what was going to jump out at us. Ben was doing the same thing nearby. Our anxiety sparked across the space to each other, feeding each other. We were caged wolves.

"Kitty, calm down," Anastasia said.

"We're not safe here."

"We killed them. They're not coming back."

"But what else is down here? Another one of those

nine-tailed foxes? Or those guys could come back as zombie werewolves. What'll we do then?"

"I hadn't thought of zombie werewolves," Ben muttered.

"There's no such thing as zombie werewolves," Anastasia said, and if you couldn't believe an eight-hundred-year-old vampire about something like that, who could you believe?

"Says you," Cormac said. I stopped and looked.

He set one of his silver daggers in the middle of the chalk design, stood back, and waited. After a breath or two, it trembled, all on its own, metal scraping against concrete. Slowly it turned, like a compass needle. The dagger's tip passed one marking, then another. We gathered closer, watching to see where it rested—and if that would point to the way out. But it never rested. It rotated a full circle, wavered, reversed course and did the same in the opposite direction. Almost as if confused, it turned one way and the other, rattling harder, making more noise as it skittered on the hard floor. It seemed sentient, the way it searched and grew more erratic when it didn't find its goal.

Corman finally stepped on it, trapping it. "It's not working."

I paced again. Cormac picked up the knife, dusted it off, and scuffed out the chalk marking with his boot.

"Now what?" Anastasia said.

"This was supposed to be your party, why don't you come up with something?" Ben said.

"I just wanted the pearl. Chen was supposed to be here, the pearl was supposed to be here, I didn't count on any of *this*." She shook her head, squaring her shoulders and resettling her dignity. "We should wait for Chen. She'll return to find us."

"Not if she's smart." I stalked away from them, down the straightaway. "Even if we can't find the same door there's got to be another way out of here. We can't just sit still and be targets."

Ben and the others followed a few paces behind. I could sense them, the sound of their footsteps and the odor of their sweat, their anxiety. Anastasia had returned to her usual composure—cool, detached. I couldn't read her at all.

Ahead, the corridor branched. I stopped at the intersection and waited for the others to catch up. "Well?" I said. "Left or right?"

"We could toss a coin," Ben said.

"It hardly matters," Anastasia said.

"Left," Cormac said.

I glanced back at him. "Is this some kind of magical hunch?"

"Just a hunch," he said. "The regular kind."

"Why not right?"

"Turn right if you want to, doesn't make a difference to me," he said, expressionless as always. He held the lantern low in his hand. The light shadowed his face so it looked like a skull.

I kind of wanted to keep poking him until he got angry. Just out of curiosity, to see what he would do. Instead, I turned right and kept walking. When I glanced over my shoulder to see if the others followed, Ben smirked at me, the expression he used when he thought I was being irrational. But if it didn't matter, it didn't matter, right?

And how had I ended up in the lead?

These tunnels seemed to go on an awfully long time without turning, breaking, or revealing any features. We were under San Francisco, there ought to be underground cables, water pipes, sewer lines. As long as we'd been walking we should have been under the bay by now. I shouldn't have felt like I was in the stone dungeon of a medieval castle. I caught a faint whiff of incense. I tried to follow the trace of the scent, thinking it would lead us to a door, a room, anything but the maze of tunnels.

A break in the stone wall revealed a smooth plywood door. It didn't have a lock.

Like other doors we'd encountered, this one also had a sign on it, a vertical length of paper with Chinese characters.

"What's it say?" I said, looking back at Anastasia.

She studied it a moment. "It's a warning." As if she hadn't expected anything different.

I snorted a short laugh. Of *course* it was a warning.

It was a pocket door, the kind that slid sideways into the wall, but it seemed to be spring loaded, or stuck, because I couldn't get it open. I grabbed the fingerhold carved into one side and shook—it rattled in its frame as if jammed. Maybe I could wrench it loose.

After figuring out what I thought was the side that opened, I worked my fingers into the gap until I found the edge of the door. The door frame scraped my skin, but I also felt a sense of hope. I could do this, get it open, and get us all out of this place. Standing back and leaning over, I braced my legs and put my weight into pulling back on the door, shaking it hard every now and then to try to loosen it. When it budged a quarter of an inch, I grinned and pulled harder, until it jumped another six inches.

"Ha!" I announced in victory.

"Where's it go?" Ben asked.

"Dunno." I put my face to the opening; the hallway appeared to continue on in darkness. Ahead, a faint white light glowed. An emergency light in a room, maybe, or the exterior light over a doorway? A streetlight and freedom?

I jammed my shoulder into the opening to force it wide enough for me to slip through.

"Are you sure you should be doing that?" Ben asked, hovering. He put his hand on the wall next to me and peered over my head through the gap. "I can't see anything in there."

Exhaling, I flattened myself as much as I could, pushed against the door, and popped on through. I stumbled away from the gap.

"There, see?" I said. "No problem—"

The door slammed shut behind me.

"Kitty!" Ben shouted through the wood. He banged on it; the sound was muted.

This side didn't have any kind of indent to use as a handle. I pushed the door, rattled it, tried to get my fingers into the gap, but this time, the door didn't budge, didn't offer a centimeter of purchase.

"Kitty!"

"I'm okay, but I can't see how to open it."

The banging against the door became deeper, steadier. Ben was throwing his whole body against it; the vibrations pounded against my hands, which I'd been holding flat against the wood. When the door started to bow toward me, I backed away, expecting him to splinter through it at any moment.

I stumbled and fell before I realized that the floor behind me suddenly sloped downward. Even then I would have recovered, flailing a bit before regaining my balance, except that after a few feet of sloping, the floor dropped away entirely, and I fell into an open pit. I was too surprised to even scream.

Chapter 10

AFTER HITTING THE hard concrete bottom of the shaft, I lay on my back, blinking into darkness. My Wolf's vision had adjusted to the distant, pale light that still shone and I made out shapes, sensing the closeness of the walls, the stuffiness of the subterranean room. The tunnel was a faint, glowing circle above me. That had been a hell of a fall. My heart was racing, my breaths came in gasps, but even Wolf was shocked and quiet.

When I finally tried to sit up, stabbing pain slashed down my right hip and thigh. I groaned and lay back again. I hoped this didn't mean what I thought it meant—something was seriously broken. No matter how I tried to catch my breath, I couldn't seem to slow it or my heart rate down. Panicking, I let out a groan.

I waited for Ben's voice calling down to me. It didn't happen. I couldn't hear him banging on the door anymore, and I wondered if he managed to break through. I pulled my cell phone out of my pocket, thumbed it awake—and nothing happened. I'd just charged the thing that afternoon, but it was dead. Like Cormac's flashlight, like the gun.

The pain was spreading, a deep throb up and down my right side.

I'd been shot once, with a non-silver bullet. The pain from that had vanished surprisingly quickly. I'd been cut, clawed, mauled, and slashed more times than I could count in various werewolf battles—all surface wounds that had closed and healed in a matter of minutes, growing healthy pink scabs while I watched. This was different. This was deep, invisible, and it didn't fade.

I'd always wondered what happened when a werewolf broke a bone. I assumed the rapid healing still played a part, but I had no idea how long it would take or if it would even heal the way it was supposed to. I couldn't guess what exactly was broken, or what had shifted around inside. I was afraid to move.

Gritting my teeth, I let tears fall. I wanted my pack. I wanted my mate. "Ben!" I shouted, hands around my mouth, focusing my voice up the shaft. "Ben! Cormac!"

Nobody answered. Which meant they hadn't busted through the door, they weren't in the corridor, and they had no way of knowing what had happened to me. They had to know that something had happened when I stopped answering their calls, but as far as they could tell, I had just vanished. And as far as I could tell, they'd vanished.

Maybe they needed help as much as I did. What did I

do then? I had to find a way out of here on my own and get back to them.

I gave myself ten or fifteen minutes, though my sense of time was growing wonky. I felt like I'd been in this bizarre maze for hours and that dawn ought to be approaching. Maybe the time between when Grace had opened the door and now had only been an hour. Between the pervasive dark and my racing heart, I couldn't tell.

The pain lessened, but I didn't know if that meant the break was healing, or that I was succumbing to shock.

Happy thoughts . . .

I braced myself, held my breath, pushed up on my arms. And gasped as a new shock wave of pain hit me. After waiting for that to subside, I tried again, rolling to my good side, getting my left leg under me. Another stabbing pain racked my right leg, and I felt nauseated, and also like I was getting used to it. Just as long as it didn't get any worse than this, I'd do okay.

Trying to stand would certainly be interesting. But dammit, the leg had to start healing sometime. Carefully, I bent both legs, and was encouraged when the pain didn't spike. Even if it didn't improve. Reaching out, I found a wall and leaned against it. Keeping all my weight on the good leg, I stood. And didn't pass out.

I could see the wall in front of my face but not much else. Creeping forward, I leaned on the wall, shuffling, trying to use the right leg without moving it. It hurt, the whole thing throbbed, but I must have been getting used to it, because I managed to make some progress. Progress toward what, I couldn't tell.

This seemed to be a room made of brick, wide and round. I didn't encounter anything like a door, but at one point the wall gave way to a rudimentary staircase, wooden slats built into the brick on a rickety frame—it had no railing. But it did go up, toward the light and escape, I hoped.

I started climbing, which was harder than walking, but I kept my shoulder to the wall and took it one step at a time. Pondering why anyone would put a big hole in a corridor, have it drop into a room that seemed to be self-contained and serve no useful purpose, and then build a staircase that led right back to the original corridor, gave me something to focus on. It made me angry, since I was beginning to think I was the butt of someone's practical joke. I'd get to the top of the stairs, and Ben would be waiting for me, and Grace would be there to explain what was going on. Everything was going to be *just fine*.

Fighting through the pain left me flushed and sweating. Even if the break was healing and hurt less, I wouldn't be able to tell.

Finally, I reached up and touched the edge of the shaft back in the hallway. Just a few more steps brought the rest of me to the top. I slumped over and dragged myself away from the stairs, then lay gasping, whining with every breath like the hurt Wolf I was. My hands and face were scraped and sore from the climb. My hip and leg felt like someone had tried to rip them apart by slowly twisting them in opposite directions. Lying on my back, I looked around.

I wasn't in the hallway.

The room was dim and cramped, like Grace's video store, but bare. The floor was concrete, the walls painted off-white. I smelled ginseng and restaurant cooking, as if I was back on Grant Avenue in Chinatown. It almost seemed normal, except that I wasn't supposed to be here. I didn't think I had gotten so turned around. I'd kept the top of the shaft within sight the whole time. At least I thought I had. But I was somewhere else now. Ben and Cormac would never find me. I'd never find them. Maybe if I howled, Ben would hear me and come running.

I tried my cell phone again, and hallelujah it worked this time. This meant more than having my lifeline back—it meant I was out of the tunnels, out of the maze, and back in the real world. When I called Ben, though, he didn't answer. Because he was still in there somewhere. When the voice mail clicked on, I took a deep breath to try to keep my voice steady. "Ben, I need help. I'm hurt. I don't know where I am. I'll try to figure that out and call you back. I hope you're okay." I took another deep breath to keep from bursting into tears. Time to get moving and figure out where I was. I needed to get outside and find a street sign.

In the front half of the narrow room, opposite the pit I'd just climbed from, a light was shining from a bare bulb suspended from the low ceiling. There looked to be some kind of apartment here—a minimal kitchen, cupboards built against the wall, a wash basin, table and chairs, even a cot.

A man was sitting in a chair, leaning back, studying me with an amused grin on a youthful face.

I rushed to sit up, clamping down hard on the throbbing bursts still racking my hip. I managed to get both feet under me and lurched upright, sticking my arms out for balance. I swayed, but didn't fall over. So far so good.

The nearest door was on the other side of the guy in the chair. I wondered if I could inch around him and get away. That would have meant limping, which would have showed weakness. Wolf wanted to stand her ground and challenge him. I agreed with her this time.

"Are you okay?" he said.

I almost collapsed with relief, because he sounded so friendly, so concerned, so genuine. But Wolf held me steady. I stared at him, waiting, wondering if my leg would hold me if I had to run, if I had to attack him.

"Do you want to come over and sit down?" he said, gesturing back to the oasis of light. A second chair sat near the card table next to him. He was slender and had a controlled poise—he seemed relaxed, but his muscles were ready to move. I couldn't smell any kind of emotion off him. Just maleness—jeans and black T-shirt a couple of days old, a meal with ginger and soy sauce lingering. He had a shock of black hair, an easy smile. He carried what looked like a bag over his shoulder, the strap lying across his chest. It reminded me of Grace's bag.

"I'm fine," I said.

"You don't look okay," the guy said. "You're covered in blood."

"It isn't mine."

"I'm sorry if that doesn't make me feel any better." He said it lightly, almost laughing. He didn't sound worried, which made me nervous.

"Can you do me a favor and not call the cops?" Although I maybe should have called an ambulance. My leg was feeling better, I was sure it was. I could convince myself of that. But I didn't want to have to explain the blood to anyone in a uniform.

"I wasn't going to."

I still had the feeling the guy was laughing at me. "And why are you avoiding the police, then?"

He grinned. "You really want to ask that kind of question?"

Falling from a supernatural underworld into a criminal underworld seemed like an improvement, considering.

"Where is this?" I said. "Where am I?"

"You're safe," he said. "Trust me."

"I don't even know you." My voice came out rough, growly.

"I'm just trying to help. You're the one who fell into my monster trap."

"Wait, monster trap?"

"Yeah. You never know what's going to come crawling through some of these doors."

He said this with a complete lack of irony and humor. As if he expected monsters to invade as a matter of course, and was only mildly surprised to find a bedraggled blond woman in the pit instead. Or rather, in addition.

"Does that sort of thing happen a lot? Monsters crawling through the door, I mean," I said cautiously, testing to see if he was serious or speaking metaphorically. Metaphorical monsters, sure.

"Not too often. Not anything I can't handle, at least. But you're not a monster, right?"

I stared. How to answer that question? I should have brushed him off. Unfortunately, I wasn't thinking too straight. I blurted, "I'm a werewolf."

He pursed his lips thoughtfully. "Really?"

Was this guy on something? Whatever it was, could I have some? "Yeah."

"Then see, the trap works! You look like you're about to fall over—why don't you come over and sit down? I was about to make some soup—are you hungry?"

On the contrary, I still felt like I was on the verge of being sick.

"You might feel better if you had a little soup. Sit down and catch your breath," he said. "You can hang out here for as long as you want. I'm not going to hurt you."

I laughed, a short, anxiety-ridden burst. If he hurt me, I probably wouldn't even notice at this point. He couldn't kill me, unless he happened to have a stash of silver bullets or bombs, neither of which seemed likely.

Pulling myself as straight as I could, I hobbled to the corner living space with as much dignity as I could manage. Which wasn't much, as it turned out. My face was stiff, locked in a grimace of pain. My right leg took some weight but throbbed with every step. My whole body was sore from bracing against the injury. But I could walk, slowly.

The stranger reached to help me; I shrugged away.

"Seriously, what happened to you?" he said.

"I fell."

"In a butcher shop or something?"

"Yeah," I said.

In the light, I got a better look at him. He was Chinese, built like Bruce Lee—lean, powerful, nothing but muscle. He probably had the training and reflexes to go with them. His expression was wry.

"You want to wash up? Here." He found a washcloth in the cupboard and ran it under the faucet in the basin. "Sorry I don't have a regular bathroom. I usually use the one in the dim sum place next door, but it's closed right now. I don't spend too much time here. Just a couple of nights a week, you know? I think I might have an extra T-shirt for you."

He found it after some more digging in the cupboard. It was black, just like the one he was wearing, and only a size or so too big. He politely turned his back on me while I took off my gore-soaked shirt and tried to scrub off some of the blood. Taking off the grubby, scratchy shirt and putting on the clean one felt pretty good. It made me feel just a little more human. But wearing it made me smell wrong.

In the meantime, the guy had begun cooking, gathering implements—pot, cutting board, knife. A minifridge sat next to the cupboard, and he retrieved a stack of ingredients from it. In a few moments, a broth was boiling on a hot plate, giving off a fresh, warm scent. Green onions, ginger, and noodles.

I found a trash can to throw the bloody washcloth and shirt into and went to the table, which had a couple of chairs next to it. I leaned on one of them and sighed; I wasn't ready to sit.

In a surprisingly short amount of time, he had produced two large bowls of a wonderful-smelling soup. The hot, domestic scent of it helped my muscles finally unclench. He set the two bowls, along with two wide ceramic spoons on the table.

"Go ahead, sit down," he insisted.

Finally, I sat. If I leaned back and kept my right leg out straight, it didn't even hurt too much.

This was all so strange. It could all be some kind of trick. "Is this safe?" I asked.

"Of course it is," he said. He was already eating, spooning up mouthfuls of the soup. "Why wouldn't it be?"

I tried to explain as simply as I could, searching for

words for concepts I wasn't entirely clear on. "There are stories about . . . I don't know. Other places. Like Persephone in Hades. Like the fairies under the hill. That if you eat anything while you're there, you'll be trapped for seven years. Or trapped forever."

He chuckled. Had he ever stopped smiling? "It's just a building. It's just soup. You saw me make it." And the phone worked. I wasn't trapped anymore, I had to keep reminding myself. The guy scarfed down his own meal.

"Sorry," I said. "I've had a very strange day."

"I believe it. Oh—I'm Sun, by the way. Does that help?"

He had a name, now. So technically, we weren't strangers anymore, right?

"I'm Kitty," I said.

His smile widened. "A werewolf named Kitty? Really?"

"That was an accident," I said, and he chuckled.

Carefully I leaned forward, shifting my weight to keep it off my right hip. I took up a spoonful of the soup and smelled it. It was spicy but subtle, warm ginger and tangy green onions. Steam curled up from the surface. My stomach growled with hunger, which was the last thing I expected after the previous couple of hours. A half an hour ago I'd been in so much pain I'd wanted to vomit.

I sipped a tiny bit of the soup. Which tasted exactly like soup—a standard vegetable broth, a little salty, with a blend of spices. It was warm and comforting, just like soup ought to be.

After a few bites, I looked at my cell phone again, as if I could have missed it ringing and needed to check for messages. No one had called.

"You expecting a call?" he said.

"I don't know. I keep hoping my friends will get in touch."

"Because you're lost."

"Yeah."

"Maybe I can help—point you in the right direction if you tell me where you need to get to."

I didn't even know where I needed to get to. I needed to get to wherever Ben and Cormac were. And where was that? If all else failed, maybe it was time to start over.

I asked, "Do you know someone named Grace Chen? She works at the Great Wall Video Store on—" I didn't know what street the shop was on.

Wonder of wonders, the guy nodded. "Yeah, I know her."

The relief was a warm wash of sunshine in my blood.

"The video store," I said. "I need to get there."

Chapter 11

"A RE YOU SURE you don't need any help?" Sun asked for the third time.

I was hobbling, but I was sure I was hobbling faster than I had been when I first pulled myself out of the hole in the floor. The monster trap. Who the hell puts a pit in a room specifically to trap monsters? This guy, obviously— so who was he again?

Before we left his—apartment? shop?—I limped to the edge and looked down, hoping for some clue about where I'd come from and how I'd gotten turned around. The stairs I'd pulled myself up looked like a normal, rickety set of cellar stairs, and they descended through what seemed to be a trapdoor cut in the floor, leading to a musty basement room. The whole thing, from the doorway to the stairs to the room itself, looked a lot smaller than it had before.

I wasn't sure I could trust any of my perceptions from the moment I stumbled over the edge and fell.

Sun led me out the door of his kitchen onto a narrow alley. The building we'd left was brick, eighty or so years old, decorated with fire escapes and signage with Chinese characters. The alley had a canyonlike quality. A set of trash cans had been put out, and a nondescript car was parked a block away. It was full night, dark and chilly—midnight, according to the phone. The sky above seemed hazy. The air still smelled like San Francisco's air.

We walked down the street, turned a corner, then another. I looked for street signs and tried to keep track of where I was. We were still in Chinatown—a lamppost across the street had a dragon sculpture climbing up it. Everything was locked up, steel doors and grilles pulled over the fronts. We were the only ones out.

I walked as fast as I could, even when Sun tried to slow down for my benefit. "I can keep up," I said.

"I thought it'd be a little easier on you if we took it slow."

"Time's an issue here. I'm fine."

"What's really going on? How's Grace wrapped up in this?"

"How well do you know her?" I said.

"It's not like we're best friends or anything. I just know her. Is she in trouble?" He sounded curious rather than concerned.

I couldn't explain it all. It was too complicated, and I didn't understand much of it myself. "It's nothing, never mind."

"You seem pretty worried."

I almost snapped at him, a wolfish gesture. Maybe I'd feel better if I Changed. Maybe it would help my leg. Yeah, Change and do what? Go where? Track Ben by scent? Run down and maul Sun while I was at it? He didn't deserve that.

"I'm fine," I muttered yet again.

When we arrived on the street with the video store, I didn't recognize it—I'd only seen the place from the back. A big yellow sign over the front said Video, along with some Chinese characters; faded posters hung in the windows.

"Here we are," Sun said. "Is Grace supposed to be here?"

"There's a back door in an alley," I said. "Do you know how to get around to the back?" I could probably find it. We had to be near where we met Anastasia in the first place.

"If you told me what was wrong, I might be able to help you."

"I don't think I can do that."

"If it's a secret—"

"No. I just don't think I'm capable of explaining the last five hours to anyone."

When I drew the next breath, I caught a scent, a familiar flavor at odds with the city smells around me. Wild, fur—werewolf. Turning around, I tipped my nose up to find where it was coming from and how far away it was.

The scent was strong, getting close fast, and it wasn't another attack. My Wolf leaped in response. Warm, familiar, perfect—the smell was Ben. His wolf—a sleek shape of gray and tawny fur, narrow snout and long, rangy legs, tail out like a rudder, ears pinned back—raced up the street, taking huge strides, claws clacking on pavement. It should have been incongruous, seeing a large wolf running through the middle of a street in San Francisco. I should have been worried that Ben had shifted alone in the city, but I was too happy to see him. I stepped into his path.

Instead of coming to me, he angled toward Sun. His lips pulled back in a snarl, a challenge. He thought Sun was an enemy.

"No, Ben, it's okay!" I ran to intercept him, diving at him because what else could I do. He was too fast; I didn't tackle him like I wanted to, but managed to grab his leg and gave a good hard yank. And I yelped as another wave of pain racked my hip.

Whirling, he snapped at me, then dipped his head and tail and snuggled close. I wrapped my arms around his neck, burying my face in his ruff. He was so warm, and he smelled so much like home, I could have breathed in his scent all night.

"It's okay, he's not hurting me, he's helping. Shh, I'm okay, I'm okay." I wasn't, because I'd wrenched my hip again, landing hard on the street and acquiring more bruises, and I was worried and tired and confused. But

Ben was here, no matter what form he was in. For now, I was okay.

Deep in his throat, he whined. Nuzzling toward me, he pushed my face away from him so he could start licking, warm, soft swipes of his tongue up my chin and cheeks. He cleaned away the tears that were falling.

He leaned against me and I wrapped my arms around him. It was as close as we could get to a hug. His mouth was open, panting worried breaths, but his hackles had flattened.

Sun watched us. I expected him to run screaming at the sight of the big slavering wolf. Most people would have. But he didn't flinch. Maybe he wasn't even surprised.

"That's a pretty big dog," Sun said.

"It's not a dog, it's my husband!"

"Huh. That's progressive."

"Shut up, he's a werewolf, too."

"Yeah? Hi there." Sun waved.

Ben glared at him over my shoulder—his eyes were amber, challenging. I had to take care of him, get him someplace safe where he could go to sleep and shift back to human. Where he wouldn't hurt anyone. He was probably thinking he had to take care of me, protect me. We were deep in unknown territory here, and all we had was each other.

I rubbed him hard, burying my hands in his thick fur, wrapping myself around him to take in that warmth.

"What are you doing, Ben? What happened? You shouldn't be like this."

But of course he couldn't answer. Not in words. His emotions poured off him, though, in wolfish body language. He was anxious, relieved to find me. He wouldn't stop pressing himself against me, and I didn't want him to stop. I'd disappeared, so of course he'd come to find me. We were in trouble, we had to protect each other—everything else was secondary.

Ben had found a way out of the tunnels—or his wolf had, animal instincts cutting through the magic. Had the others been able to follow? I didn't sense any sign of Cormac, Anastasia, or Grace. But Ben was here.

"You okay now?" Sun said.

"Yeah, I am," I said.

"You want some advice?"

"I'm not really in the mood for advice," I said.

"You ought to get out of here, go home, and stop messing with things you don't understand," he said.

Ben licked my face, as if agreeing with the sentiment.

"I'll consider it," I said.

"Well, good luck then." Sun waved as he walked away.

Ben curled his lip, his hackles rising again, and his muscles going rigid.

"Shh," I murmured at him. He started to lunge after Sun, and I held him, bracing my weight against him to keep him from attacking. Ben made an uncertain noise—part growl, part whine—in his throat.

I only glanced away a moment while trying to settle Ben. When I turned back to the street, to take one more look at Sun, he was already gone, ducked around some corner or into some shadow. I couldn't even smell him on the air anymore, except for his scent lingering on my borrowed T-shirt.

As soon as we found Grace I was going to have to ask her about that guy. Now, about finding Grace . . .

Ben was still acting like we were surrounded by enemies—watchful, nervous, braced. Part of me wanted to join him—turn Wolf so the two of us could run, just get out of here and find safety wherever we could. Golden Gate Park had to be around here somewhere, didn't it? At any rate, I was done with Anastasia and done with the Dragon's Pearl, Roman, and whatever weird magic was operating around them. It wasn't worth killing ourselves over.

I scratched his ear and kissed his furry cheek. "We have to find Cormac and get out of here. Where is he? Where'd you leave him?"

He pulled away from me and trotted back the way he'd come. At the end of the block, he stopped and waited. Sighing, I hauled myself to my feet. I had to be healing because it was easier than the first time I'd tried it, after climbing out of the pit. But I'd never been so sore, all the way to the bone. However much I wanted to run, I could only manage to shuffle, wincing with every step.

When Ben saw me limping, he loped back and nudged

me, whining, worried. His nose tracked all over me, searching for what was wrong, poking at the hem of the shirt until he found skin. His nose was cold and wet. I rested on him, lacing my hand into the fur of his neck. He came up to my hip and made a perfect crutch.

"I'm okay," I said with another sigh. Together, slowly, we made our way to the end of the block and around the corner.

The alley ended ahead, and I recognized Grant Avenue. Ben put his nose down and sniffed, looking for a trail. I tried to imagine what had happened. Even through all the fighting we'd done, he hadn't shifted. He'd kept it together. This time he'd either made a conscious decision to shift, or something had finally pushed him over the edge, and he'd lost control. I wanted to get him someplace safe and quiet, convince him to sleep instead of protecting me, and ask him what had happened.

But first, we had to find Cormac.

All the trails I sensed were old. My nose was pretty good, but Ben's wolf's nose would be better at this, and he was crossing back and forth, aimless, trackless. Ben had been back this way recently, but Cormac and Anastasia hadn't, not since we first came here right after dusk. No sign of Grace, either. He trotted on to the end of the alley, made another pass, back and forth a couple of times—still no trail to follow.

I tried calling Cormac on my cell phone and wasn't surprised when I got voice mail. I left a message. "Hey, we're trying to find you. Ben's here, we're both okay. Call me as soon as you can." Not that leaving a message would do any good, but it couldn't hurt.

The street was empty; no one was around, not a car, not a traffic light, nothing. Seemed odd for a big city, even in the middle of the night.

When I tipped my nose to the air again, a cold thread of scent touched me. A familiar chill, it stabbed through the city's background mist of cool air coming in off the water. A vampire—cold, undead. Not Anastasia. My imaginary hackles rose, my shoulders stiffening.

I looked behind me, down the alley we'd just left. A figure stood there, part of the shadows, visible only because he was backlit by some distant light diffused through the mist. He was male, with close-cropped hair and an angular shape to his features. He stood with his arm crooked, as if he rested his hand on the hilt of a sword hanging on his belt. But the stance was an illusion. He wore an overcoat. From a block away, he looked like a statue.

I knew him, I recognized him, that smell, that posture, the way I could feel him staring at me even when I couldn't see his eyes. I stepped toward him, until my vision resolved his features and I was sure.

The vampire turned and walked away.

Ben whined. Back at the curb, he was looking back and forth, pacing, agitated. I went to him. "Ben?"

Roman—the figure I thought had been Roman—was

out of sight now, but I still smelled the chill of vampire on the air. Ben loped to my side, brushing his flank along my thigh. I gripped his fur. He looked up at me with amber eyes, full of energy and determination. *Run?* he seemed to say.

Two vampires—different vampires—approached us along Grant from either direction. We'd be cornered in moments.

"I can't," I said, despairing. I squeezed my right hip, feeling the still-deep bruising. I wasn't about to try to hobble away and get caught from behind. I'd rather face them.

Ben flattened his ears and tensed for battle.

The two newcomers strolled on the sidewalk as if they were average ordinary pedestrians. One of them even wore jeans. I tried to remember—had I ever seen a vampire wear jeans? He wore an embroidered Havana shirt with the jeans, and looked like he should have been drinking something out of a pineapple. The other wore a black turtleneck and gray slacks. They looked like a couple of young twenty-something hipsters. But they were still vampires, and they were coming after us. Ben and I stood side by side, our backs to the brick of the building behind us, and stared our challenges.

"We had word that some rogue wolves were running loose in town," the Havana shirt guy said. "You must be it."

My words caught behind a growl; I couldn't talk. I

wanted to shift and run away with my mate. Ready to rip and tear, claws burned inside my hands, which I clenched.

"What are we going to do with them, Joe?" Havana shirt guy said to turtleneck guy.

"Boss says haul 'em in." His voice was low, calm, businesslike. He had no doubt about his ability to complete the task before him.

"Are you working for Roman?" I said, despair tightening my voice. I sounded close to tears. "Did he send you?"

"Roman?" the first vampire said. We blinked at each other. I ducked my gaze quickly, to avoid looking in his vampiric eyes. And because I was confused. He suddenly seemed bored, like this was a chore he could have done without. Which didn't seem like Roman or one of his minions.

"So. You going to come quiet or make it hard on yourselves?" he said.

Ben's face wrinkled, lips pulled back, showing his teeth in an epic snarl. All his fur stood on end, and he was braced to leap.

"Ben, no," I murmured, clinging to his fur.

He jumped out of my grip and sprang at the vampire in the turtleneck, claws out and open jaw aiming for his throat.

The vampire was ready. He stepped aside, and Ben overshot his target and went sprawling on the street beyond. His claws scrabbled on the pavement as he worked to recover, change direction, and try again, but the vampire was too fast, too strong. In a stride he was on top of the wolf, digging a knee into his ribs, holding his front legs away with one hand and clamping down on his neck with the other, pinning him to the street. The wolf's head was tilted up and away, leaving his jaws and teeth useless. No matter how he kicked and thrashed, he couldn't break free of the vampire's grip.

I attacked, because what else could I do?

Scrambling forward despite my injury, I made to tackle Ben's captor. The other vampire was there to grab me from behind. I hadn't even seen him move. He wrenched my arms back and dropped me to my knees. Despite the pain stabbing in my shoulder, I kept lunging forward, futilely trying to break free and reach Ben.

"We don't want to hurt you, really," the vampire holding me said. "Please just come with us."

The please did it. I stopped struggling and nodded, because my voice still wasn't working right. All Wolf wanted to do was growl.

"I let you go, you stay calm?" he said. "You'll tell your mate to stand down?"

I nodded again.

"Can you even talk anymore?"

I swallowed, concentrated very hard on human words, and said, "I'm having a really bad night."

He let me go. I slumped forward and rolled my shoulders, working the kinks out. "Ben, please. It's okay. It's going to be okay."

The wolf settled. The other vampire cautiously lifted his hands and backed away. As soon as the pressure was gone, Ben lurched to his feet. He stared at the vampire a moment and seemed to debate about risking another attack. Then he lowered his head and trotted to me, pressing close, twining himself in my arms. I hugged him hard, and he licked my face.

The first vampire was talking on a cell phone. A moment later, a shiny black Cadillac pulled around the corner and stopped at the curb. I couldn't see the driver through the tinted windows, but I assumed it was another vampire. And Rick said the Family here was laid back.

The first vampire, the one in the Havana shirt who still hadn't given his name, opened the back door and gestured us inside. The other, Joe, opened the front passenger-side door and climbed in.

I didn't want to go. Ben stood between me and the car like a wall—he didn't want to go, either.

"You're from the San Francisco Family," I said, stalling, trying to get my bearings.

He looked at me and sighed specifically to demonstrate his frustration, it seemed. "Yes. My name is Henry. Now will you please get in so we can get off the street?"

I looked at Ben, cupping my hands around his face, smoothing back his fur. "What do you think?"

He licked my chin. Leaving it up to me. Leaning against him, I pulled myself to my feet and hobbled to the car.

"You're hurt," Henry said.

"I said I've had a bad night."

"Broken bone?"

I glared at him. "I'm fine."

He shrugged. When Ben and I were inside, he closed the door after us. He got in the front with Joe, and the car drove smoothly away.

Chapter 12

THE DRIVER WAS human. Living, breathing, though tainted with the scent of vampire. A human servant, then. Average size, he had pale skin and wore a designer leather jacket. Both Henry and Joe sat in front, even though it had less room, leaving the back to us. I had to admit I felt safer this way. I had room to breathe—and a possible escape route. Ben found an awkward position, sitting braced across me, still protecting me, and half twisted forward so he could keep the vampires in view. His lip stayed curled, showing sharp teeth. I rested an arm across his back and breathed in the warmth of his fur.

Henry was tall, meaty—almost stout. He had the build of a retired athlete. Joe had Mediterranean features. His dark hair had curl to it, and I would have called his skin tanned if he hadn't been a vampire.

"You two are a long way from home," Henry said.

"Not so long," I answered.

"What brings you to the city by the bay?"

"The sights."

"Which is why you're gallivanting around Chinatown at midnight."

"Ghost tour. We got separated from the group."

Joe craned around. "Do I know you from somewhere?"

Such a loaded question. I wasn't sure if my identity would make things better for Ben and me, or worse. Complete toss-up. "That depends. You listen to much radio?"

The looked of recognition dawned. "You're Kitty Norville."

Henry looked at him. "What? Are you sure?"

"Yeah. It's not the voice so much as the sarcasm."

I rested my head on Ben's back. We were so doomed.

"Why didn't you say something?" Henry said.

"Because saying something is just as likely to get me shot in some circles as not," I said.

They both chuckled. The driver glanced at me in his rearview mirror, and even he was smiling.

"Boss is going to love this," Henry said.

I hugged Ben.

We drove for maybe fifteen minutes. I couldn't see out the tinted side windows, so I tried to watch out the front windshield. We'd entered a neighborhood of Victorian-looking townhouses with bay windows, on pleasant, tree-lined streets.

"Where are we going?" I asked.

"The Haight," Henry said. "We own a few buildings here."

"Like, Haight-Ashbury?"

Henry nodded. At another time—during daylight and with no injuries, for example—I'd have been excited. Site of the Summer of Love, home to icons of psychedelic rock, I'd have loved to just wander, to see if anything was left of that old hippie atmosphere or if it had all been swallowed by twenty-first-century commercial tourism. But right now all I wanted to do was go home.

Finally we turned down a sloped driveway into an underground garage and stopped.

"Everybody out," Henry said.

I leaned around Ben to open to the door, and he jumped out ahead of me. Again, we stood side by side, to face whatever came next. The garage looked as if it was used for a motor pool of some kind. A couple of other sleek sedans were parked here, along with a zippy red sports car and a big SUV. The place was lit with flickering fluorescents, which made my eyes hurt. The driver waved at the vampires and went into an office. Joe opened one side of a set of double doors and gestured inside. Henry led the way.

Past the doors, a hallway led to what must have been the building's basement, which meant we were entering a vampire's lair. Underground meant no windows, and no sunlight. And no exits. Joe closed the door behind us and followed.

The place reeked of vampires—cold and stale blood, not a hint of fresh life. Keeping one hand on Ben, clinging to his fur, I walked. Ben stayed pressed against my hip. His steps were slow to match mine, and his claws clicked on the linoleum. I kept telling myself that if they'd meant us harm, they wouldn't be saying please, and they wouldn't be letting us walk under our own power. They just wanted to talk. Vampires did this kind of thing all the time—they had to be the ones in control, they had to talk on their own turf. I was still nervous, and the muscles on Ben's shoulders and back were stiff. They might have given us champagne and fresh steaks and we'd still be nervous.

The hallway opened into a room, the tile gave way to thick, rich carpet, and the fluorescent lighting was replaced by the soft glow of low-wattage, shaded lamps in the corners. The sofas were leather, and there were plush armchairs, polished wood coffee tables, and hidden speakers playing soft music, light and jazzy. All the colors were dark, giving the room a sultry, denlike atmosphere. Someone should have been handing out cocktails. I took a breath, surveyed the room's smells, and counted four vampires in addition to Henry and Joe. They wouldn't be drinking any cocktails. One of the four was Anastasia, standing apart, arms crossed, looking annoyed. There was also a mortal human, living and breathing, carrying the distinctive scent of a worn leather coat. I knew that smell. Beside me, Ben whined a long, soft note; he recognized it, too.

"Kitty!" Cormac called. He was off to the right, next

to Anastasia, in front of a trio of vampires lounging on sofas. In a couple of strides he was in front of me, holding my arm.

I gripped his arm in turn. "Are you okay?"

"Are you?" he said.

Ben's sleek wolf maneuvered between us, leaning against my legs and nudging Cormac's hip with his muzzle. At the contact, Cormac stepped back, and we broke apart. He watched the wolf warily.

"He gets a little territorial," I said, resting a hand on Ben's head.

Ben looked back at Cormac, nose tipped up, staring, but not doing anything further to threaten. The hunter pursed his lips, his expression closing down. I didn't think he'd fully reconciled himself to the idea that Ben was a werewolf, even though he was there when it happened. It was hard to see the animal sitting in front of you and remember the man he usually was. Even when you looked him in the eyes.

"Come here, let me have a look at you," said the man on the sofa. The three local vampires arranged on the chairs and sofas studied me with interest. Two were men, one a woman, and like Joe and Henry seemed to be hipsters, unassuming upscale urban types—but from the Jazz Age rather than the current era. They'd set up shop in the 1920s and stayed there. One of the men wore a double-breasted suit with a silk tie. His brown hair was slicked back, his smile was wry. The one on the sofa wore a suit without the jacket—red suspenders stood out against the white starched shirt. His gaze was inquisitive, and I had to work not to meet it. The woman wore a clinging gown, black, beaded, with spaghetti straps, and had her honey-colored hair in a perfect bob. Together, they looked fabulous, like something out of a movie. Exotic, even. Strange and intimidating all at once. I squeezed Ben's coat for comfort.

Cormac returned to where he'd been standing. I limped over to join him, Ben stepping carefully at my side. He was watching the limp, along with Anastasia. I itched under their gazes, hating to show so much weakness. I was getting better, I really was. Ben stood tall and proud beside me, matching each of their gazes in turn as if to say, *I'm looking out for her, don't get any ideas.* I leaned on him a little more, grateful for the support.

"What happened?" the hunter asked.

"I fell," I said, my voice low, hidden. "I think I broke something."

"But it's healing."

"Yeah, slowly."

"Are you okay?"

It was the second time he'd asked in as many minutes. I still didn't answer. "What happened to you guys? How'd you get out of the tunnels?"

"We followed Ben. His wolf side didn't seem to have any trouble."

"Why'd he shift?"

"You were gone."

The door had shut, I'd shouted at him from the other side, he'd pounded on it, trying to get to me—and then I'd fallen. Vanished. Maybe they'd even gotten the door open but couldn't find any sign of me on the other side. Or they'd kept shouting through the door and got no answer. And Ben had lost it. I stroked the thick fur along his back, and he turned his head back to give my hand a quick lick.

I couldn't figure out the situation. Anastasia seemed unhappy but not nervous. Cormac was cautious, like he always was. His right hand rested in his pocket—clutching a cross, I'd bet. The stake would be hidden up a sleeve. Had the vampires even searched him for weapons? Joe and Henry stayed behind me, near the door, and seemed amused. I glanced over my shoulder trying to keep them in view. Then there were the three new vampires in front of me. One of them was no doubt the Master of San Francisco. Anastasia's old ally, or her old nemesis? This felt like a tribunal of some kind, like we were being brought here to face some kind of reckoning. I couldn't identify which one of them was in charge. All three seemed confident, and none showed deference to any other. I was used to seeing hierarchies among vampires, as much as I did among werewolves. Joe and Henry had talked about a boss—who was it?

"You're Kitty Norville?" the one on the sofa, the suspenders-no-jacket guy, said. He leaned forward, resting his elbows on his knees, making him seem even more like a Prohibition-era gangster.

"Hi," I said, waving my hand. "And you are?"

He waved the question away. "This is your mate?" He pointed at Ben, who growled.

I pressed his shoulder, quieting him. "Yeah."

"Well. Thanks for joining us."

"Did we have a choice?"

He smiled broadly, and the muscles across my shoulders twitched. "I have to ask, what are you doing in my territory?"

"Ask her."

He glanced at Anastasia, his expression souring before he looked back at me. Maybe checking for confirmation, or fishing for a reaction. "Then you do serve a vampire? The gossip about you says you don't serve anyone."

I straightened, tipping my chin up in a show of pride, hoping to demonstrate that the gossip was right. And there was gossip about me? What gossip? What were people saying about me behind my back anyway?

"Actually, I'm really pissed off at her right now," I said.

Everyone except me looked at her for a reaction; she didn't oblige them, only spoke calmly in a cold, creamy voice, "She doesn't serve me. She's here as a favor. As an ally."

"What the hell did you do for her to deserve a favor like this?" he said to her.

Anastasia and I glanced at each other, trying to egg

each other on. For a moment I even thought, what *had* she done for me? But that wasn't the issue. Favors weren't currency you could line up and trade, one for one. At least, not to me. I was here because we both wanted to take down Roman.

I had to tell her about the figure in the alley, the imperious spy.

We were at some kind of stalemate. We'd answered questions, but the vampire—I had to assume the one in suspenders was the boss—wasn't happy with the answers. They didn't seem likely to let us go, but they were also treating Anastasia with kid gloves. Was this the Master who had taken power in the 1920s? It seemed likely. At any rate, this was Anastasia's bailiwick, and I didn't know the rules here. I ought to let her do all the talking. What were the odds?

When he didn't get an answer, he shrugged. "Well then. Welcome to San Francisco. It would have been nice if you'd called first. You're from Denver, right? Who's running things there now? Rick, isn't it? You could have asked him, gotten an introduction, made it all official—"

"He said you wouldn't mind it if I just passed through."

"Did he? He's either getting senile in his old age or he has a lot of confidence in you. Which is it?"

I tilted my head. "How old is old? All of you," I said, glancing at each of them, even Joe and Henry behind me. "Rick says you've been running San Francisco since the twenties, so that's at least a hundred."

The members of the vampire entourage wore crooked, amused smiles. The woman had blood-red lips.

"It's rude, asking vampires about their age," said Boss.

I shrugged. "Yeah. I keep doing it anyway." I was getting my groove back. I came as close as I could to staring at him without looking him in his hypnotic eyes. He had a slight hook in his nose. "I have some questions. You've been running San Francisco for almost a century, so you were here during the sixties. Summer of Love and all that, right? You ever meet Janis Joplin? Jerry Garcia? Country Joe? Any of those psychedelic guys?"

"What if I said yes? What do you expect me to say about any of them that hasn't already been said?"

"Maybe I just wanted to see if you had any concert bootlegs."

Ben bumped my hip with his nose and whined a little. Yeah, maybe I was talking too much. But what if he'd said yes? And what if he'd actually given them to me? It never hurt to ask.

Boss raised an eyebrow. "You are definitely Kitty Norville."

"So that's a no?"

"You'll have to ask Henry, that was more his scene." Behind me, Henry gave a little wave.

The thing was, as long as we were all talking, nobody was fighting. If I got Boss to like me, or at least to not think I was a threat, he'd be more likely to let us all go. He might even help us. If he'd known we were all in town, maybe he knew that Roman was in town. Maybe when Henry said he'd been looking for rogue wolves, he'd been looking for Roman's gang. Maybe they could tell us something.

He turned away from me. I'd been surveyed, and I wasn't a threat, apparently. I was sorry I'd missed what he'd said to Cormac before we got here.

"Where were we? Right. Anastasia, you're back after what, eighty, ninety years? I'd wondered what happened to you. You left so quickly after the coup."

Anastasia said, "I didn't see a need to stay. You didn't need my help—at least not anymore."

He opened his hands in agreement. "Begs the question, though—why are you back?"

"I'm here on an entirely unrelated matter."

"Still, the last time you were in San Francisco, you helped stage a coup against the former Master."

"That's not what happened and you know it."

"All I know is you do things to suit yourself and no one else. You could have put yourself in charge here. You could have made yourself Mistress of a dozen cities the world over, collected all that power, but what do you do instead? You meddle and move on. What's the story now?"

What do you know—we had the same opinion about Anastasia.

"I wanted to see the old stomping grounds," she said.

"You could have called me for a tour."

"I didn't want to trouble you."

"You were in Chinatown with a mercenary." He gestured at Cormac. "What were you looking for? Or what did you already find and are trying to hide from me?"

She strolled a quiet step forward on her heeled shoes. Her eyes narrowed, and she caught Boss's gaze. "Nothing you need to bother with," she said softly.

He straightened, leaning back to regard her, his brow furrowed. The other vampires were frowning now, looking back and forth between their Master and the stranger.

Maybe Ben and Cormac and I could get the hell out of here while they had their standoff.

"Anastasia," Boss said, his voice low, threatening.

We were wasting time, so I dropped into the conversation to tip the balance. "Roman is here," I said.

The mood snapped back. Boss blinked and looked away from Anastasia, at me. "Roman?" he said, much the way Henry had, as if I was muddying the waters on purpose.

"Dux Bellorum," Anastasia murmured.

Well, that made the air go out of the room. Boss's mouth opened—he even showed fangs. The male vampire companion gripped the arms of his chair and leaned forward. Joe stepped closer. All five of them looked shocked. Anastasia frowned at me.

"Really?" Boss said. He shifted his gaze from me to Anastasia. "Why didn't you tell me?"

"This isn't your battle," she said.

He raised a disbelieving eyebrow. "It isn't? Because it's *your* battle? Because you think you can handle him all by yourself?"

"I know him," she said with conviction.

For once I wanted to keep quiet, because I wanted them to keep talking. I wanted to learn more. But nobody said anything.

"How?" I said. "How do you know him?"

She didn't answer. What else wasn't she telling me?

Boss settled back into his seat and donned an air of calm, but he also looked sad. As if he was facing the inevitable; as if he'd faced it many times before. His expression was at odds with the offhand manner he'd shown so far. I bumped up my estimation of his age another hundred years. This guy had been around.

When he spoke, he spoke to me. "My predecessor belonged to Dux Bellorum—Roman, I guess is as good a name as any. Some of us"—he gestured to his four colleagues—"didn't like that she bound us to someone who wasn't one of us. That she swore fealty to a Master outside the Family. We wanted our Family to be a family. Not some . . . platoon in someone else's army."

Dux Bellorum was how Roman named himself, when he wasn't being sneaky: the leader of war. The general.

"We're losing, Anastasia. In the last hundred years we've gained what, San Francisco? Denver? But how many cities have we lost? After you left I assumed you were out there, doing more of the same. Subverting his lieutenants, putting better Masters in their places. But I never heard a word. Meanwhile, Dux Bellorum has dozens of agents everywhere, all working to bring more cities in line."

"Agents," I said. "Like Mercedes Cook?"

"You know Mercedes?" Boss said.

"She came through Denver a few years ago." And instigated the war that brought Rick to power. She had intended for Rick's predecessor to destroy him, but Rick was better than she expected. He'd surprised a lot of people that night.

"Rick booted her out?"

"Yeah."

"I always knew I liked that guy. You're working for Rick?"

"Rick is my friend. I've met Roman. If there's a war coming, I won't be on his side," I said.

"It's been a long time since the werewolves had a leader step forward," Boss said.

I rolled my eyes and sighed with frustration. "I'm not leading the werewolves, I'm not working for anybody, I'm just trying to do what's right."

"Then you've bitten off way more than you can chew, dear."

I growled under my breath. I was ready to get out of here. Ben licked my hand, comforting me. As long as we stuck together, things couldn't be so bad.

Boss turned to Anastasia. "So you're here because

Roman is here. Is my Family, is our place controlling San Francisco, in danger?"

"No," Anastasia. "I'd have come straight to you if that were the case, I swear it."

"Then . . ." He gestured, indicating that she should continue.

"There's an artifact in Chinatown. The Dragon's Pearl. Roman is looking for it. I need to find it first. He can't be allowed to have it; it's too powerful. This is bigger than you, or your Family, or San Francisco."

"You should have come to me anyway, Anastasia. The city's changed since you were here. I can help you."

"You can't defeat Roman," she said.

He chuckled. "No, of course not. But I can protect San Francisco. It's what I've promised, it's what I'm able to do. Roman won't find a foothold here. Maybe I can help you find this pearl of yours, since when the boys found you none of you looked like you were doing too well."

Anastasia was stubborn. Her dignity was like armor. I had to wonder if she just didn't like other vampires all that much. At least, the ones she didn't create herself.

"Ask him about Grace," I said to her. "It can't hurt."

Sighing, she nodded. "There's a young woman, a magician named Grace Chen. She was helping us before we ran into some of Roman's soldiers. We don't know where she is now, and I need her to find the Dragon's Pearl."

"You want me to find her?" Boss said.

"If you can."

"I'd be happy to help you, Anastasia," he said, opening his arms. "Give us a couple of hours."

"It's only a few more hours until dawn," Anastasia said.

"It's the best I can do. Feel free to wait here. Make yourselves at home." He stood, and his companions stood with him, flanking him. Boss waved at Henry. "You stay, keep an eye on things." Henry nodded, straightened, and stood solid as a tree, his hands crossed before him in a clear bodyguard posture. The posse departed, leaving the room quiet.

Were we trapped? Prisoners? Could we leave? Was there a shower somewhere? A bathroom maybe? Anastasia wasn't offering commentary. She seemed to be focused inward, stewing. Cormac was in "wait-and-watch" mode. Since they weren't saying anything, I wanted to talk to Ben, who couldn't talk. I rubbed his fur, and he leaned into my good leg.

Henry it was, then. "Are you here to guard us or to play host?"

"A little of both. Boss doesn't trust you not to poke around where you shouldn't."

"He could have just asked."

Henry only smiled.

"So. *Do* you have any Janis Joplin bootlegs?"

He chuckled quietly. "The rarest bootleg'll never be as good as the real thing, live and in person. She was one of a kind."

"Well, yeah. But . . . do you?"

Still chuckling, he waved me off, refusing to answer, which was as good as yes in my mind. Arrogant vampires . . .

That left us sitting around the living-room-slash-audience hall, waiting. Anastasia settled into an armchair. Crossing her arms, she stared at Henry, who crossed his arms and avoided looking at her. I chose a padded chair and stretched my leg out. In all the excitement, I hadn't noticed that the pain had almost faded. Now, my whole leg and side just ached horribly.

Cormac paced over and loomed. "You okay?"

"You keep asking that."

"I don't like this," he said. "We need to get out of town while we can."

"I know, but I want to make sure Grace's okay. And I'll stick around if it means getting to take out Roman."

"With everything you've told me about the bastard I'm inclined to agree."

"If you see an opening, take it."

"Absolutely."

Ben left my side and padded to the corner, where he turned in a couple of circles, lay down, and curled into a tight ball, paws tucked in, tail resting over his nose. He finally felt safe enough to sleep. Or at least, to try to sleep. He still didn't look particularly comfortable.

I leveraged myself out of the chair and went to join him, settling on the floor and resting my hand on his back. He snuggled closer to me.

Cormac said, "I'll keep an eye out."

Then Ben seemed to relax.

I dozed, leaning against the wall, my arms draped over Ben, fingers laced in his fur. When he moved against me, I awoke and drew away as the fur under my touch thinned and shrank. I watched Ben come back to me.

Cormac said he'd keep watch, but he turned away when Ben started to shift back, when the fur faded and vanished, his skin stretched and bones melted into new shapes. It happened slowly, bit by bit. The Change back to human was like a sunrise—the sky paled, paled some more. Then—suddenly, you'd swear—it was daytime. Ben, naked and chilled, lay curled up, head and shoulders tucked into my lap, arms and legs pulled protectively close.

I stayed still, quiet, letting him sleep. Absently, I touched his ruffled hair, smoothing it behind his ear.

When he was human again, Henry came over with a blanket. He kept his distance, holding it out as an offering, taking care not to startle Ben by getting too close, for which I was grateful. I took the blanket from him and spread it over Ben.

The others left us alone, and we waited.

After a time, Ben tensed—I felt his muscles tighten against my leg. His nose flared, and he flinched awake, sitting up. I waited for him to gain his bearings, to get the scent of the place, to settle. It only took a second.

He looked at me. "I thought I'd lost you."

I fell against him and we kissed. His arms closed tight around me and I pressed myself to him while our lips worked, hungry for each other's taste. I wanted to rub myself all over his skin, taking in his warmth, his scent.

"Werewolves are all about instinct, emotion. They're so full of passion. Makes them fascinating, don't you think?" Boss had returned, regarding us from the doorway. He seemed to be speaking to Anastasia, conspiratorial, as if this was a long-running vampire joke.

Most vampires annoyed me because I didn't know their ages. But to not even tell me his name? It was typical. Rick hadn't been born with that name, Roman was an acquired name, and I really doubted that Anastasia was her original name, either. They'd reinvented themselves, like shedding old skins, when they became vampires. They could choose their identities, because who from their old lives was around to remember? To call out the inventions?

I tried to imagine Anastasia as a young woman, a child, eager instead of calculating and obsessed. And I couldn't.

Joe was with Boss, and between them stood Grace Chen. Mission successful.

I rested my forehead against Ben's shoulder and sighed. For just a moment, I'd been able to forget about everything, everyone, but him. We'd had our own little sphere of perfection, however fleeting. Ben kissed the top of my head and kept his arms around me, holding me close. Yeah, we could stay like that for a while longer.

"Are you okay?" I whispered, trying to keep the conversation between us.

His breath ruffled my hair, which felt marvelous, comforting. I reveled in the smell of him. "I'm feeling kind of stupid. I lost it. Completely."

Obviously. "Why? You got through two fights without losing it. What happened?"

"When you didn't answer, I panicked. I didn't know what to do—so I lost it."

"And came looking for me?"

"Yeah."

"That's sweet, you know."

"I'm glad you think so." We kissed again, a reassuring touch of lips. "What about you? You're hurt, your leg—" He put his hand on my right hip, which twinged at the touch. But I held his hand there, not wanting him to move.

"I fell," I said. "Broke something, I think."

"But you're okay? It healed?"

"It's taking awhile, but yeah, I think so."

"We have to get out of here," he said.

"Yeah. But we can't, not yet."

"I know."

I nestled closer in his embrace, finally feeling strong enough to deal with the situation outside.

Boss was still grinning at us like he thought we were cute. Cormac was back to standing guard. He didn't particularly look like he was standing guard, but he'd put himself between the two of us—huddled on the floor, vulnerable—and the rest of the gathering. The arrangement suggested us against them.

Anastasia was talking to Grace.

"I didn't count on any of this!" the young magician said.

"Your family understood what was asked of them—"

"That was hundreds of years ago! What do you expect me to do? I wasn't going to stick around and try to fight monsters. I can't do that."

"Do you honor your ancestors or not? We've lost time, it may be too late."

"I have to butt in," I murmured to Ben, extricating myself from his embrace, as much as it pained me to do so.

"Of course you do," he said, his smile turning crooked. He wrapped the blanket firmly around him after my departure. Which was a shame. If we'd been alone I'd have stripped down to join him. Later . . .

"Anastasia, chill out," I said. "She did the right thing when she ran." Both Anastasia and Boss arced brows at me, as if surprised by my interruption. I hoped they were impressed by my assertiveness. "Roman's here. But he doesn't have the pearl or those werewolves wouldn't have been asking us for it. So we still have a chance of finding it. Don't we?"

Anastasia set her mouth in a frown—grim and hopeless. She didn't think there was a chance.

"Grace," Cormac said. Everyone looked at him, startled. He was quiet enough most of the time that he almost blended into the background. That was exactly how he planned it. "I might be able to work out a way to search for it, but I don't know what it is, what it looks like. If you can give me something to look for, we might be able to find it."

The young woman raised her arms in a gesture that was half pleading, half frustration. "Have any of you considered that if this terrible Roman guy doesn't have it, and we don't have it, then someone else got to it first—someone who put the *huli jing* in a cage? Someone more powerful than any of us? You really want to go after that?"

Anastasia frowned. "If you had not failed in your duty to your ancestors—"

Grace put her hands over her ears. "Oh, stop with that, please! You sound like my grandmother!"

Taken aback, Anastasia pursed her lips.

"Grace," Cormac said again. "You think we can do this?"

Deflating, she fidgeted, taking off her glasses, wiping them on the hem of her shirt, putting them on and glaring through them, giving the vampires surly glances. "Yeah, I think so."

"We'll need some space and quiet," Cormac said to Boss.

"Can we watch?" he asked.

"Sure. Long as you're quiet."

"This way, then." He started toward the other side of the room, where a door stood.

Ben got to his feet, keeping the blanket wrapped modestly around his waist. The look was kind of cute, showing off his lean body. I had an urge to pull his hand away so that the blanket dropped . . .

"I could use some clothes," he said.

Cormac reached to the floor behind one of the chairs and produced several items of clothing, stacked and folded—and Ben's battered semiautomatic. And that answered the question of whether he'd been searched. Boss and company obviously didn't think we were much of a threat. It was almost insulting.

"I picked up what you dropped. Some of it's kind of mangled." He handed the stack to Ben.

"You shouldn't even be *holding* this thing." Ben gestured at the gun.

Cormac shrugged him off. "Won't happen again. I thought you might need it."

"For all the good it's done so far. Anyway. Thanks." He set the gun on a table and surveyed the clothing.

"It'd be nice if you could avoid that sort of thing from now on."

"I'll put that on the list. 'Don't lose your shit.' Then you won't have to use those silver knives of yours on me."

"I wouldn't—"

Ben pointed. "You would if you had to."

Cormac looked away. So did Ben. I wondered if I should shove in between them to keep from saying anything else—something either one of them would regret.

"Sorry," Ben said finally. "I'll try to keep from freaking out too badly from now on."

Cormac shrugged him off and headed to the doors. "Let's see that room."

Boss led the way, and the others followed, leaving us alone for a moment, and I was grateful. Ben handed me the pile of clothes, taking the shirt off the top and holding it up. Sure enough, the I ESCAPED ALCATRAZ shirt was ripped at the seams, Incredible Hulk–like, as a result of Ben tearing it off rather than bothering with conventional removal. Not to mention all the blood soaked into it from the earlier fight. It showed up even against the black. We'd all had a hell of a night, hadn't we?

"Huh," he said, then wadded it up and threw it into a corner.

"At least when that happens to you you can go shirtless," I said. "I have to walk around with my arms crossed."

The trousers, boxers, and shoes were intact enough. He put them on and gave a satisfied sigh. Straightening, he squared his shoulders, indicating that he felt increasingly more human. I wrapped my arms around his middle and rubbed my faced against his chest, letting the hair there tickle my skin and taking in his scent.

He hugged back, then picked at the T-shirt on my shoulders.

"That's not your shirt," he said.

"Yeah. The last one was kind of covered with blood.

It seems to be the theme of the night. That guy loaned me one."

"That guy—the on the street where I found you? I remember him. What was up with him?"

"I don't really know," I said. "He seemed nice enough."

"That's kind of what's weird about him," Ben said. "Did he even want his shirt back?"

I looked down at myself and furrowed my brow. "Why do I suddenly want to look for a homing device stitched into this?"

"I wouldn't mind seeing you walk around with just your arms crossed," he said.

"Later," I said.

"I *knew* we wouldn't be going back to the hotel room just yet. Can't we go back just for an hour?"

"Aren't you the least bit curious about how all this is going to turn out?"

"Not at the expense of losing you," he said, smoothing my hair back from my face. "I don't ever want to get that close again."

I wanted to tell him that he wouldn't, that I'd always be all right. But I couldn't make that promise.

Hand in hand, we followed the others through the door and into the next room.

It wasn't much of a room: bare tile on the floor, off-white walls, no windows, a couple of floor lamps in the corners giving off muted light. About fifteen by fifteen, the place reminded me of a cell.

"What do you use this for?" I asked Boss.

"Time-outs," he said.

"Time-outs? Like, if one of your vampires gets violent?"

"You ever seen what that looks like?"

Until recently, I'd have said no, but the starving vampire we found near Dodge City gave me a pretty good idea of why vampires might need a room like this. A question remained: Just what did you *do* with a vampire that far gone? How did you get them back to normal, or what passed for normal among vampires? Answer: they needed blood. And what did *that* look like? I wasn't sure I wanted to know. The place smelled innocuous enough—it had the cold, clean scent of the rest of the lair. I surreptitiously hunted for stray bloodstains on the floor and didn't find anything.

We kept to the edges of the room. Cautious, Grace stood in the middle, waiting for Cormac, who paced around the room, touching walls, studying the ceiling. His lips were pursed, thoughtful.

He took off his jacket and put it on the floor in the corner. His gray T-shirt showed off his rugged frame— he'd grown up on a ranch and it showed. He let his arms hang loose, tipped his head back, took a deep breath. When he released it, he made the soft hiss of a slowly deflating balloon. He rolled his shoulders, his head, stretching his neck. Then, blinking, he gazed around the room as if waking from a nap. His scent became bookish, older.

"What's happening?" Boss asked.

"He's Amelia now," I said.

The vampire glanced at me, his expression questioning, but I couldn't explain.

Brisk now, businesslike instead of watchful, Cormac returned to his jacket and pulled a few items—small, hidden in his hands—out of the pockets. Going to Grace, he handed her a piece of red chalk. "Draw a picture of the Dragon's Pearl, right here." He gestured at the center of the floor.

"I can't draw that well. I'm not an artist."

"It doesn't have to be an exact likeness. Just a suggestion. A symbol."

Tentatively, she took the chalk from him, crouched, and began drawing. I stood on my toes and craned forward trying to see what she drew, but the image remained hidden. While she was drawing, Cormac unfolded a street map of San Francisco and spread it on the floor.

Next, he spread a layer of a fine, dark-colored powder over the map. It smelled a little like charcoal.

"What is it?" I whispered to Ben.

"Gunpowder," he said.

This ought to be good. The last item in Cormac's hands was a lighter.

I didn't know enough about magic to be able to guess what spell, incantation, ritual, divination, cantrip, or whatever Cormac was going to work. I was learning more all the time. Amelia's magic seemed to be rooted in items and in ritual. Objects she could manipulate, procedures she could perform, tapping into external symbols rather than drawing on any innate power. Apparently, in some cases magic could be learned and didn't depend on natural psychic ability. This should have been comforting—it meant anyone could control it, and it wasn't so mysterious after all, right? But for the true wizards and magicians I'd met—Odysseus Grant, Harold Franklin, and Amelia Parker—magic wasn't a hobby they'd picked up in a few classes or weekly knitting circles. They'd dedicated their whole lives to the study. It consumed them. In some ways, they became something other than human—as monstrous as I was. They no longer fit with the human community.

That wasn't such a huge change for Cormac, as it turned out. Maybe that was how Amelia had found him—or how they'd found each other. I wondered if I'd ever learn the whole story.

"Are you finished?" he asked Grace after a moment.

She sketched the last couple of lines, then got back to her feet, brushing her hands on her jeans. "Yeah. Don't know how much good it will do you." She gave him back the piece of chalk, which he used to draw a circle around both the map and Grace's drawing. I scooted forward, trying one more time to get a look at what the Dragon's Pearl looked like—she'd drawn something square with squiggles in the middle.

Cormac shot me a look. "Stand back."

I raised my hands in a gesture of innocence and backed away.

Cormac stood just outside the circle. The room was so quiet, I could hear us breathe—at least, those of us who did breathe. The moment demanded stillness. I was about to say something, unable to bear the tension of anticipation any longer, when the sometime-wizard flicked the lighter on and knelt, touching the flame to the map.

A spark flared on the paper, and a tongue of fire leaped a few inches high. Just as quickly, it vanished, leaving behind a wisp of smoke and the smell of sulfur. Cormac remained kneeling, his hand over the map, the smoke curling around him.

"Whoa," Ben murmured. We all leaned forward for a better look at what had happened.

Cormac shook a layer of fine soot off the map and held it up to the light. The flame had burned a perfect pinpoint mark into the map. X marks the spot.

"Really? It's there?" Grace said, moving to Cormac's side to look over his arm at the image.

"I guess so," Cormac said. I studied him, searching for a sign that it was really him, that he was back in control instead of Amelia. His posture seemed more like himself. He smelled like books and leather, a confusing mix that didn't tell me anything.

"That seems too easy," she said.

"Sometimes you just have to lay out what you really want," he said.

"So what," Grace said. "We go pick it up?"

"I doubt it," he said. He began scuffing out the chalk marks with his shoe, erasing the circle and then the drawing, until the whole area was a vague red smudge.

She looked confused, and I explained. "We still don't know who took the thing from the safe in the first place. I assume we're going to have to take it back from them."

Anastasia hadn't spoken through the whole spell casting. The other vampires seemed interested and amused, as if we were entertaining them.

"We'll have to move slow," Cormac said. "Scout ahead and check it out before we go in. Make sure this is even right."

That was Cormac. The hunter was back in charge. Grudgingly, I had to admit that they made a pretty good team, however weird I thought the arrangement.

"Part of the tunnel system goes there," Grace said. "We should be able to get to it, no problem."

"This time we stick together," Cormac said. "Nobody gets lost."

"That's going to depend on what we find," Grace said.

I turned to the vampires. "Anastasia?"

"I think it's a trap," she said.

"Just like last time," I said cheerfully. "Shall we get moving and get this over with?"

Anastasia turned toward the door. "Yes."

"Just like that?" Boss said after her. "You're not going to ask me for help? For an army?"

"As if you would give it."

Boss turned to his right. "Henry? You want to go with them?"

"Sure," the vampire said, shrugging.

"Ah, so now you're sending a spy," Anastasia said, glaring at Boss, sneering at Henry, who actually wilted a bit.

"Yeah. But you don't have anything to hide and he might really be able to help," Boss said.

They couldn't do a damned thing without arguing. I said, "Do vampires ever just help anybody out of the goodness of their hearts?"

"Didn't you know, we don't have hearts," Boss said, and he and his minions laughed.

Cormac looked at me. "I hate vampires."

"Yeah," I muttered.

Boss shrugged. "If you don't want Henry along, just say so and you can go on your merry way."

"He can come," I said before Anastasia could pitch a fit about it. "Thanks for the offer. I'm sure we can use all the help we can get."

Boss inclined his head, the hint of a bow, and Henry winked at me.

Anastasia pursed her lips. "Fine. But you'll listen to me." She pointed at Henry.

"Yes, ma'am," he said.

Boss sighed and shook his head. "I bet we can even find a shirt for Mr. Kitty here. You see how helpful we are?"

"Mr. Kitty?" Ben said, eyebrows raised.

"I may have to borrow that one," Cormac said, smirking.

"Don't even think about it," his cousin said.

I butted in. "A shirt would be great." We could argue about name calling later, though I had to admit I was hating Ben's reaction. *Seriously?*

Henry went to fetch a shirt.

"Well," Anastasia said to Boss. "At least you'll learn how it all turns out."

"It's my city, after all," he said.

"You never did thank me for that."

"Is that all you really want?" he said. "Well then, Anastasia dear, thank you for helping me win San Francisco."

She rolled her eyes and scowled. "Too late."

"Oh, Anastasia, it's never too late. We have all the time in the world."

Of course they did.

Chapter 13

THE SPOT BURNED into the map was back in China-town, not far from where we'd originally met Anastasia. If the Dragon's Pearl had up and wandered away, it hadn't gone far. At least, not far in linear distance. What we couldn't tell was if the pearl was accessible, resting on a shelf in a back room at street level, or if it was hidden in one of the winding tunnels that Grace and her strange key had access to. If that was the case, I couldn't quite trust the spot on the map.

Henry borrowed the car and driver to take us that far. We crammed in and rode in silence until we reached the corner that Grace picked for us to begin quest part two—Stockton Street this time, a block over from Grant, and the not-as-touristy section of Chinatown. The traffic lights hanging above the narrow intersection glowed red, but there were no cars in sight. Old brick and concrete facades stood around us like sentinels, watching, waiting to pounce.

Ben had acquired one of Henry's Havana shirts, red with cream embroidery. He was fidgeting in it; it wasn't a good look for him. I'd rather have seen him in a retro suit with suspenders, maybe a fedora. But hipster it was.

"What do you suppose he'll do if I manage to get this one all bloody?" he said.

"Thank you?" I answered, and he grumbled.

The air had turned cold—winter cold, it felt to my Colorado bones. The damp in the air made the temperature clammy, insidious. I shivered; Ben put his arm around me, and I huddled close.

Grace and Cormac consulted the map.

"I just pointed the way," Cormac was saying. "This is your show now."

"If this is a trap, it'll get us as soon as we head underground," she said.

"Do we have a choice?" Cormac said.

Anastasia glared at them. "Just find me the pearl—I'll worry about the trap."

Grace shot back, "If I'm supposed to be in the lead I'm damn well going to worry about a trap."

"Just *go,*" the vampire said.

We started walking. Grace had the map now and kept glancing at it, then at the buildings. She turned a corner, and another, and into an alley, where a set of stairs led down to a basement door. Here we go again.

"I have to admit, I'm missing my nine mil right about now," Cormac muttered.

"Not that it would do you any good against vampires," Ben said. "Or in the tunnels."

"No. But sometimes I just want to hear something go bang."

Henry acted like he was on a tour, hands in pockets, strolling along looking at all the interesting buildings. "I'm not sensing any trouble. Everything seems normal to me."

I wasn't sure I'd recognize normal any more if it bit me in the ass.

"Where are we going?" Anastasia asked.

"This is the spot on the map, at the mouth of the alley," Grace said. "But there's nothing here, so we have to go underground."

"There's not much underground here, is there?" Henry said. "The tunnel system's an urban legend. The real tunnels were all destroyed in the earthquake back in '06. The previous '06, I mean."

"I don't care how long you've been here, how long you've been alive, you don't know Chinatown," Grace said. She glanced back at Anastasia. "None of you do."

"I've known Chinatown for a hundred and fifty years," Anastasia said.

"But it's not the same. You act like China hasn't changed in eight hundred years. All you know is what you think you know, but that isn't always what's real."

Anastasia sneered at Grace, the puny mortal who had only a fraction of her years. She must have really hated needing the magician's help.

Grace wasn't done. "What about your ancestors? You keep holding mine over me, but what about yours? I bet it's been centuries since you've made any offerings to them—that's why you're having all this shitty luck. Maybe you should be heading to a temple—"

Anastasia reached and caught hold of Grace's neck. Grace gasped, and I jumped, lunging forward to grab hold of the vampire's arm.

"Anastasia, stop," I said.

She glared down at Grace, imperious and dispassionate, while Grace blinked back, struggling for breath. I squeezed Anastasia's arm. "Let go."

She did. I don't know what I would have done if she hadn't. Grace slumped against the wall.

"I have stepped outside the cycle," the vampire said. "I have no descendants to burn offerings for me, so I burn no offerings for anyone else."

"Your ancestors remember you. It doesn't matter how long they've been dead, they're still watching—"

The vampire shook her head and turned away. She murmured, "I'm sorry, Grace Chen. I shouldn't have touched you."

Grace would have been justified in walking away right there. But she reached into her bag and, frowning, said, "Let's get this over with."

We all turned to the door. Cormac tucked his cross and stake back into his jacket.

Grace pulled the candle and lantern from her bag and

handed them to Cormac, who lit the lantern while she shouldered open the door at the base of the stairs. The second oil lantern had evidently been abandoned. Once again, the candle was our only light. We entered a dark tunnel.

"Where does this go?" Henry asked, and Grace shushed him.

Grace led, and Cormac and Anastasia kept close to her; Henry, Ben, and I followed, constantly glancing over our shoulders. The flickering candlelight created shadows, in which I was sure I saw demons.

I'd have thought I'd eventually get used to the feeling that ghosts were moving at the edges of my vision; that tingling feeling had settled into my spine and it wasn't any more comfortable now than it had been at the start. This wasn't my world down here, and I got the impression that I wasn't welcome. None of us were. We'd escaped the tunnels last time—that didn't mean we would again. A rat in a maze must feel like this, closed in, only able to see the paths in front of you and behind, wishing you could somehow see above it all, to see what terrors lurked ahead.

On our last trek, we'd moved forward with some amount of purpose, confident that we'd find what we were looking for at the end of the journey. This time, we walked cautiously, uncertain that any amount of vigilance would help us. I didn't think any of us believed that we'd find the Dragon's Pearl just lying there, waiting for us to take it.

"Ben, Kitty—you guys smell anything?" Cormac called back to us.

"I need a shower," Ben said. "That's about it."

"Hm, shower," I murmured. "Incentive for getting this over with and getting out of here as quickly as possible."

Our footsteps sounded loud on the floor.

"We ought to be getting close," Grace whispered.

We turned the next corner and saw a glow ahead. It could have been anything—a stray lamp, the first light of dawn breaking through a street-side aperture. But as we approached, it took on the quality of a lantern burning— yellow, warm, dancing. Whether we found ourselves in a room, in another part of the tunnel, or in some kind of alternate reality, someone was there, waiting for us. My nostrils widened as I tried to take in as much air as I could, hoping to sense what was waiting for us. I only smelled burning wax, heat, and lingering smoke. It masked whoever was there.

The corridor opened into a room; fanning out, we all saw him at the same time. A man, pale, his dark hair shorn close, his face stern, angular. He wore conservative clothing, a dark button-up shirt, black trousers, and a long overcoat.

It was Roman. He stepped back, his eyes widening for just a moment before he donned his stony, superior mask. I'd have sworn he looked surprised to see us.

"You do have the pearl!" Anastasia said.

"Anastasia," he said simply, flatly. He might have been

greeting her as they passed one another on the street. "It's been a long time."

She hissed at him, teeth bared, fangs showing, furious. When she sprang forward, Henry grabbed her, moving in front of her to force her back. At the moment, she didn't look like a cool and collected player. What showed on her now was hatred. Henry had to wrap his arms around her and lean into her to keep her in check.

Roman looked at each of us in turn. I had an urge to grab Ben with one hand, Cormac with the other, and run hard the other way. Get me and mine out of there. Save ourselves while we still could. If this was a trap that Roman had set, we had little chance of escaping.

Then, I *really* looked.

Five candles burned in a circle around him, and he'd drawn symbols on the floor in red chalk. He, too, had a map of San Francisco spread before him, but his was drawn directly onto the floor, and I only recognized it by the shape of the coast. The streets were all different, wrong—twisting and haphazard, branching oddly and ending in wide blocks or dead ends. It was a map of the phantom tunnel system. Roman wasn't just a vampire, he was also some kind of magician. He'd had lots of time to pick up hobbies here and there, one gathered. He was casting a search spell as Cormac had, to try to find the Dragon's Pearl.

We hadn't found the pearl at all. We'd found him, also searching for the pearl.

"Cormac?" I murmured, in lieu of a more useful question. His spell had gone awry, evidently.

"Huh," he said. "Weird."

Ben's hand closed on my arm, transmitting his tension. Were we going to run? Fight? Those were the wolves' choices. My choice was usually to talk. I had to swallow a couple of times, because my voice stuck.

"So, have you found it?" I said finally.

Roman cocked his head, and I couldn't tell if he was amused or annoyed. Maybe he was trying to decide. "The elusive Katherine Norville," he said. If only he had a handlebar moustache to twirl.

"Not really. I'm pretty easy to find."

"Yes," he said. "You keep throwing yourself in front of avalanches."

Yeah, about that . . . "I guess this means you haven't found it, either." Roman—not omnipotent. I should have been pleased.

"It's mine!" Anastasia shouted. "I'll find it! You'll never get it, you'll never have its power!"

"You were my slave, and you're still little more than that, aren't you?" Roman said to Anastasia, dismissing her with a glance, without a wasted emotion. "It's only a matter of time. One of us will find it. If you do, I'll simply take it from you."

Someday, I would get the long and sordid story about those two and all the centuries they'd been at each other's throats. But enough of the witty banter. I squeezed

Ben's arm. "It's time to go, I think. Henry, get her out of here."

"Henry, wait," Roman said.

Henry stopped. His attention turned to Roman, drawn as if on a thread.

"Bring her to me."

Henry moved toward him, steps slow and heavy. He tilted his head, and his expression turned pursed, confused, as if he could not understand why he was obeying. And yet he kept moving.

"Henry, stop," Anastasia said, and he did. But he didn't let her go.

"It's all right," Roman said. "It's going to be fine. Bring her here."

The anxious lines in Henry's face went slack as his will vanished. Anastasia struggled, pulling against his grasp as he dragged her forward.

This wasn't happening. I didn't care if Roman thought he was god-emperor of vampires, this wasn't happening. I sprang at Henry, hoping to knock him off balance enough that Anastasia could break free. Then I hoped she'd have the sense to get herself out of here instead of going after Roman again.

I slammed my weight on his arms to break that grip. Instead, we all crashed into the wall. I didn't have much that worked against vampires, but I tried, jamming my elbow into his throat and biting a meaty bicep. I didn't want to hurt him, I just wanted to rattle him. Shake him loose from Roman's control. I had no idea if it would work.

Anastasia wrenched free with a snarl, and I scrambled away from them both.

She was getting ready to pounce at Roman again. I grabbed her arm.

"Go, get Grace out of here," I said. "You guys have to find the pearl before he does." Her expression twisted with the indecision—stay to fight her nemesis, or be the first to get the artifact. The big-picture goal must have won because she took Grace by the hand, and together they ran. "Henry?" I said, hoping to get through to him. "Henry!"

He was staring at Roman, still entranced, waiting for the next instruction.

"Kill the wolf," Roman said to him, and Henry looked at me.

So much for that.

"Ben," I hissed, looking for my husband. I didn't have to look far—he stood behind me, shoulders hunched, ready to attack. I grabbed his arm and pulled him toward the doorway. "We gotta go."

I thought Cormac was right with us, on the same page—escape and regroup. But during the commotion, Anastasia's outburst, and Henry's enslavement, he'd clung to the wall and worked his way around the edge of the room. He was going to do something stupid; it wasn't going to work. I kept my wide-eyed gaze on Roman, hoping not to draw any attention to the hunter, who had slipped Wyatt Earp's polished stake into his hand.

He lunged, stabbing the stake down toward Roman's back. The strike was perfect—the careful stalking, the patient waiting, and the pounce that came without warning, without a flinch. Any wolf pack would be proud of such a hunt.

Roman saw it coming anyway.

The vampire pivoted back, arm raised, cracking his fist into Cormac's face. The hunter fell, limbs loose, crumpling to the stone floor. Blood streamed from a split lip.

Ben and I sprang to protect our family. Hunting as a pack now, we went low and high, me for Roman's legs and Ben for his throat. Not that either target would have any impact on the immortal undead. If we chewed long enough maybe we could rip his head off. If only Roman would give us the opportunity.

The vampire punched, putting his whole body into the strikes, one fist into Ben's face, the other into mine, in almost the same movement. I hit the floor and saw lights. Roman stood, immovable as stone. We were never going to win this fight, and in my gut Wolf whined, kicking with an urge to flee.

Roman moved before the doorway, blocking our exit while the three of us were still picking ourselves up off the floor. This would be the perfect chance for someone standing in the doorway to put a stake in the guy's back, but Grace and Anastasia had fled; the hallway behind

Roman was empty. Well. At least they'd gotten away. Roman didn't appear willing to give us a chance to do the same.

In the absence of any targets directly in front of him, Henry had paused, looking at Roman and waiting for the next command.

"Henry!" I called. "Henry, please, wake up! Help us!"

"Henry, sleep," Roman said. The younger vampire closed his eyes and slumped against the wall, not even bothering to fall all the way to the floor. He seemed suddenly childlike and helpless. How could I ever think of a vampire as helpless?

The walls felt like they were getting closer.

"Cormac?" I whispered. I sounded hoarse, Wolf's voice on the surface. Still holding the stake, he nodded. If we could distract Roman, we might get a second chance. Roman couldn't fight all three of us at once, could he?

Actually, he could.

He moved too fast, and his senses were too good. No matter how we tried to game it—one or two of us attacked from the front while another of us waited to ambush from behind, or all of us tried to jump him from three different directions—he was always ready. To strike first, to step out of the way, to grab one of us and slam us into the other. He'd survived for two thousand years. He knew *a lot* of tricks.

We were getting pummeled, but we kept going because we could take a lot of pummeling. My injured leg had gone stiff, throbbing with pain. Cormac—he'd slowed down and half his face was bloody. He couldn't take much more of this, but how did we stop it? Roman was playing with us, catlike.

Get Roman away from the door, grab Henry, then run. That was the plan. I gave Ben a nod, hoping to communicate this to him. He was panting for breath, and his own wolf glinted gold in his eyes.

Someone whistled, a high, sharp note that hurt my Wolf's ears. It sounded close, right behind me even, but I couldn't see who made the noise. I didn't dare look away from Roman, who was glancing behind him, also searching for the source. None of us saw it. Our breathing echoed harshly; Roman was silent.

The whistle came again, and we all looked, watchful and ready to pounce. I wouldn't have been so worried except that Roman didn't seem to know what it was, either. His brow had gone furrowed, anxious.

The attack came from the shadows in the hallway. A long, wooden staff struck at Roman's legs, toppling him. He hadn't seen it coming. I was in awe.

Roman rolled to his back, looking for his attacker, and Sun sprang over him, smacking him back with the end of the staff.

Now if only it had been a sharpened stake able to puncture his chest.

Sun seemed content to slap the vampire around. He was grinning, like this was fun. I just stared and wondered where he'd come from and why he thought beating up an evil vampire—rather than staking him—was a good idea. Did he even know Roman was a vampire? And how the hell was he able to beat him up in the first place? Roman dodged the blows from the staff, but he wasn't able to get to his feet, much less get in a strike of his own.

Their speed seemed impossible. Sun's next blow came even as Roman dodged the last. Though Sun never stopped moving, striking, none of the subsequent hits landed. They were two perfect warriors.

Meanwhile, something had happened to the room— the candles flared brighter, and the chalk lines on the floor had taken on some of their own light.

"Cormac?" I asked.

"I see it," he said. He was holding his side and wiping his bloody face on his sleeve.

Sun seemed to have a strategy that may not have involved destroying Roman. Instead, he was leading Roman away from the door—giving us an escape route. I grabbed Ben to get his attention. Together we helped Cormac to his feet. Cormac moved sluggishly. He was fine, I told myself, heart racing. He'd be fine.

The candles were sparking now, hissing with fire. I had to squint my eyes against them.

"Wait a minute," Cormac said, his fingers digging into my arm as he tried to wrench out of my grip, to turn back. "His spell, it's reacting—the pearl, it's here, *it's here*!"

We stopped. Roman heard him, too, because he looked at us.

"What are you talking about?" I hissed, because it didn't make any sense. The pearl hadn't been here when we got here, I didn't see anything that looked like a pearl now—what had changed?

Sun. Sun had arrived.

The young man had backed off. Planting his staff on the floor, he leaned on it and regarded us with a big goofy grin, as if he'd just delivered the punch line of a really awful joke. His breathing wasn't labored, though sweat gleamed on his hairline.

He hooked a thumb around the strap of the bag he wore over his shoulder and said, "You want this? I don't think so."

Roman turned to him with a look of such hunger and determination, his craggy face had gone slack. Sun smiled like it was a game.

"Sun, get out of here!" I called, my voice thick with desperation, despair.

"You get out," he said. "I've got it covered."

Roman lunged for him.

"Ben," I said, clinging to him.

"I don't know why he doesn't just run," Ben said.

"He's got something in his hand," Cormac said.

"Who, Sun? Or—"

No. Roman had pulled something from his pocket and threw it in the space behind Sun. The powder hit the flares along the ring of candles and exploded, knocking Sun off his stance. He hit the floor, rolled—didn't drop his staff, but ended up on his back, with the vampire looming over him.

I lunged forward. "We have to help, we have to stop—"

Again they were too fast, and I was too slow. Sun swung to block Roman. Roman ducked and slashed with the knife he held in his other hand, slicing through the strap of the bag.

The vampire grabbed it, strode away, and came face to face with me. Ben was at my shoulder. I sure hoped Cormac was conjuring some spell to counter him.

From under my shirt I pulled out the cross Cormac had given me, back at the beginning of the night, eons ago. I held it up to him, sure that it wouldn't do any good, but needing to try.

Sure enough, Roman's lip curled, mocking me. "You know I can destroy you."

"You can't have it," I said, nodding at the cloth sack in his hand. Something heavy inside it bulged.

"Yes, I can."

I threw the cross at him. He ducked without effort and flung his arm at me in a backhanded strike. I fell before it landed—Ben pushing me out of the way. We both hit the hard stone floor.

Roman tossed out more of the flammable powder, which burst in a wall of flame that filled the room. Sun had picked himself up, but had to duck again. I curled up, arms around my head—I could smell my hair burning. Ben crouched over me. I hoped Cormac and Henry were okay—

Smoke burned my lungs and made my eyes water. I couldn't see or smell anything. The bursts of fire and smoke were magicians' tricks. Roman had baffled us with bullshit, as they say. When I could raise my head again, when the room had cleared, Roman was gone. Maybe Grace and Anastasia could stop him. But I rather hoped he didn't find them at all.

"You okay?" Ben asked, helping me up. His hair was singed, his skin flush with the heat, but he seemed uninjured. I squeezed his arms back.

"Think so. Cormac?"

"Fine," he said, brushing himself off. He'd crouched by the wall. "Roman's gone, though. With the pearl."

I looked at Sun, crouched in a defensive posture, staff braced across him. At least his smile had turned sheepish. "Yeah. Um, oops?"

"*Oops?*" I said. "Just who are you?"

"The guy with the Dragon's Pearl? At least, I was."

"*You* took it from the safe?" I said.

"Yeah. When we found out so many people were looking for it, it seemed best to move it. To keep it safe."

I glared. "You did a hell of a job of it!"

"You needed help," he said, pointing the staff at me.

"That's beside the point!"

Ben touched my arm, interrupting. "Kitty? Where's Henry?"

The wall where Henry had slumped was empty. I thought of all the fire, looked for a pile of ash where he used to be—nothing. The room looked desolate. The chalk marks were smeared, the candles had melted to puddles of spent wax.

"Roman took him," Cormac said.

My injured leg, weak and throbbing from the fight, finally gave out. Ben and Sun both caught me as I fell. I sat there a moment, sprawling, both of them hanging onto me, and fought back tears. So, the worst vampire ever now had the super magical thingy. And Henry, whom I'd been getting to like. And we were once again stuck in the impossible tunnels without our guide.

What was Sun, really? I stared at him. "We need to find Grace and Anastasia. But *you* get to tell her what happened."

"Aw, her?" he said. "She's really a big old softy on the inside."

"Let's go," Ben said before I could scream.

With Cormac hobbling in the lead, Ben and I leaning on each other, and Sun bringing up the rear, we left the scorched and smoking room and made our way down the corridor. The walls seemed to glow with their own green phosphorescence. I squinted; Wolf's vision saw everything as shadow.

We came to a T intersection.

"Which way?" Ben asked.

"The others went left," he said, and so we went left. "Oh by the way, nice to see you again. Human this time, even."

"What?"

"We met earlier, but you were furry then."

"Huh—"

"Have you been watching us?" I said. "Following us?"

"Maybe a little," Sun said.

"Who are you? *What* are you, some kind of ninja?"

"Um, no."

The musty corridor continued. Ahead, Grace's candle shone, but the light seemed dampened. Maybe it was just my outlook.

Ben and Cormac pulled up short; I almost ran into them. Sun was behind me, looking back. He held his staff in both hands, blocking, waiting for attack.

Ahead of us, Grace stood in the middle of the hallway, and Anastasia leaned against the wall. She looked exhausted and still fuming, like she wanted to run right back to take on Roman.

"You waited," I said to Anastasia, startled.

She nodded at Grace. "Chen wouldn't let me leave. What happened?"

We all looked at Sun, who scuffed a sneaker on the stone floor and winced. "Well. First I had the pearl—I took it from the safe to protect it. Then I lost it." He shrugged.

I was used to seeing vampires as calm and imperious,

moving serenely through the world, which crashed like waves around them. Pillars of stone, unmoving and unfeeling.

Anastasia closed her eyes and wilted. Shoulders slumped, head bent, face drained of what little life it had. "Then it's over," she whispered.

"No," I said, shaking my head. "There has to be a way to find him. We can still get it back, we can still stop him. We got away from the cabin in Montana, we can get away from this."

"Kitty—" Anastasia breathed.

"We can kill him, we have to—"

"Are you sure he *can* be killed?" Ben said.

Anastasia railed. "None of you understand. None of you know what we're up against."

"I'll go after him," Sun said. "I'm the one who lost the pearl, I'll get it back, no problem." He leaned casually on his staff as if it was an extra, familiar limb.

"What can you *possibly* do?" Anastasia spat.

Sun waved a confident hand. "Leave it to me. That way the rest of you can get out of the tunnels entirely. Go home, have a cup of tea, and forget you were ever here. And you—" He pointed at Grace. "You should know better than that, bringing these people here. You know what's down here, and I'm not talking about crazy Western vampires."

Grace had been staring at him, mouth working like she wanted to say something but couldn't decide what. She finally shot back, "Who are you?"

I looked at him. "I thought you said you knew her."

He shrugged. "I said I knew her. I never said she knew me. But I think she does—she just doesn't know it yet."

Riddles, conundrums, secrets. I hated it. We'd had our chance to finish off Roman, and we'd lost it. We'd tried to fight him, and we couldn't. We'd lost Henry. It was time to go home, circle the wagons, and hope Roman didn't come after us. I went to Ben and Cormac, who slouched against the wall, looking terrible. Ben guarded him. I touched their arms, as much for my comfort as for theirs.

Anastasia lunged toward Sun, hand outstretched and pointed as if dispensing a curse. He stood his ground.

"How old are you?" Anastasia said to him.

"*Really* old," he said. She stared, but her vampiric gaze had no effect against him. "Older than you, even."

"All right," I said, turning on them. "What the hell are you? You're not a vampire. What else is that old?"

"Yeah, that's the question, isn't it?" he said, his smile growing broad. Still smiling despite everything. Made me want to either punch the guy, or laugh.

Anastasia backed away, suddenly fearful. I'd seen that expression on her before—when we'd seen the nine-tailed fox in the cage.

While Anastasia showed fear when regarding Sun, Grace showed wonder. Maybe even a little hope. "Sun Wukong."

He lifted the staff, twirled it once, and gave a playful bow. He seemed pleased. "I knew you'd know me."

"What are you doing here?" she said.

"What I always do, Grace Chen. I'm protecting what must be protected. Getting into trouble." He winced at this last.

I drew close to my pack of three. Cormac was watching the exchange through a swollen eye. Red and puffy now, it would turn impressively black in a day or two. He was still holding his side as if ribs were broken. We needed to get him someplace safe to rest.

He gripped my shoulder. "Sun Wukong. The Monkey King."

I'd heard the name before—a Chinese folk hero, a character in a story. I still didn't know what that meant in terms of the man standing before us. He seemed so . . . ordinary.

"Am I talking to Cormac or Amelia?" I said.

He frowned and gave a curt shake of his head. "He never should have attacked that vampire. I tried to tell him it was useless but he wouldn't listen. He so rarely listens."

That was Amelia, speaking with Cormac's voice. Berating him with it.

He shook his head again; this time the gesture was tired. "She's never hunted vampires, not like I have. She doesn't know what she's talking about."

And that was Cormac. This was weird, even by my standards.

"You two are arguing like married people," I said.

"You should hear it on the inside," he answered, and I didn't know who was talking that time.

"I've helped you about as much as I can—and caused enough trouble, I think," Sun said. "This isn't your fight, not anymore. Anastasia, you're blinded by your own history. You need to let it go. Be at peace for once in your life."

"Don't feed me your Buddhist drivel!"

Sun shook his head. "That's the trouble with you vampires. You step out of the world and think it makes you free."

"But you don't understand, if Roman has the Dragon's Pearl—"

"It's not the end of the world. Trust me. Go home and rest."

His words were persuasive. They were meant to be, to ease us out of this crazy underground world and back into the mundane one. Back to my normal werewolf life. This wasn't my problem. Larger powers were at work here, and I wasn't one of them. Didn't I keep saying that?

Ben and Cormac were both looking at me, as if they could tell what I was thinking. As if they knew I wasn't going to let this go. Neither of them argued. I ran my hand over Ben's head, brushing my fingers through his hair. He nudged my hand, wolflike. More in-depth communication would have to wait. I so wanted the chance to curl up in his arms and believe that we were going to be safe.

"We have to try to find Henry," I said.

"He's just a vampire," Sun said. I glared at him.

"That's not the only problem," Grace said. She'd started pacing, only a few steps in the confines of the passageway. "How did that vampire—what's his name?"

"Roman," I said.

"How'd he get down here?" she went on. "How'd he find his way into the tunnels, much less through them, without getting lost? Who's his guide?"

Sun's expression didn't change, and Grace looked grim, but Anastasia had turned apprehensive again—as if she knew exactly the shape of the world outside her control.

A sound reached us, muffled, blocked by a wall or a door, but close enough to track. I held my breath and listened—it sounded like a baby crying. I knew that sound; the hair on the back of my neck prickled, and my gut turned cold.

Sun moved toward the sound. "Uh-oh."

"What do you mean, 'uh-oh'?" Ben shot at him.

Sun turned back to the rest of us. "Someone wants to meet us."

Sun—Sun Wukong, the Monkey King—gestured, and we looked to see the nine-tailed fox sitting at the end of the corridor, shining ruddy in a small patch of light. It opened its mouth to make that eerie, too-human noise of a hungry infant. Instead of being attracted to it this time, I was horrified. Wrong, this was all wrong. I wanted to run, to flee. I reached for and found Ben's hand, and he squeezed back.

"Who?" Anastasia said. "I won't go until you say who has summoned us."

"Do we have a choice about this?" I said.

"You know who the *huli jing* belongs to," Grace said, wondering. She seemed entranced as she stepped toward the creature, which then jumped to its feet and twitched its tails, waving them. The bundle of tails blurred, it seemed to move so quickly, the red fur sparking in the dim light.

Grace went toward the fox, and I followed with my pack because I didn't want to leave her alone. Anastasia hesitated, but Sun gestured, and she went forward. He brought up the rear.

The fox bounded ahead and stopped at a side door that I swore hadn't been there before. This one had Chinese written directly on the wood—another blessing or a warning? The fox yipped—this time, the sound was like a child's sharp laugh. Standing on its hind legs, it put its paws on the door as if hoping to push it open, but it was too heavy. Grace went to help it, and Sun joined her. With the three of them pushing together, the door creaked open, wood scraping against the concrete floor, dust shaking from the hinges. A warm light shone from the room behind the door.

I held back, feeling like I was stepping into someone else's story. I didn't understand the rules and symbols that were being shown to me.

"Grace?" I asked softly.

"Just watch," she said. "And be quiet. Be respectful. You think you can do that?"

Normally, I could never promise to be quiet. Somehow, I didn't have much of an urge to speak just now.

"What's happening?" Ben said. I shook my head, so he turned to Cormac.

"Never seen anything like it. Neither of us," he said.

We entered the room.

Chapter 14

T HE NINE-TAILED FOX bounded forward like a puppy greeting its favorite person. Its final leap took it into the lap of a woman, middle-aged and full-bodied, seated in a chair, ornately carved and lacquered in black and gold. Cooing, the woman gathered the animal close, scratching its ears, rubbing its flanks, bringing her face close so the fox could lick her chin and nose, which it did joyfully, and the woman laughed.

The woman—she must have been of average height, of normal size. But she seemed to fill the space. Her face was kind and beautiful, though what must have been smooth porcelain features when she was young had softened to make her more approachable, more motherly. Her thick hair, black and shining, was twisted into a knot and held in place by sticks carved from a milky green stone—jade, maybe. The robe she wore over a multi-layered gown was silk and shining, royal blue, with dense images embroidered in gold and silver, belted around her waist with a braided gold cord. She smelled like incense and peaches.

Her chair's arm on the right-hand side was carved in the shape of an angry, bulging-eyed tiger, its stripes painted like daggers. The left-hand arm was shaped like a dragon, body twisted around on itself, slender whiskers trailing from a mouth full of teeth. On the back of her chair stood a large black bird, a crow. It hopped back and forth, snapping its beak and shaking its feathers at us. It had three legs, three sets of claws to scrabble at the wood.

The chair sat on a wooden porch overlooking a night-time garden, however impossible that should have been. We were in a room, in a tunnel system under downtown San Francisco. And yet, a pond spread out from the porch, its surface dark and glasslike, reflecting back the image of a blossoming tree that grew from the shore nearby. From the branches hung red paper lanterns that gave off a peaceful light. Across the pond I thought I could make out buildings, carved railings around more porches, lit windows, tiled pagoda roofs that didn't seem out of place here—an entire palace complex.

I smelled fresh air and the scent of peach blossoms. My mouth watered.

Grace knelt, her hands pressed flat together and touching her nose, her eyes tightly shut—praying hard, keenly devout. She may not even have been breathing.

Anastasia stared, and her expression altered, slack wonder pulling into grief, lips pursed, brow furrowed, eyes narrowing until I thought she might cry. Finally, she covered her face with her hands and sagged.

Behind us, Sun quietly closed the door.

We waited. No one could hurry this woman or make demands. She could ignore the tableau before her forever, and that would be fine. And what a tableau—two Chinese women who obviously knew who and what she was and were awed into immobility; and three white-bread American tourists, rude and ignorant, cowboys in a china shop, as it were. If we didn't move, maybe we wouldn't break anything.

Then there was Sun Wukong, who looked on her as a friend. That look made me relax a little.

Finally, she kissed the fox on the top of its head and urged it away, stroking the length of its body, including the batch of tails, as it hopped off her lap and took up the position of a sentinel under a pedestal table next to the chair. It wrapped all its tails around its feet like a big fur stole.

She straightened, regarded us all, then focused that regal gaze on Sun. "Well, Sun Wukong, I gave you a simple task and look what happens. Always trouble with you!"

"And yet you keep trusting me. Look, I had everything under control—"

She raised a hand, and he stopped. She turned her gaze on the rest of us. I suddenly wanted to apologize. This felt like I'd been brought to the principal's office.

"Grace Chen," the woman on the throne said, her voice

gentle. Grace, her nut-brown skin flushed with emotion, bowed even lower.

The woman began speaking to her in what I assumed was Chinese. I didn't understand, but the tone was kind, not at all accusing like it had been a moment before.

I glanced at Anastasia, hoping for a translation, but her eyes were tightly shut.

Sun saw my look and translated. "Xiwangmu is telling her that her family has done well, guarding the Dragon's Pearl for these centuries, but the task is finished now. She's releasing the family from its vow."

Grace was looking up at her now, smiling.

"Xiwangmu?" I whispered.

"She is the Queen Mother of the West." Sun raised a hand to silence my next question and watched.

Anastasia stepped forward, shocked and appalled, her hands closed into angry fists, and spoke a sharp sentence in Chinese. Sun jumped to stand between her and Xiwangmu, blocking the vampire's way with his staff. Anastasia hissed at him, and he laughed, at which she snarled and turned away.

The woman on the throne regarded her a moment, then spoke. I didn't understand the words, but the tone was reproachful. Anastasia didn't turn around, but as the lecture went on, her back bowed, her shoulders slumped, and she seemed like a child being punished for something horrible that she'd done.

Maybe this wasn't my world and maybe I didn't belong here, but I had to find out what was happening.

"Um, I'm sorry, excuse me . . ." My voice sounded wrong and startling. I inched forward. The fox sitting under the table flattened its ears and bared its teeth, and the woman on the throne, Xiwangmu, flashed her dark gaze at me. If the door behind us was still open, I'd have been tempted to flee. "I know Anastasia's kind of obsessed, but she's my friend, sort of, and . . . I want to help." I didn't know how I could help when I was in so far over my head. But that was why I asked. If that elegant woman told me to leave, to forget about all this, what would I do then?

She studied me, and in my belly Wolf curled into defensive huddle, cowering at the scrutiny. Ben was standing behind me; I could feel his warmth, and that settled me. But this so wasn't our territory.

When the woman smiled—a slight, amused curl of her lips—my knees went wobbly with relief.

"This is not your battle, child," Xiwangmu said.

Encouraged, I said, "Anastasia asked me to help, so it is. Her enemy—the one who has the pearl now, and Henry—is my enemy, too." *And your enemy, as well.* None of us alone could stop him. Well, maybe *she* could stop him by herself. I got the feeling she could do anything she wanted.

Everyone else was watching me with the air of witnessing a wreck. Quiet and respectful, Grace had ordered. Hey, I'd tried . . .

The woman leaned back in her throne. "Do you know why she hates Gaius Albinus, the one called Dux Bellorum?"

Anastasia flinched at the name; I glanced at her, trying to read her, but she was trapped in her storm of emotion.

"Not exactly, no," I said.

Xiwangmu turned to Anastasia. "You've not told anyone your story, have you?"

"No one," Anastasia said, stifled and hoarse. "Not even you."

"And yet I know it, for you were mine before he made you his."

I looked at Anastasia, trying to parse what Xiwangmu had said, considering the implications. It changed the meaning of everything Anastasia had ever said to me. I'd never guessed. Maybe I should have.

"Anastasia? Roman made you a vampire?" I said. She didn't answer.

I tried to imagine the scene, eight hundred years ago, Anastasia—except she wouldn't have been Anastasia then, she would have had a different name, a different life—standing in sunlight, in some farm or town or village in the middle of China. Roman had started as a soldier, part of an occupying army on the eastern Mediterranean. How had he traveled thousands of miles east across deserts and mountains to find her? What could possibly have happened?

Xiwangmu spoke with the slow cadence of telling a story, full of depth and consequence. Her tone held both kindness and pity. "Li Hua was the young daughter of a prosperous merchant in the city of Changzhou. Then the barbarian raiders came—Mongols from the north. The city resisted the invasion, and so the Mongols slaughtered everyone. Only a few survived. When they came to Li Hua, they said, 'Look, this girl does not cry. How strange.' But she could not cry—everyone was dead, with no one left to bury them, no children left to light incense at the altars for the ancestors, whose ghosts were wailing. What good was crying in the face of that? They took her prisoner, made her a slave, and brought her to Kublai Khan. They made her a concubine, a prize of the great empire of China—the girl, the beautiful flower who never wept. That was the end of the Song Dynasty.

"Our two worlds, East and West, were beginning to discover one another. The Silk Road, the trade routes across Asia, were strong. This was the time of Marco Polo. That was how Dux Bellorum came to China, seeking power, magic, and allies. The mysterious trader who traveled only at night and who never feared bandits fascinated all who met him. In the court of Kublai Khan he found a slave, a strange young woman who barely spoke and who troubled many with her cold gaze. Who knows what Dux Bellorum thought when he saw her, except that he believed he had some use for her, so he bought her from the Khan for an ingot of gold and a pair of Arabian horses.

"She served him for years, learned what he was, learned of his plans—and began making plans of her own. The General needed lieutenants. Sure of her loyalty, he turned her, made her one of his army. But she was always stronger than any of her captors knew. When she'd gained that part of his power, she escaped. Broke the bonds between them, smashed his token, and fled. That was how Li Hua came to the West and became, eventually, Anastasia."

She had probably looked a lot like this, standing before Mongol invaders, her city burning around her, her anger and sadness buried deep, showing only a hard mask to the outside world. Xiwangmu had revealed the story to us all, and she might as well have stripped Anastasia bare, the way the vampire bore it. Her air of elegance and poise was suddenly a pretty, decorated facade disguising an edifice of tragedy. I wanted to weep, and I wanted to murder Roman for doing this to her.

From a pocket in her trouser, Anastasia drew out what looked like a pendant on a chain and held it out to Xiwangmu. Whatever design had once been on it, it was now smashed, flattened, and crossed with a dozen hatch marks carved into the bronze. I still had the one we'd flattened earlier; this one was hers.

Xiwangmu took it from her and clasped her hand. "I have watched you all this time, child," she continued. "The spirits of your ancestors begged me to watch over you, and so I have, as much as I could."

Anastasia whispered, "I remember holding my mother's hand when we went to your temple to light offerings and pray to you. I have tried to remember her, to honor her—"

"She knows."

"Is her spirit safe? Contented?"

"She is," Xiwangmu said.

Anastasia bowed her head and finally, after all this time, tears fell. "My spirit will never join with my ancestors. No one will ever light offerings at my grave."

"You have a different path," Xiwangmu said. Anastasia—Li Hua—nodded. She had probably known that from the beginning.

Grace stood and tentatively went to the vampire and touched her arm, a brief offering of comfort. I held my breath, waiting for Anastasia to turn her back, isolate herself. But she took Grace's hand and squeezed it before letting it go.

Xiwangmu straightened, shifting moods, tones—no longer a matron telling a story, she became a queen making a pronouncement.

"The Dragon's Pearl is gone. Now, we must decide how to build defenses against the one who has taken it. How to oppose one with so much power."

"Wait a minute," I said, and I could see Grace and Anastasia both flinch. "That's it? What about trying to get it back? What about getting Henry back?"

"Do we know that Roman is just going to leave town now that he has it?" Cormac said. "Not come back and try to finish you off?" He nodded at me and Anastasia. Finishing us off—it was what Cormac would have done.

"Be quiet," Grace hissed. "Let Queen Mother speak!"

Xiwangmu had cocked her head, listening, turning her gaze to me. "How would you oppose the Roman?"

I swallowed a lump in my throat at the sudden, intent scrutiny. I hadn't thought about the how of it, just that it needed to be done.

"There has to be a way to find him," I said finally. "Trace him, track him, something. Grace said he has to have a guide in the tunnels, someone who's been helping him. Maybe we find who that is, and from there find Henry and the pearl."

"Henry is gone, Kitty," Anastasia said softly.

"I don't want to have to tell Boss that," I countered.

"*I'll* tell him," she said.

Xiwangmu raised a hand, and Anastasia settled. "This guide, the one who is helping Gaius Albinus. I think you are right, and that we should discover who this is. For our own protection, if nothing else." She folded her hands before her and narrowed her eyes in thought. After a moment, she glanced at Sun, who was leaning on his staff, looking back.

"Do you have any ideas?" she asked.

"I do. You won't like it, though," he said.

"Yes, indeed." Sighing, she said, "To oppose us, it would have to be one of us."

"One of you?" I said. "What does that even mean? You're not vampires, you're not demons or spirits. What are you?"

Sun laughed. "What, is this so you can go home and

look us up in your encyclopedia? Check another category off in your supernatural guidebook?"

I flushed. I was usually the one taking the piss out of everything. "I just want to know."

"Of course you do—you're a nosy American."

I rolled my eyes.

Behind me, Ben said close to my ear, "You're never going to get a straight answer."

I never did.

Sun came over to me, planted his staff in front of me, leaned heavily on it, and grinned. "Surely you can guess what we are, can't you? You must have some idea."

If I did, my conscious mind was shying away from the knowledge, because it was impossible. It couldn't possibly be right.

Xiwangmu leaned an elbow on the arm of her throne. The look in her eyes was part amused, part impatient. The look a teacher would give a slow student. She said, "Katherine Norville called Kitty—we're gods."

Chapter 15

I'D BEEN CAUGHT up in events over my head quite a few times over the years. Just when I thought I was getting pretty good at treading water and keeping stable, a new wave came up to knock me over. A bigger one. The waves were getting very big these days, and I was less sure of my ability to stay afloat than ever before. There was too much to know. I'd never learn it all. I would never learn half of what I needed to know. Yet somehow I had to keep trying—and hope.

Of course they were gods. Anastasia had worshipped this woman since she was a child, eight hundred years ago. Because Xiwangmu had earned such worship.

Still, I shook my head. "No. I've seen a lot of crazy stuff and met a lot of weird beings. But this is where I draw the line."

Sun said, "Take everything else that you know is real— vampires and werewolves and ghosts are the least of it. Why not this, too?"

"But that would mean everything is real," I said.

Sun raised an affirming brow.

I had always drawn lines. Before I became a werewolf, I had assumed—blithely, confidently—that I knew what was real and what wasn't. The world was solid and logical. Then I'd been attacked by an oversized wolf late one night, and a lot of assumptions turned inside out. Werewolves were real, and I'd stepped through a certain kind of looking glass. Then I'd met vampires, were-jaguars, were-tigers, psychics, wizards, ghosts, djinn, fairies. With each encounter I erased the line and drew it a little further out. Like, maybe Bram Stoker's *Dracula* had been based on a real-live—real-undead—vampire. Maybe a lot of those stories had their roots in reality. But that didn't mean that some ultrapowerful guy named Zeus ever turned himself into a swan to try to pick up girls. It didn't mean that when you prayed there was actually someone out there listening.

Did it?

"I don't understand," I said simply. Maybe it was *don't*. More likely it was *can't*. I was caught in a cosmic tsunami.

"It's best if you don't think about it too hard," Sun said.

That was the problem—I didn't trust what I couldn't think about and pick apart. What was I supposed to do, knowing that the world was *that big*? How did you strip down and take a shower knowing that some omnipotent god somewhere might be watching? Answer: you lived very, very softly, to make sure no god took an interest in you. I thought about this, regarded the Monkey King and Queen Mother of the West, and realized I was pretty much fucked, wasn't I?

Ben loomed protectively nearby. He put his arm across my shoulders, pulling me into the shelter of his body, kissed my head above my ear and stayed there a moment, his lips pressed against me, his breath stirring my hair. I closed my eyes and focused on that touch, because that was my answer—you clung to what you loved, and that kept you going.

"We need to discuss," Xiwangmu said. She clapped twice and a pair of girls appeared from the shadows, dressed in elaborate silk gowns, their hair done up with pins and charms. They carried trays stacked with bowls and saucers and a steaming pot of what smelled like earthy, spicy tea. They spread a cloth on the floor and began arranging tea service for seven.

"Do we have time for this?" I said. "It must be getting close to dawn."

"It's an hour away," Anastasia said.

I didn't have a watch; our phones had gone back to dead, and we had no way of telling time. The night seemed to have gone on for days already. It had gone on forever. But clearly Anastasia knew exactly how close sunrise was. Not that she seemed worried about it—she'd gone back to her poised, superior self. She was also staying close to Xiwangmu, within reach of her throne, as if she planned on kneeling at the goddess's feet at any moment. She and Grace both stayed close to her, like an honor guard.

"This is a war council," Xiwangmu said. "Now, sit."

The serving girls had vanished when I wasn't looking. Xiwangmu left her throne to take her place in the circle, and Anastasia and Grace sat on either side of her. The nine-tailed fox crept out from under the table and pressed itself to its mistress's side, and she clicked at it and scratched its ears. I sat across from her, flanked by my own escort of Cormac and Ben. Ben was looking growly; Cormac looked like he wanted to take notes. He still had a bruised eye and cuts from his fight with Roman, but he didn't seem to mind. The injuries were fading, as if just being here had a healing influence. Maybe it did.

Sun Wukong dropped his staff, which vanished. I was looking right at it and it vanished. He let go, it should have fallen to the floor, but it never did. He flopped cross-legged in the spot between Grace and Cormac, the two magicians. I kept staring.

"What?" he said.

"Where'd it go?"

He tilted his head and smirked, clearly admonishing me for asking such a silly question.

Xiwangmu raised an apple-size bowl of tea and sipped. The rest of us followed suit. I didn't know what I expected the tea to taste like—something magical and divine, probably. Exotic and full of sparks and fireworks. A tea that would fill me with enlightenment and reveal the answers to all my abstract questions.

It was just green tea, maybe with a hint of mint. It tasted very good, maybe the best green tea I'd ever had—perfect leaves harvested at the perfect time and brewed perfectly in exactly the right temperature water. But I couldn't sense anything magic in it. I wasn't sure I was supposed to.

Xiwangmu said, "You seem disappointed."

"What? Oh, no, it's fine. It's really good. It's just I wondered if maybe you'd spike it with the nectar of the gods or something." I shrugged and ducked a sheepish gaze. Anastasia frowned at me, and Grace gaped at me, appalled. "Stupid idea. Forget I said it."

Sun laughed, but it was good-natured, not mocking. Friendly. He said, "You want the Elixir of Immortality from her, you have to steal it."

"You would know, wouldn't you," Xiwangmu said to him darkly, hinting at a story between old, old friends. The kind that neither party would ever let the other forget. For all their power, for all their talk, they seemed like friends. Like people. Which made it even harder to believe in gods.

The council began.

Xiwangmu had known what she was doing with the council. We hadn't stopped, rested, eaten, drunk anything, done *anything* but hunt, fight, seek, and flee for hours. Even ten minutes of sitting, sipping tea and nibbling on little rice crackers that the young women brought out, made me feel better—a little more ready to head back into the tunnels and face what was there.

But only a little. We were talking about confronting Roman, after all.

"How do we know he's even still here?" Ben said. "He's got the pearl, why do you think he's going to stick around?"

"Because Anastasia's here," I said. "He wouldn't pass up a chance to finish her off."

"Or you, really," Anastasia said.

Yeah, I supposed there was that, though I didn't like to think of being that high up on Roman's hit list.

Sun said, "I'd *really* love to know who's helping him."

"Yes," Xiwangmu said. "So would I."

Ben said, "There's still the problem of where exactly he is, and what you're going to do once you find him."

Sun chuckled. "Oh, I'll take care of that, don't worry."

As to how to find him, I had an idea. "What do you do when you want to draw someone out?" I said. "You lure him. Your fox taught us that."

The creature yipped and opened its mouth wide; Xiwangmu scratched its ears.

"So, what, we use you as bait? No way," Ben said.

Cormac said, "We've got his tokens. We ought to be able to track them backward."

"But they've been neutralized," Anastasia said. "The magic in them is gone."

"Maybe it is," he said. "They still came from him."

The idea seemed chancy, but it also gave me a little hope. If Roman was still around then so was Henry, so was the pearl. All wasn't lost, yet.

"We have to try," I said, pulling the coin from my pocket and giving it to Cormac.

The vampire closed her eyes, and for a moment was so still she seemed truly dead. Her chest was still, her skin lacked color. I could push her and she'd fall over.

Finally, she opened her eyes and said, "I would love to see that devil gone. Forever, so he can never hurt anyone else."

Xiwangmu said, "I agree that Gaius Albinus will look for a chance to destroy you. You can use that desire against him."

Anastasia nodded. "Yes. Let's catch Roman."

We made a plan.

The problem was, we didn't know anything about Roman's guide. He or she was Chinese, most likely, to know the secrets, tricks, and magic of the tunnels. Sun Wukong and Xiwangmu seemed confident that he or she was a god. They also said there were hundreds of Chinese gods and goddesses. "Even we need books to keep track of them all," Sun said, laughing. Still joking at a time like this.

Whoever it was, Roman had kept the guide hidden.

We didn't know what its powers were, or its weaknesses. Now, had Roman hidden the guide because he/she/it was weak? Or because he was a powerful ace in the hole that Roman would only use in an emergency? Like if, say, Sun Wukong showed up again?

Assuming we could draw them both out—assuming that Roman hadn't decided to flee since he had the pearl and he didn't need to bother with Anastasia—we had to hope we had enough firepower to get the pearl back and drive them both off, if not destroy them entirely.

It would be such a relief to drive that stake through Roman's heart here and now, and never worry about him again.

We didn't have much time to gather supplies and organize. Dawn was close—I was afraid that Roman had left Henry senseless on street level in full view of sunrise where he'd go up in flames at the first hint of daylight. Cormac made a whole list of items he wanted—a crossbow, wooden bolts, holy water, stakes, crosses. Sun Wukong found him a crossbow, and Cormac looked at it askance—it was old, the wood weathered, the mechanism stiff and unwieldly, as if it hadn't been used in a century. I think he was hoping for something big and modern, made of plastic and steel.

Grace had a bag full of charms, spells, and unlikely weapons—sticks of incense, bells and rattles, firecrackers. "Noises drive off demons," she explained.

"So I could just scream real loud?" I wasn't helping

very much. All I had were my convictions. And teeth and claws, if it came to that.

Xiwangmu was our ace in the hole, which meant she was staying here. It seemed somehow unfair. I was in awe of her, but also perplexed. I didn't know how to act around her. Maybe she really was a god and not some powerful sorceress with delusions of grandeur. But she wasn't *my* god. The world may have been stranger than even I ever imagined, but I wasn't going to fall on my knees before every being who came along claiming to be divine. Seemed like a person could get in a lot of trouble doing that.

"My warrior days are behind me," she said, seeing us off at the doorway to her garden.

"I thought gods were supposed to be eternal. Once a warrior, always a warrior," I said.

Her smile was amused—and way too human. She didn't match my idea of divinity—austere, distant, unknowable. Metaphor and literary invention. Obviously, I was going to have to think about this.

"We live our lives same as anyone else."

I pursed my lips. "Does that mean you can die?"

"You ask too many questions."

"Yeah, I get that a lot."

She folded her hands before her, so they were hidden in the sleeves of her robe. "I will be here, if you need refuge."

If this went badly, we'd have someplace to flee to. But

if this went that badly, I wasn't sure we'd have the opportunity.

Sun Wukong's job was to deliver the Dragon's Pearl to Xiwangmu. If our trap failed, if Roman turned it back on us, he would do everything he could to retrieve it and then flee. That was his priority. He would help us if he could, but we weren't as important as the pearl. They hadn't actually said that, but the implication was clear, and Anastasia and Grace had seemed to take the conclusion as a matter of course.

I wasn't so sure that was the best strategy. I had my own plan, unspoken to the others: to protect my pack, Ben and Cormac, and get us out of there safe. If we could bring down Roman, fine. But I wouldn't do that at the cost of my pack, and I wouldn't defend the pearl at the cost of my pack. A wise wolf gave up a difficult hunt. You didn't want to spend more calories than you'd get from the kill. Simple economics.

Six of us went into the tunnel, which closed us in darkness as soon as the door shut. Grace lit her lantern, and with her leading, we traveled down the tunnel to find our battleground. Cormac walked a step behind her, both Anastasia's and the Dodge City coins in hand. Amelia had some kind of spell planned for them. We'd see.

Only Grace's footsteps scraped on the stone floor. The rest of us were hunters, warriors. I watched, eyes and ears straining, for any hint of our enemy. Tipping my nose up, I breathed deep to take in as much of the air, as many scents, as I could. All I smelled was stone and incense.

Ben and Cormac stayed within reach; I always knew where they were.

The tunnel opened into a room, not terribly spacious—twenty by twenty, maybe. Large enough to move in, small enough to be defensible. The problem was, each of the four walls had an open doorway leading to another tunnel. This was a crossroads, and Roman could come from anywhere.

"I don't like this," I said. "Too many ways to sneak up on us."

"No, we can use this," Cormac said. He produced tools and items, the ones he'd used for the compass spell earlier. He drew the chalk circle and design on the floor, set the mangled coins—both Anastasia's and the one from Dodge City—within the circle, then set a silver dagger in the middle.

Holding my breath, I watched.

The dagger scraped on the stone floor as it began to turn. It inched clockwise, then slipped counterclockwise, more confidently, turning until it stopped—pointing solidly at one of the doorways.

"So he's there?" I said.

"Yes," Anastasia said. "He's coming."

Oh. Well then.

"Let's go, then," Cormac said, scooping up the objects and scuffing out the chalk markings. He then went to one of the corners, set down his bundle of stakes, and worked to draw the crossbow.

Ben squeezed my hand. We stood in the center of the room, side by side, facing the doorway the dagger had marked. The tunnel beyond looked like a black throat.

Grace was laying strings of firecrackers around all four walls. If she had to set those things off, it was going to get real loud in here. My ears hurt just thinking about it.

Anastasia waited in the middle of the room, placing herself in the line of fire as bait. Sun Wukong stationed himself in the opposite corner as Cormac, where he smiled over the proceedings, leaning on his staff, which had reappeared as inexplicably as it had vanished. His otherworldly sense of amusement was starting to wear thin.

Finished with the firecrackers, Grace lit four sticks of incense and set them in each corner. After that, I couldn't smell much from the tunnels, just the spicy-sweet reek of the burning sticks.

"Is that really necessary?" Ben said. She'd blinded us, scent-wise.

"Yes," she snapped back.

My shoulders were bunched, my hackles raised. I had to wonder, had we set this trap for Roman, or had he set it for us?

"Keep it together," Ben whispered, pressing his shoulder to mine. Funny, I'd been just about to tell him the same thing.

"He may not even come, this close to dawn," Anastasia

said. This had to be nerve racking for her—she wasn't any safer this close to dawn than Roman was. Her last apprentice—a gorgeous woman, very young in terms of both her age and the length of time she'd been a vampire—died when she was exposed to sunlight. Anastasia had to be thinking about her. I certainly was—I'd watched it happen, and I never wanted to see that again.

"It'll be all right," I said to her. Somehow, it would. We were underground—she'd be safe, surely.

"Heads up," Ben said, leaning toward the doorway, his head cocked, listening.

The room fell so quiet I could hear the muted fizzle of the smoldering incense sticks. From the doorway to Cormac's right, a set of shuffling footsteps sounded—heavy, clumsy. Like someone big and drunk was dragging himself along the wall. It certainly wasn't Roman. We'd never hear Roman coming, which was a big part of the problem with setting a manually operated trap for him.

Right then, Roman didn't matter: *something* was coming toward us.

I kept my breathing steady and settled myself more firmly into my body, my legs, my muscles—ready to spring in any direction, to leap in an instant, and fight.

Henry stumbled through the doorway, as though the darkness had spat him out. Swaying for a moment, he blinked in confusion. He looked unhurt physically—only his expression was odd, dazed. He wore a bronze coin on a chain around his neck—one of Roman's binding coins.

He looked at me, opened his hands, and scattered a few dozen small objects on the floor between us. They flashed in the light and tinkled like bells when they hit the stone. Then he collapsed on his side.

I started to run to him, but Ben held me back. "Kitty, look."

The objects Henry had thrown looked like jacks, a children's toy. Studying them revealed their sharpened points, like twisted knives—caltrops. And they were silver. If one of them even scratched us, we were done. Clinging to each other, we moved back. Roman had immobilized us without even touching us.

"I hate this!" I growled.

Grace went to check on Henry, touching his face, his arm. How did you tell if a vampire was okay? Feel for a pulse? Make sure he was breathing? No and no. He looked dead—pale and cold, unmoving. Of *course* he looked dead, he was a vampire.

"Grace?" I said. "How is he?"

Grace rolled him onto his back, smoothed the hair away from his face, and pulled back an eyelid to check his eye. He seemed to be sleeping—except for the not-breathing part. He had to be alive, or whatever the vampire equivalent of alive was. He was still here, he hadn't disintegrated. So that was something. His clothes hadn't been mussed or altered—even his shirt was still in place. He'd just appeared. Or rather, he'd been shoved in here as a distraction.

"I think he's okay," she said, but sounded uncertain.

"Anastasia, what's wrong with him?"

"Incoming," Cormac called before she could answer. He held the crossbow ready, aiming at the opposite doorway from where Henry had appeared. He had a clear shot through the middle of the room.

Grace pulled Henry into a corner, and I reflected on the irony of trying to protect an undead guy who was essentially immortal. If said undead guy was unconscious and possibly injured, how would we ever know? Was there a vampire doctor we could take him to?

I was constantly astonished by the absurdity of it all.

"What are we going to do about this?" Ben said, nodding at the silver knives scattered on the floor. We braced, wolflike and ready to pounce—but away from danger, away from the silver.

All I could smell was the stupid incense, and the hallway appeared darker than it should have—my wolf eyes should have been able to make out *something*. Something had caught Cormac's attention. Movement flickered in the shadows, or in my own imagination.

The thing that crept in through the doorway made no sound. At first glance, he was a man, incredibly tall, as tall as the doorway, and bulky, stout and full of muscles. He wore nothing but worn trousers and went barefoot. At second glance, however, the details became uncertain and impossible. The figure moved hunched and low, like a wrestler approaching an opponent. As if he was sizing us up. Except his eyes were sewn shut. Two rows of vertical, swollen stitches marked where eyes should have been. Black stitches also marked his nostrils, mouth, and even his ears—he didn't really have ears, just crusted stitches crisscrossing holes on the sides of his bald head.

I didn't know how he could sense anything—I didn't know how he could *breathe*. Yet he kept on, stepping carefully, flexing his hands as if preparing to strike.

If he didn't breathe, could we stop him?

Grace gasped as if she recognized the creature, which would have been great, because then she knew what it was and would know how to stop it. But she didn't say anything. Maybe he was mortal, human. Maybe we could just beat him up. But that didn't explain the ruin of his face or how he could function without four of his five senses.

The crossbow fired and a bolt whistled past me, smacking into the monster's neck. The shaft stuck out of sickly grayish skin, quivering. Behind me, Cormac cranked back the crossbow for reloading.

Not that it would help, because the monster didn't much notice. He grunted, swiped at the bolt, pulled it out, and tossed it away. A bare trickle of blood ran from the wound. So, he was a near-invincible kind of otherworldly monster. Check.

Cormac slung the crossbow over his shoulder and began rummaging in his coat pockets.

"What are you doing?" I said.

"Not going to waste ammo I'm going to need for the vampire," he said.

Anastasia stared at it with awe and doubt.

"What is it? Who is it?" I shot at her.

"Hundun," she murmured. "God of chaos."

Of course he was; we had to get one of those in the mix.

"I don't know—I thought the guy was dead," Sun said.

"Wait a minute—if he's a god how could he be dead?" I called out.

"Oh, gods die all the time."

I would have to parse that later. "That means we can kill him, right?"

He didn't answer.

Common sense—Wolf's common sense—told me that I didn't know enough about this enemy to be able to fight him. He wasn't prey, and this wasn't a hunt. We weren't cornered—we could escape through the doorway behind us, avoiding the silver caltrops. We could run. We ought to run. That was common sense. But I couldn't leave the others. And I couldn't help.

The creature had paused a moment, seeming to look at each of us in turn, noting us, marking us. Then he almost nodded, a single tip of his head, which he swung around to focus on Sun Wukong as if identifying him as the most dangerous among us.

With what seemed to be a sense of a joy, Sun took a running start and leapt forward, meeting the blinded monster head-on. Holding his staff with both hands, he jabbed upward, aiming for the creature's chin—but the thing, this strange god of chaos, sidestepped and whirled to slam his fists into Sun's back. The creature's speed belied his size and apparent lack of senses. Maybe the thing really could see, somehow, and all the stitches were there for horrifying effect.

My common sense was failing me.

Struck hard, Sun stumbled forward, but was able to quickly spin to once again face his opponent, and in the same movement he struck again, cracking his staff against the monster's head. The being shook off the blow and swung a punch at Sun, who dodged it by jumping *over* it. It all happened in a blur.

"Sun, you must break him!" Anastasia called. "Break *through*, remember the story."

"I can handle it!" he called, and she hissed as if she didn't believe him.

"Cormac, the crossbow, you must aim for his eyes, open his eyes!" Anastasia yelled.

The creature lunged again, punching with both fists.

"I'm feeling so useless," Ben said. We were still on the sidelines, watching a fight that would have been amazing if it had been in a kung fu epic. Being able to smell the sweat in the room made it too real.

Cormac hadn't heard the vampire. He—Amelia—was still rummaging for whatever protective or defensive spells they had. I was furious that Ben and I had been sidelined by toy-size hardware.

Then I saw him, in the shadows of the same doorway

Henry had come through, aiming a crossbow of his own at Anastasia.

I didn't think. I took a running leap and sprang over the stretch of spilled caltrops, hoping, reaching, *praying* I'd make it.

"Kitty!" Ben snarled after me. Then he called, *"Cormac!"*

I crashed onto clear floor and kept going, straight into Roman, tackling him. We both slammed into the wall. He growled and shoved me aside.

Wolf kicked and I let her come to the surface, allowed her instincts to fill me. Curling my fingers, I dug them into the vampire's arm, raking, kneading, gouging. I might not be able to kill him, but I could keep him from using his weapon.

He swung me against the wall, cracking my head against brick. I saw stars, and Wolf bared her teeth at him.

"Kitty, the bag!" Anastasia called to me. "The bag!"

The words sunk in through the fighting haze. Roman was wearing Sun's cloth bag over his shoulder, the strap repaired with a simple knot.

He wouldn't drop the crossbow, which meant he couldn't effectively get rid of me. I was hanging on him, tearing at him. The stitches in his silk shirt tore. I put my hand on the strap of the bag. I could rip it, take it away from him—

Air whistled past my ear. A crossbow bolt.

Roman made a noise, like the air going out of him. But

he was still here—the bolt had landed in his left shoulder, inches from his heart. Inches from my *face*. But hey, I'd heal, Cormac had probably been thinking. In the center of the room, he was loading a bolt for another shot.

I'd found a tear in the strap and was breaking through the cloth.

Roman had had enough of all of it, because he spun into the room and swung me down to the floor, toward the pool of silver caltrops. It happened too fast. I would hit them, they would bite into me in a dozen places, and the poison would burn through my blood to my heart.

Then came wind. A fierce, fast wind, like the kind that blasted the plains in Colorado, scoured the room and swept the caltrops away, into the opposite wall.

Sun Wukong stood in a fighting pose, sweeping his staff along the floor, bringing the wind with it, until the silver was all gone. Hundun batted him in the head and he went flying.

I landed on the floor, Roman landed on me, and I rested, unhurt but for bruises.

Roman scrambled to his feet and fled back to the hallway because Cormac was pointing his crossbow at him. He fired; I didn't see if he hit or not.

I was holding the bag, weighed down with what I hoped was the Dragon's Pearl.

"I've got it," I breathed around panting breaths. Wolf was clawing at my gut. *Can we run now?* Yes. Yes we could. "I've got it!"

"Then go!" Sun said, picking himself up, readying his staff. "I'll take care of this one!" He went back to fighting Hundun, blocking the creature with his staff while he dodged blows.

I'd have been worried about Sun and his ability to keep fighting, except he was wearing this big silly grin like he'd never had so much fun in his life. In fact, his blows seemed particularly nonfatal. He'd knock the monster on the side of the head to rattle him, trip up his feet with the staff, make him hop and dance as he avoided the hits, and Sun jumped out of the way in time to avoid the monster's blows. The creature didn't look any more frustrated or angry than he had when he entered the room. He simply kept going, his head low, jaw set, determined. They were two actors playing their roles.

Then the room blew up.

It began with a few pops and white sparks, then turned into an explosion that raced around the edges of the room— fire traveling along the strings of firecrackers, igniting them all within seconds. Grace must have set hundreds of them. They cracked, banged, bounced, flew, threw multicolored sparks, and trailed clouds of acrid gray smoke behind them, until the room filled with the stench of the stuff, stinging my eyes and burning my nose. Not to mention the noise, which turned my head to cotton.

The eyeless, earless creature moaned in agony, the sound muffled by his sealed mouth. How could he even tell what was going on?

Someone grabbed my arm. I almost whirled and took a swipe at the person, my fingers bent like claws. Then Ben came close, bringing himself nose to nose with me. Even that close I couldn't smell him for all the smoke and burning. My lack of senses put me on the edge of panic. The firecrackers were still going off, like sporadic pops of popcorn. Still loud, still producing smoke and fire. Something pounded against the walls hard enough to shake them and make the floor tremble. Mortar and dust shook from the ceiling.

I grabbed Ben's hand; he'd be my anchor.

"Where's Roman?" I hollered.

"Ran," Cormac said. "Let's go that way." He pointed to the opposite doorway from where Roman had been.

The smoke cleared some, drifting out of the doorways. The monster held his wounded head in his hands, groaning as he crashed into the walls, looking for a doorway, trying to escape. Again and again, he slammed against the stone, rattling the room. Sun Wukong stood back, holding his staff defensively in front of him, watching.

"Go," he said. "I'll be fine, really!"

Who was I to argue?

More debris rained on us.

Coughing through the dust and smoke, Ben and I made our way to Grace and Anastasia. Henry still lay near the wall. His clothing seemed scorched by the fireworks, but he seemed otherwise okay. I pulled the chain with Roman's coin over his head and threw it away.

"We're going," I called, and Ben and I took charge of Henry, grabbing his arms and pulling them over our shoulders. He seemed much lighter than he should have. We hauled him across the room after Cormac, who led the way, jacket and stakes in hand. Grace and Anastasia were right behind us. The vampire was looking ashen. Like the sky outside, if we had a window to look out.

As the room cleared, the blinded monster's senses seemed to come to focus, and he turned to Sun and roared. The Monkey King faced him, staff in hand.

We fled down yet another brick and stone corridor. I had Henry on one arm and the bag with the Dragon's Pearl on the other.

Chapter 16

WE KEPT MOVING.

Henry didn't twitch a muscle. I was hoping he'd wake up after Ben and I bounced him around in our efforts to keep from dropping him. But no, he was dead weight. No pun intended. Since I was a little shorter than Ben, Henry's head kept flopping toward me. He smelled like himself—not any more ill or damaged than I would have expected. Maybe charred from smoke and firecrackers.

Behind me, Anastasia stumbled. She recovered quickly, putting a hand on the wall to steady herself. But she should never have stumbled in the first place.

"Anastasia?" I said, trying to glance over my shoulder at her. "How close to dawn is it?"

"Very," she said, with astonishing calm. "The sun is rising."

"At least that means Roman's not likely to come back," Ben said. He had a point.

"Grace," I said. "We need to get back to Xiwangmu."

"There's no time," Anastasia said.

"Okay, then we have to get to a room, someplace with just one door and no windows, no access to sunlight."

"And defensible," Cormac added.

"I can't just *find* a room like that instantly," she said. "I'm not Sun Wukong."

Anastasia slumped against the wall. "I need to rest, just for a moment."

"Just a few more steps," I said blithely, staving off panic.

If she collapsed here, we could stop and try to protect her. At least there wouldn't be any sunlight—I hoped. I didn't see any vents or storm drains. But in the open corridor, anything could find us. We'd already been awake all night, and we hadn't been completely rested when we started. I wasn't looking forward to trying to guard anything for another eight-plus hours. The monster's grumbles still echoed down the corridor.

Ahead, Cormac stopped. A narrow wooden door was set into the wall. Grace pushed forward, fumbled in her bag for a moment, and drew out a ring of keys, which she began fitting, one by one, into a rusted lock. Her hands were shaking.

"Take your time, Grace," I murmured.

"I wasn't ready for any of this, I didn't agree to any of this, my *ancestors* didn't agree to any of this, they had no *right*—"

"Careful, girl," Anastasia said. "They're watching."

Grace's shoulders slouched. "I'm sure they knew what they were doing. But—times are different, it's not like I have Mongol hordes to battle, it's just *me*. I run a video store. I'm not strong enough."

"You are, and you honor them," she said.

After pausing a moment to draw breath and maybe say a prayer, Grace returned to trying the dozen keys on the chain.

Meanwhile, Anastasia slumped against the wall and slid to the floor.

I helped Ben prop up Henry and knelt at her side, hand on her shoulder. "Anastasia—"

She shook her head weakly. "I really didn't think I'd go out like this."

So, she agreed that if we stopped here we were done for. "It's not over yet."

"I should have let the pearl go. It isn't worth all of this. All of you. Kitty—thank you. For what's left of my life. Thank you."

Maybe we should have all cut and run a long time ago. Like, at sunset. Momentum had carried us all night long.

"Anastasia, we got the pearl back, it's going to be okay."

"Li Hua now, I think . . ."

The door popped inward with a high-pitched squeak of rusting hinges. A cloud of dust rattled loose from the frame. Cormac pushed past Grace and entered the room. He held up the quartz crystal from his pocket, which glowed, blinding. The candle lantern was long gone.

"Everyone in," he said, stepping back out a moment later.

"You got him?" I said to Ben. He grunted an affirmative as he pulled Henry over his shoulder in a fireman's carry. I drew Anastasia's arm over my shoulder. She tried to pull away, attempting to stand on her own while propping herself against the wall.

"You called me asking for help, let me help," I grumbled at her. That she didn't grumble back worried me.

I glanced back down the corridor; Sun Wukong still had not joined us.

"I wouldn't worry about him," Cormac said.

"Because he's a god?" I muttered, saying it like it was a joke.

"Because he's a hell of a fighter. Get in."

All six of us were in the room. Cormac closed the door behind, and Grace locked it with the key.

Our only light was the glow of the quartz crystal, which he had muted with a handkerchief. That was a good thing, I told myself. It meant no sunlight would creep in. But I could really have used some sunlight right about then. The crystal's light was fading.

"Anastasia?"

"I'm all right," she whispered, but she was slipping, her head lolling, like a child fighting sleep and failing. Ben had settled Henry against the far wall. I lowered Anastasia to the floor next to him. She was gone, her skin cold as ice, no different from a dead body. I had to tell myself she wasn't dead, not really.

The room was small, cozy with the six of us in it,

with unadorned stone walls and a cold floor that felt like slate. We might have been in a concrete basement or a castle dungeon—it was all the same. And we were here until sunset.

"Kitty, you gave me a fucking heart attack back there. Don't ever do that again," Ben breathed. I grabbed his hand and pulled myself close to him, and he wrapped his arms around me, squeezing me to him. His body felt like a blanket. Pressing my face to his shoulder, I took a deep breath of him. He smelled of sweat, grime, and exhaustion. It made me hug him harder.

"You okay?" he whispered close to my ear.

I started to shake my head, then didn't. It wasn't like he could do anything about it. "I love you," I murmured instead.

"God, I love you, too."

"You still have that chalk?" Grace asked Cormac.

He fumbled in his pocket a moment and handed it over. With it, she started writing on the walls—the door first, then moving clockwise around the room, stepping over the vampires' bodies. She made a column of Chinese characters on each wall.

As she drew the final line of the last character, the remaining bits of it disintegrated in her hand. She brushed her hands together, wiping the last of it away.

"Is that some kind of protection spell?" Cormac asked.

"No," she said. "They're prayers."

And on that cheerful note . . . The corridor outside remained silent, and the room seemed safe.

Grace turned to me. "The pearl—you got it," she said, dragging me from my warm cocoon of Ben.

I finally had a chance to look inside the bag we'd fought so hard to get. I held it out as if it contained snakes. Poisonous snakes.

"That's it, huh?" Cormac said. "Why don't we have a look."

We all sat on the floor and gathered round.

A button flap closed the sack. Carefully, I unfastened it, opened it, and reached inside. Nothing snapped at me, but I wouldn't have been surprised if it had. My hand touched a rectangle of cool stone, which I drew out and set on the cloth.

It was a rough tablet of polished jade, pale swirling white and gray in its depths. A half dozen Chinese characters were carved into the flat surface. Beautiful, it would have been at home in a museum display. It seemed so innocuous.

"That's it?" I said. I didn't mean to sound disappointed.

"You weren't expecting an actual pearl, were you?" Grace said.

I shrugged. "You know, maybe, yeah."

Cormac moved closer to study it. "It's not a thing, it's a spell, isn't it? Worked into the stone, made permanent." He was stroking his chin, as if he was getting ideas. Amelia was probably loving this.

"Does it really work?" I said.

"I'm thinking it does," Cormac said. "You notice the coin Henry was wearing?"

"I noticed he was wearing one," Ben said.

"I'm thinking he already made himself a batch of the things," Cormac said.

If only I had a few dollars in my pocket, or maybe a granola bar. My stomach growled, still hungry despite tea and cakes with the goddess. It must have been close to breakfast.

I said, "Does anyone have something to eat? Granola bar maybe?"

"Don't tell me you're hungry," Cormac said.

"No. I want to try something."

He pulled a Power Bar from an inside breast pocket of his leather jacket—a jacket with very deep and infinite pockets, apparently—and tossed it to me. I managed to catch it without fumbling. Small victories . . .

I put the jade tablet back into the bag, along with the Power Bar, and closed the flap.

"What are you doing?" Grace asked.

"I just want to see if this is worth all the effort we've spent on it," I said.

"You can't—" she said, horrified. I stopped her with a glare.

"So. How long does it take to work?" I said.

"I don't know," she said. "I have no idea how it's supposed to work."

"What *do* you know about it?"

"The magic that made it is lost. That's why everyone wants it so badly."

Too curious to wait and unable to keep my hands off

it, I lifted the flap of the bag. Which was filled with Power Bars. I scooped them out, all of them, at least a dozen, which made an impressive pile on the floor. Then I just stared at them, afraid to touch them, because they couldn't be real, could they?

"Okay, that's weird," Ben said. "Isn't there something in the law of physics that says this should be impossible?"

"Yeah," I murmured.

Cormac said, "Might be some kind of dimensional door or pocket. It got the mass for it from *somewhere*."

"Huh," I said. "Anyone have a twenty? A fifty?"

"No," Grace said, scrambling forward to yank the bag away from me and hug it close to her. "No screwing around. This is serious."

Oddly enough, I felt better, because this had all been worthwhile. We couldn't let Roman have this. We couldn't let *anyone* have this.

"Don't tell me you're not even a little bit tempted," I said, poking, just a little. Grace rolled her eyes at me.

"Don't try it with any cash until you know you're not going to end up with a stack of twenties with the same serial number," Ben said.

"You're all ruining my fun," I said. "So. Is anyone hungry?" I gestured to the stack of Power Bars.

No one was.

BEN PICKED a wall—well away from the corpselike vampires—and sat against it, huffing perhaps a little more dramatically than he needed to. I curled up next to him, pulling my legs close and snuggling against him, more wolfish than I usually was. I was tired, and I needed the comfort that the warmth and scent of my mate's body gave me. He draped his arm across me and sighed.

Across from us, Grace sat, hugging the bag with the pearl close, propped against her own bag, looking particularly young and lost. Cormac took off his jacket and handed it to her. Accepting it, she smiled thinly and used it as a blanket.

Next to Ben and me, Cormac sat with his back to the wall, within view of the door and the vampires, the loaded crossbow propped on his bent knee. He seemed to be waiting for an invasion. He wasn't going to be getting any sleep, either.

I nodded at the crossbow. "Do you really need that? Roman's not going to show up for a while."

"What do we do when those two wake up hungry?" He nodded at Anastasia and Henry.

"I trust Anastasia. She wouldn't hurt us."

"That chick is batshit crazy," he said.

I sat up. "You would be, too. And you're one to talk, what with the Victorian wizard-lady living in your brain."

Hugging herself, blinking through her glasses, Grace watched us. I settled back and promised myself I wouldn't argue anymore. Much.

"It's not like I can just get rid of her," Cormac whispered.

"So she is possessing you. Holding you prisoner."

"She saved my life," he said.

The silence stretched. I would have appreciated a ticking clock. As it was, I felt as though we'd fallen out of the universe. Grace's written prayers seemed to glow in the muted light of Cormac's magicked quartz.

"What happened to you in there?" Ben asked. Meaning prison. What had happened to change Cormac so much in two years?

Cormac gave a short chuckle. "Place had demons."

"Most people would think you meant that figuratively," I said.

"Demons, gods—the world's full of all kinds of shit," he said.

"But Amelia saved your life?" I said, to confirm it in my own mind as much as anything. The more I tried to pry the story from him the more surly he'd get. But I wanted to be sure of that much.

"Yeah."

"Then I guess I'll stop bitching about her."

I could see his wry smile, even in the semidarkness. "She and I both appreciate it."

"I've just been worried about you," I said.

"You don't have to worry about me," he said, matter-of-fact, instantly—like a defense mechanism.

"Yes, I do," I said.

"Get used to it," Ben said, amused. "You're part of the pack."

"The pack?"

I hesitated, then said, "Pack of three. That's what I've been calling us. I figure we have to look out for each other."

"Huh," he said, settling himself against the wall, adjusting his grip on the crossbow. I kept waiting for him to say something else, but this was Cormac. The strong, silent type.

After another long moment, Ben said, "When they say they're gods, they don't mean *literally* gods, do they? They're something else and they're just *calling* themselves gods."

Nobody said anything, until the silence itself seemed the answer.

Cormac said, "It's a hell of a lot to take in."

"No, you're right," I said. "They can't literally be gods, because that would mean . . ." I took a breath, swallowing a lump that was threatening my voice. "That would mean religion, everything they said in church—"

"I wouldn't go that far," Ben said. "People say all kinds of crap in the name of God, doesn't mean they're speaking for an actual higher power. It's like you're always saying, there's real and then there's *real*. There've been plenty of two-bit psychics who claim they're channeling Cleopatra when they're doing no such thing. That there may really be something out there just gives that many more people a chance to try to make a fast buck on big claims."

"Ben, you remember that freak of a preacher your mom used to listen to on the radio?" Cormac said.

"Which one?"

"The one who said NASA ought to stop going into space because it was blasphemous trying to get too close to heaven."

"Geez, yes," he said, chuckling. "That was right after that guy who was all about how 'God will call me home' if he didn't get a million dollars or something. No, I'm sure that's got nothing to do with any capital G god."

I squeezed Ben's hand and settled his arm more firmly around me. "That's the real power, you know. That televangelist got the money he asked for, did you know that? There doesn't have to be anything magic there if you can use the concept to manipulate people."

"But how do you know?" Ben said. "When Anastasia evokes a promise Grace's ancestors made hundreds of years ago to scare Grace into helping her—how do you know there's not really something there?"

"You don't," I said. "That's why it works."

Cormac sounded frustrated when he said, "But Grace's got something going on, those two are really vampires, you two are really werewolves, I've got Amelia, and that Sun guy is *not* human."

"We could talk ourselves in circles and still never figure it out."

"It's like running a race: you just keep your eye on the path in front of you," Cormac said.

"What happens when you find yourself right back where you started?" I said.

He didn't answer.

Grace had fallen asleep. She was huddled against the wall, wrapped in Cormac's jacket, her breathing deep and even. I wished I could sleep; Wolf wanted to pace. I tried to settle her—Cormac was part of our pack and keeping watch. Nothing could make Cormac *not* keep watch. We were as safe here as we'd been all night. Sighing, I thought maybe I could sleep for a little while.

Ben was playing with a strand of my hair, stroking the tangles out of it, curling it around his fingers, over and over. I looked at him. "You okay?"

"On what scale? At the moment, I'm okay. I hope I can still say that in six hours or so."

I turned my head to kiss his shoulder.

Still watching the door, Cormac said, "Look, I want you two to know, if something happens and we don't make it out of here—"

"We'll make it out of here," Ben and I said together.

"Damned optimists," he said with a huff, rearranging his seat against the wall, adjusting his grip on the crossbow, and settling into silence.

We shouldn't have interrupted him. I'd never find out what he'd been about to say.

BEN WASN'T going to let himself sleep, either. His muscles under me were tense. With all this vigilance around me, I should have been able to nap a little. But I'd drift off for a few minutes, then start awake, convinced I heard the sounds of battle right outside the door. Every time, Ben would touch me, comforting me.

I still couldn't get over how much the two vampires lying against the far wall looked like corpses.

"Should have learned Chinese," Cormac murmured, breaking the quiet. Only it wasn't him, because he wasn't looking at the door anymore; he was studying the characters Grace had written on the wall. "It was next on the list, after Arabic and Hebrew. But I never got 'round to it. I suppose I can, now."

It sounded like Cormac, but as far as I knew he'd never harbored any ambitions of learning any foreign languages. I might accept what had happened, but I would never get used to hearing Amelia's words spoken in Cormac's voice.

"Amelia, I think we need Cormac here," I said. "Just until we don't need the crossbow anymore."

He/she sighed. "I used to be reasonably handy with a crossbow. But you're probably right."

After blinking a moment and rubbing his eyes, Cormac returned to looking at the door.

"I didn't drift off there, did I?"

"No. You handed the wheel over for a few minutes," I said.

"Ah." With no other reaction than that.

We couldn't see how close the sun was to setting. Now that I was still and thinking about it, I could have really used a restroom. I could not *wait* to get back to the hotel room. A hot bath, some takeout, some alone time with Ben . . . It made a worthy goal to work toward. We'd get out of this. We would.

Henry twitched. Just a spasm in his hand.

We all jumped. Cormac swung his crossbow around.

"Don't shoot!" I hissed, holding out my arm in front of him. He didn't move, keeping Henry in his sights. I was sort of offended. Not like a bolt would kill me, but it was the principle of the matter.

Grace started awake. She sat up, looked around, a hand on her head as if she had a headache.

"You okay?" I asked.

She seemed to need a moment to focus on me. "Yeah, just some really weird dreams. You didn't see a five-inch-long dragon in here at any point, did you?"

"No. I think that was a Disney movie," I said.

"God, this is the worst night of my life," she muttered.

Oddly enough, this had not yet reached the level of being the worst night in *my* life. It might not even rate in the worst three. But we weren't quite finished yet.

"You have another candle?" Cormac said to Grace. "The light's about out." The quartz crystal was sputtering. Grace dug in her bag and found another stub of a candle, which Cormac lit with a lighter. I squinted and turned away from the sudden flare. Ben made an unhappy growl.

Henry was definitely waking up, an arm shifting to rest on his chest, head tilting—asleep now, not dead.

My sense of relief that he was moving—no longer unconscious or under Roman's spell—was tempered. When he woke up, would he still be Henry? Would he recognize us, or would he be in some monstrous, blood-fueled frenzy?

I crouched, balanced on one hand, waiting to see which way I'd have to jump.

"Henry?" I prompted, cautious.

The vampire moaned, an oddly Frankenstein's monsterish sound. I could almost hear Cormac's finger twitching on the trigger. No, just another second, just to see.

"Henry?" I prompted again.

"Yeah?" he said tiredly.

I smiled. That single coherent word was hugely reassuring. "You need to sit up or say something intelligent before the vampire hunter gets even more twitchy."

He sat, propping himself against the wall and looking around. He blinked at the shadows, appearing confused.

"What happened?" Henry said. "Where am I?"

I glanced back to see if Cormac had lowered the crossbow; he hadn't.

"What do you remember?" I asked.

His expression grew thoughtful. "That was Dux Bellorum, wasn't it?"

"Yeah. He kind of took you over."

"I don't remember. As soon as he looked at me—I don't remember anything." He rubbed both hands through his hair as if he could draw the memories forth, an oddly vulnerable, human gesture. "We're not supposed to be able to influence each other like that. Only the one who made you should have that kind of power over you."

"Roman's learned a lot of tricks." Anastasia had woken and pushed herself up, sitting with her legs bent to the side, ladylike.

Henry chuckled, but the sound was bitter. "Dux Bellorum's a scary story Boss uses on young vampires. A 'You think I'm bad' kind of thing. I didn't think I'd actually meet him. He's not supposed to be real." He was pale and seemed to be shivering. When he noticed his hands shaking, he balled them into fists and crossed his arms. If he'd been human, I'd have said he was about to faint.

I started, "Henry—"

"I'm fine. I'll be fine. I just have to get back home."

Anastasia looked at me, her expression wondering. "You did it. You kept us alive. You got the pearl."

"You sound surprised," I said.

"No," she said, smiling as she ducked her head. "I'm not. But only in hindsight. Grace, may I see it?" She held out her hand for the bag with the Dragon's Pearl.

"Kitty was messing with it," Grace said, handing it over.

The pile of Power Bars was still in the middle of the floor. "Yes, I see."

I blushed but resisted the urge to apologize.

Anastasia took the bag and kneaded it in her hands, feeling the shape of the tablet inside. She closed her eyes, and all tension left her expression. She nearly glowed with relief.

We were all awake. Exhausted, weak, cranky, but awake, sitting up, and glancing at that doorway. It might have been my imagination, but the chalk characters Grace had written seemed faded, as if they'd been partially rubbed out. As if their work was finished. A strange notion.

"What do we do now?" Ben asked.

I smiled a wolfish smile, showing teeth. "We get the hell out of Dodge."

Chapter 17

ORMAC GESTURED TO Grace. "Open the door and stand back. Keep that light low."

She shaded the light from blinding us. Cormac stepped into the corridor first, leading with his crossbow, looking both ways, then moving out. We followed, steady and watchful. Guided by Grace, Cormac led. Ben and I stayed in back. While he kept watch on the corridor behind us, I surreptitiously kept an eye on Anastasia and Henry. They seemed all right. Then again, they were surrounded by four juicy, blood-filled bodies. Maybe they'd keep it together, maybe they wouldn't.

Anastasia, I noticed, rested her hand on Henry's arm. Henry had stopped shivering.

We walked for a time, back the way we'd come, toward the room where we'd fought the eyeless creature. At least, I thought we were heading that direction. I also hoped Roman wasn't waiting for us there. I could have wished for a faster way out of the maze. Some handy escape ladder leading back to the streets of San Francisco.

Ahead, the air smelled of sulfur and burned powder. Sure enough, we emerged into a room with a doorway on each wall. The shredded paper of spent firecrackers littered the space, and black streaks of soot marred the floor. I breathed deep, but I could only smell burned gunpowder. I sneezed.

"Look," Cormac said, nodding at the floor. He kept the crossbow aimed at the other doorways.

A large body lay before us—the monster with the stitched-up face. He was on his back, unmoving—apparently dead, though you never could tell with this crowd. The stitches had been cut, and jutted out like thorns from loose skin. Gashes crossed his eyes, ears, nostrils, and mouth. His jaw hung open, slack; he didn't seem to have any teeth inside. Traces of frothy pink fluid leaked from the newly opened orifices.

Next to the body knelt Sun Wukong, his head bowed, holding his staff upright.

"Sun?" I prompted, relieved to see him, but hesitant to break the funereal silence.

"I didn't mean to kill him," he said. No longer grinning, his expression was pinched, sad. "Just knock him around a little. But the stitches broke. He's not meant to have eyes, you see. It's what killed him the first time."

As if that explained everything.

"Are you okay?" I said.

"My old master would be very upset with me," he said.

"Because you killed him?" I said.

"Yes."

"But—"

Anastasia put a hand on my arm, silencing me. "Sun Wukong is a good Buddhist. 'Victorious Fighting Buddha,' isn't it?" she said.

He chuckled, but the sound was sad. "I never could stay out of a fight."

The vampire knelt by the creature's body. "Poor Hundun. Always being used, always at others' mercy. No wonder he's so angry."

I hunted around on the floor where Henry had lain, and by kicking through the ash and torn paper found what I was looking for—the coin I'd taken off Henry. I held it out to Sun and Anastasia. "We probably ought to do something about this."

Standing, Sun held out his hand for the coin, which he dropped on the floor, then pounded his staff end-first on top of it. It landed with a bone-rattling crack of thunder. The impact produced a puff of smoke and a scattering of dust, and the coin was gone.

"Stay sharp, people," Cormac said. He was looking through one of the doorways. The darkness there was solid.

"Cormac?" I prompted.

"Someone's there," he said.

"Roman?" I said, tensing. We all backed into defensive stances.

"Dux Bellorum no longer has a guide through the tunnels." Xiwangmu spoke, emerging from the tunnel on the opposite side of the room. The nine-tailed fox stood at her side, flicking its tails and staring down its whiskered nose at us. The three-legged crow perched on her shoulder, beak slightly open as if about to speak.

The sight of her made me lightheaded, then made me smile. Grace knelt as she had before. Sun also seemed happy to see her. The others—Ben, Cormac, and Henry—blinked, nonplussed.

Anastasa's relief seemed even more heartfelt. Approaching the goddess, she bowed her head and got down on her knees. Drawing the bag with the Dragon's Pearl over her shoulder, she offered it to the goddess and spoke in Chinese.

Xiwangmu answered, and I thought I recognized Anastasia's name—her real name, Li Hua. They conversed. Anastasia became agitated; Xiwangmu was never anything but kind.

I approached Grace and whispered, "What are they saying?"

"I don't know. They're speaking early Mandarin and I only know Cantonese."

"The Queen Mother is refusing to take back the Dragon's Pearl from Li Hua," Sun Wukong announced.

Xiwangmu glared at him. "This wasn't your conversation to pass along, Sun Wukong." He just shrugged, and the goddess sighed, as if she expected nothing different from him. Turning back to Anastasia she said, so all of us could understand her this time, "I will protect the Dragon's Pearl, Li Hua, but I want you to carry it for me, and come with me as one of my handmaidens."

The vampire stared, baffled. "But I have so much work to do here. Someone has to stand against Roman. No one else knows him like I do. I'm the only one who recognizes his tokens—" She gestured back to the coin that Sun had smashed.

"And now others do, too."

She shook her head. "You've seen what he can do—"

"You have allies now who can do the work for you."

The goddess looked at me. And then everyone was looking at me. The weight of the attention made my shoulders slouch.

I shook my head. "No, I can't do it, I don't know enough, I'm not powerful enough—"

"Kitty," Xiwangmu said, and her eyes sparkled when she smiled. "You have been battling demons for a long time now, and holding your own among gods. You're powerful enough." Beside her, the fox barked, as if to say *yes*!

Well. I didn't know how to respond to that. I'd survived this long, hadn't I? That had to count for something. I just had to keep on doing it, one way or another. I could only stare at her, blinking dumbly.

Xiwangmu turned to Anastasia. "You, on the other hand, have been battling for a very long time. Come with me and rest for a little while." She smoothed back

Anastasia's hair, brushing it behind her ear. Anastasia touched that hand, holding it, and for a moment she seemed like a little girl whose mother had just kissed away some hurt.

For that moment, the scene was perfect—safe, gentle, and full of love. I wanted the credits to roll.

Sun said, "Queen Mother, it's time to go, I think."

"Yes. You can lead the others out of the tunnels?"

"I can."

The goddess said, "Li Hua, are you ready?"

The vampire stood and came to me. She even looked younger, as if eight hundred years of life and cynicism had fallen away.

Earnest now, she said, "Stay vigilant, Kitty. Stay watchful. Roman isn't finished."

"I don't exactly need an archvillain in my life."

"It's a little late for that."

I shook my head. "I don't know why you think I can do this. I don't have your contacts, your experience."

"Just do what you've been doing. Find allies."

Build the army to stand against Roman's army. I was going to need to get myself a new Rolodex.

I reached out a hand, and she shook it. "Take care of yourself," I said. "I don't know what's ahead for you, but, well, be careful."

"I don't know what's ahead, either. I think I like the feeling." She actually smiled—a genuine, open smile, full of hope. Maybe her first in a very long time.

She squeezed my hand, then turned her shining smile back to Xiwangmu. After giving each of us a look and a quick nod—a blessing, maybe—the goddess walked side by side with Anastasia back through the doorway and disappeared into the shadows of the tunnel.

I had a feeling that if I ran after them, I would find the tunnel empty. I didn't try, and so saved myself another round of bafflement.

"Who was that?" Henry asked, a tad awestruck.

He'd missed that little bit of the previous night's adventure. "Queen Mother of the West," I said, unable to explain beyond that.

"Who?" he replied.

"Where are they going?" I asked Sun.

"Into the West," he said. "The Queen Mother's realm."

"But where is that?"

He gave me a look, like I should know better than to ask such a question. *There are more things in heaven and earth, Horatio . . .*

Heaven, earth, and how many places in between?

"We should get this one home," Sun said, nodding at Henry, who was hugging himself and looking longingly after Anastasia, who'd been his anchor.

"Henry?"

"I'm fine," he murmured, not seeming altogether present.

"Yeah," I said to Sun. "Let's go."

Grace was standing with her head bowed, eyes closed.

"Grace?" I said, tentatively touching her shoulder. "We have to get going."

Sighing, she pulled herself from the wall and joined us. Now to find that escape ladder.

Sun Wukong gave the monster's body one last, sad look before leading us down a different hallway than the one we'd come from or the one the others had left through. We continued on in semidarkness. Our lantern seemed to grow dimmer, and the shadows more pervasive. I reached, and found Ben's hand reaching for mine. We walked together, shoulder to shoulder, as wolves do. Cormac kept glancing behind us.

Finally, Sun stopped and put his hand on the rusted rung of a ladder climbing up toward a grating. What do you know? An escape ladder.

I regarded it wryly. "Can I have a pony, too?"

"She doesn't want a pony," Ben said.

I frowned. "Why can't I have a pony?"

"What are you going to do with a pony?"

Eat it? Wolf helpfully contributed. Maybe Ben was right.

"The grate should pop right out," Sun said. "Here is where I leave you."

"Just like that?" Grace said.

"I'd have thought you'd have had enough of the tunnels," he said.

"Yeah, and my whole life I'm going to wonder when someone else is going to come along needing a guide. Don't send them to me, okay?"

"I can't make that promise," Sun said, grinning.

"That's it, I'm out of here," Grace said, and started climbing.

We waited until she got to the top, and as Sun had said, the grate swung up on well-oiled hinges, and Grace pulled herself to the sidewalk, where she was lit by the orange-ish glow of a streetlight.

"Henry?" I said.

He still looked far too pale, even for a vampire, but he set his jaw, nodded, and started the climb. I turned to Cormac next, but he shook his head.

"I'll cover the back."

That was his role—watching our backs. I would never be able to argue him out of it.

I looked at Sun. "If you give me a phone number I can get you your shirt back."

"Keep it. Consider it a souvenir," he said. So much for my underhanded attempt to find a way to track him.

Next he held his hand out to Cormac and said, "But I will be taking back that crossbow." Cormac just stared. "It's a priceless antique," Sun said. "I can't let you keep it. Sorry."

"Priceless?" he said.

Sun chuckled. "You're a funny guy, you know that?"

Cormac handed it over.

After that, all I could do was hold my hand out. "Sir, it's been an honor."

I wasn't sure he'd shake my hand. But he did, flashing me his grin. "Good-bye, Kitty Norville."

I climbed the ladder, about twenty feet to street level. It seemed like we should have been much farther underground, for all the darkness and weirdness we'd encountered. We should have been in another world entirely. Yet here we were. Ben came up right behind me—I could feel him, sense movement close to my feet. Finally, up came Cormac. When he was off the ladder, he swung the grate closed, then stomped on it a couple of times for good measure. He might as well have muttered "Good riddance."

We were in an alley. The night was still early, and the street a few yards away was busy—cars passing, pedestrians walking in clusters heading for dinner or an evening out. Restaurants were still open, though other stores had closed the grilles over their fronts. Traffic flowed, and a car radio playing very loudly passed by. The noise, the sights—the astonishing normality of the scene—was jarring. Part of me was still in the tunnels, waiting for mythological creatures to appear.

The five of us looked at each other, bemused. Had it really happened? Or had we been standing here all night?

Grace walked to the end of the alley and looked out, tentative, as if she wasn't sure that the world we'd emerged into was the same as the one we left. But she turned back to us, smiling. "We're right at the store. And Chuck didn't come in to open. Of course." She sighed. "I gotta get going."

"Just like that?" I said. "After all . . . that? You just go to work?"

"What else am I going to do? Somebody's got to open the store."

"Kitty likes to debrief over coffee," Ben explained.

"What's there to say?" she said.

I sputtered, because I couldn't get all the words out at once. "I need to know what happened down there. I need to know what all that magic was, and who those people were, and where they come from, and what's it all mean, and what's going to happen to Anastasia, and what's going to happen next—"

"You think I know all that? I got roped into this, just the same as you. I can't explain it."

"You have a better chance than any of us."

She stepped close to me, her jaw set, and her words were fierce. "You expect me to be able to explain all of Chinese culture and mythology and folklore to you in a couple of hours? China isn't a culture—it's hundreds of cultures. I don't speak the same version of Chinese as half the people in Chinatown right now. Every religion that came into China got incorporated. What's the point in talking about God? We have hundreds of them, and they all have their own temples, their own stories. Sun Wukong is a Buddhist hero. Xiwangmu is a Taoist goddess, but they both end up in the same story about the Monkey King stealing the Elixir of Immortality from her. And there are stories about her way older than that, so I don't know where she comes from. Now that I've met her, I see she's got a little bit of all those stories in her. Hundun is part of an old story that got wrapped up in a Confucian parable. I'm not the person who can explain all this. I inherited some tricks and spells and a set of keys and a bunch of promises my ancestors made. I didn't think I was ever going to have to use any of that, then it all shows up to bite me in the ass. What else you want me to say?"

Like I expected her to be a sage dispensing wisdom. Like even if she did explain it, it would all make perfect sense. But she was right—it didn't matter how much explaining she did, it would never make the kind of sense I wanted it to.

"Maybe I just need to talk it out to make sure it all really happened."

She put her hands on my shoulders and squeezed, shaking me a little. Completely unconcerned that I was a werewolf. Unafraid of monsters. "It really happened," she said. "Now, go home. You still have a life. We all still have a life.

"Call me at the store later if you still want to talk."

She hopped off the sidewalk and crossed the street during a break in traffic as though she couldn't get away from us fast enough.

"Now what?" Ben asked.

I frowned. "I can't decide what I want first. Dinner, a shower, a bathroom, or a really stiff drink."

Cormac dug into his pocket, but instead of drawing out some magical implement, he held his cell phone. "*Now* it works. Figures."

I tried mine. Eight o'clock. Was that all?

"May I borrow it?" Henry said, hand out to Cormac. "I can get us a ride." The vampire, so pale he almost glowed, was leaning against the wall. He looked tired—he'd had to work to draw the breath that allowed him to speak.

Cormac didn't seem inclined to hand anything over.

Henry's lips parted, showing the points of his fangs, and he stepped toward Cormac.

Cormac held the polished stake in his hand; he'd kept it hidden under his jacket all this time. When Henry moved, the hunter raised it so the point of it rested against Henry's chest, ready to plunge it home. Henry stopped. I held my breath, but Cormac didn't strike.

"Here, use mine," I said, slipping between the two of them and handing it over. Cormac lowered the stake.

Henry called Boss, and in about ten minutes, the Cadillac arrived and parked by the curb with its emergency lights blinking.

Joe stepped out of the front passenger seat and barely glanced at us before moving straight to Henry. "When you didn't come home this morning we just about wrote you off. What happened?"

Henry put his hand on the other vampire's arm and leaned. "It's a very long story."

"Hell, you're a mess." Joe propped him up.

Henry nodded in agreement.

Joe turned to me next. "Kitty. Boss was hoping you'd survive so he could talk to you."

"Yeah, I just bet," I said.

"So. You coming?" He nodded back to the Cadillac.

I looked at Ben and Cormac, my pack. Neither of them seemed thrilled.

"This wasn't what I had in mind for a debriefing session," Ben said.

"I think I have to warn him," I said, and Ben nodded. "Will there be coffee?" I asked Joe.

"I think we can manage that," he said.

Chapter 18

JOE SAT IN front with Henry and the driver. The three of us sat in back, quiet and dubious. Henry was pale, glassy-eyed; Joe kept a hand on his shoulder. Their mood had the quality of one friend driving another to the hospital for stitches after a minor mishap. Some amusement, which was mostly to mask the palpable concern.

We drove north through Chinatown to the next neighborhood. Abruptly, the signs stopped being in Chinese, the streets widened, and the dim sum restaurants turned into Italian bistros and bar and grills.

The car turned a corner and pulled into a parking alcove hidden behind a low brick building. The front showed the blue and red neon lights of what looked like a popular bar—a line of people waited to get in. We went through a back door and down the stairs to a private club.

The place was nice, kind of retro. Red color scheme, polished wood trim, brass fixtures. A jazz trio played on a tiny stage off to one side. The bar was long, lacquered, and a mirror reflected lights off hundreds of liquor bottles. The clientele seemed well-to-do, dressed up and drinking expensive-looking martinis and wine, and relaxed. Most of them were human. I wondered if any of them knew a vampire ran the place?

Boss occupied a leather booth in the corner. Tonight he wore the complete ensemble: suit and tie, tapping a fedora on the table in front of him. Master of all he surveyed. His two previous companions were with him. The bobbed-hair woman wore a clinging red silk number tonight. Jaw-dropping, really. None of them had drinks. Thank God.

"Have a seat," Boss said, while Joe guided Henry to an unmarked door in the back.

"Is he going to be okay?" I said, nodding after them.

"Joe'll fix him up. He'll be good as new in half an hour."

Cormac said, "You have voluntary donors or what?"

He must have had some kind of professional need to ask. I wondered where he was hiding that stake and if he planned on doing anything with it.

Boss quirked a grin. "Nobody dies feeding me and mine. We don't even raid the blood banks like some people."

Cormac's expression didn't change. He studied the trio of them as if he was still considering using that stake.

"Nice place you got here," I said in a blatant ploy to interrupt whatever standoff was developing.

"Thanks," Boss said. "The kitchen makes a very nice rare steak. Interested?"

My mouth started watering. I hadn't eaten anything since Xiwangmu's rice crackers the night before. A bunch of Power Bars were still piled up in a hidden room in Chinatown's nonexistent tunnels.

I glanced at Ben, who had such a look of hunger in his eyes it was almost lustful. "I think that's a yes," I said, glancing over his shoulder to Boss to accept his invitation.

Fifteen minutes later, we had three rare steaks, two beers for the guys, and a glass of pinot noir for me. All in all, not a terrible way to round out the evening. The three vampires watched, amused.

There was a price for the meal. "So, what happened?" Boss asked. "What happened to Henry?"

I explained, in summary. We went underground, found Roman, lost the Dragon's Pearl, lost Henry, went after them both, managed to get them both back, and then were trapped. We emerged after sundown, when it was safe for the vampires. I didn't mention the Chinese gods. I wasn't sure Boss would believe me.

"Where's Anastasia?" he asked when I'd finished.

I didn't feel like that was my story to tell. "Her work here is done," I said, shrugging. "She rode off into the sunset."

It was even true. Henry couldn't contradict me when he told his side of the story.

"What exactly did Roman do to Henry?" Boss asked, concerned.

I shrugged. "Put him temporarily under his control, I think. Nothing else, as far as I could tell. Cormac?"

Cormac had pocketed the original two destroyed talismans, the smashed one from Dodge City and Anastasia's defaced coin. All that was left of her in this world, I thought, with some sadness. We had to carry on. He brought them out now and gave them to me. I put them on the table, and Boss leaned forward to look.

"Roman uses these to mark and keep track of his followers, his minions. There may be more to them than that, they may have some controlling element to them, I don't know. Henry was wearing one when we found him, but we got it off. They look like Roman coins, but erasing the markings seems to nullify their power."

"So I see one of these, I need to destroy it?"

"Yeah, pretty much," I said. Now Anastasia wasn't the only one who knew about the coins. Now, everyone would know.

"Where is Roman?" Boss asked finally.

"I don't know," I had to answer. "Can I hope that he got caught in daylight and went up in a poof of ash?"

Boss shook his head. "A two-thousand-year-old vampire? Not likely."

I was afraid of that. The thought dulled the taste of the steak and wine.

We finished our meals, made small talk, and ended the

meeting. Boss made me promise to send my regards to Rick, which I assured him Rick would be happy to receive, and sent us back to our hotel in his car. We'd worry about fetching our car in the morning, after some sleep.

Flush, alert, and happy, Henry reappeared in time to accompany us on the drive.

"Are you okay?" I asked him as we piled into the Cadillac.

"Yeah, just fine," he said, shrugging, but his expression was muted. "I'm not sure I remember everything that happened. I seem to remember . . . there were a couple more people there, right at the end, weren't there? The Chinese woman, the guy with the staff. It's not real clear."

I smiled. "I know what you mean. It's like something out of a story."

"Yeah, maybe," he said.

On the block where our hotel was, the car pulled over to the curb. Henry looked at us over the backseat.

"Kitty," he said. "It's been interesting."

"In the Chinese curse sense, right?"

He ducked his head and chuckled.

"Hey, Henry. Want your shirt back?" Ben asked, tugging on the Havana shirt that was looking a little the worse for wear.

"Naw, keep it," he said.

"Damn. The one shirt I can't seem to get rid of," he said. I leaned into his shoulder and giggled. The shirt had stopped smelling like Henry and smelled like all Ben, which was fine with me.

Ben, Cormac, and I piled out of the car and waved good-bye.

Finally we could get back to our rooms, I could have a long, hot soak in the tub and work all the knots and cramps out of my injured hip and leg. I didn't even want to know what color the bruises had turned.

In exhausted silence we rode the elevator up to our floor. We'd have to talk about the last couple of days sometime— debrief from our debriefing. But we all seemed to agree that could wait until after a good scrubbing and a long nap.

The elevator doors opened, and we exited and turned toward our rooms. At the far end of the hallway, a figure stood and turned to face us. He looked like he'd been waiting.

Roman wore his long overcoat, and the understated shirt and tailored slacks he always did. His hands were in his pockets, and he regarded us, frowning. The lines in his face seemed set in stone. The hall seemed too bright for him; I'd always seen him in shadows. His face looked even more severe in the light.

Ben leaned forward, baring his teeth, clenching his hands like claws. Cormac reached into his pocket, presumably for his cross, stake, or both. I nearly jumped over Ben to get at Roman. I wanted my paws around his throat. His skin would feel so soft and buttery under my claws . . .

And then we froze, because he hadn't reacted. He wasn't afraid of us. He could stop us before we did anything. Maybe one of us could get him while the other two distracted him. And then what? Vampire smackdown in the middle of the hotel? How would we clean that up? So we all just stood there.

"May we talk?" Roman said. As if this was just a chance meeting among friends.

"I think I'd rather we didn't," I said.

Roman arced a brow.

"What do you want?" Cormac said. His jaw was set, angry—he held a stake tucked back against his arm; he wasn't even trying to hide it, and Roman didn't seem at all concerned about standing before the hunter.

"The Dragon's Pearl. Where is it?" Roman asked.

"Anastasia has it," I said, frozen, unblinking.

"And where is she?"

Slowly I shook my head. "I have no idea."

"No idea at all?"

"None," I said, smiling a little because it felt like a victory.

Roman pursed his lips, all the anger he was likely to show. "You have an opportunity to walk away," he said. "Stop these games, these quests of yours. Stop getting involved, and I'll let you alone. You'll never see me or mine again. The war will be over for you. Here and now, we'll call a truce."

Wasn't that exactly what I kept saying I wanted? Just

walk away, stay in Denver, stay safe, look after my own little world. Think about starting a family. Anastasia had left me a very large mantle—eight hundred years of fighting this man who stood before me. But I didn't have to take it on. I couldn't fight Roman. We both knew that.

But if not me, then who?

"You wouldn't be asking for a truce if you weren't worried about me, at least a little," I said, pulling out all the alpha attitude I'd learned over the last few years. Stand tall, stare hard, and show a little bit of fang.

He bowed his head, hiding a smile. Normally, looking away from my stare would have meant that he was conceding a point—recognizing my strength, bowing out of a challenge. But with him, I couldn't be sure that interpretation was the right one. Even staring at him, I wasn't meeting his gaze—I hadn't made a real challenge. I got the feeling he was laughing at me.

"I'm just trying to save myself the trouble of dealing with a nuisance," he said. "You're a nuisance, Ms. Norville. Nothing more."

You have been battling demons for a long time now, and holding your own among gods.

"Then you obviously have nothing to worry about," I said.

"You wolves are slaves. You've always been slaves. In the end, you'll see that you're no different."

"Thank you for the history lesson," I said.

"You're welcome," he said.

Behind us, a door opened. Next to me, Ben flinched, turning and snarling at the new threat. Cormac shifted to try to look at the door while keeping Roman in view.

A few doors down, an older Hispanic woman, her graying hair braided behind her, leaned out, squinting into the light. She held a blue terry-cloth bathrobe closed at her throat.

Closing his coat around him, Roman glanced over us one last time, then strode to the doorway at the end of the hall, leading to the emergency stairs. He went through, and the door thudded closed behind him.

I smiled an apology to the woman, who ducked back into her room, shaking her head, muttering.

Shivering, I squeezed shut my eyes and hugged myself. I'd been holding myself up by sheer force of will, and now I turned into a puddle of melted nerves. Ben put a hand on my arm and drew me into an embrace, which I slumped into. Cormac was staring at the door, after Roman. He still held the stake ready.

"Why doesn't he just kill us all?" Cormac muttered finally.

For the same reason we couldn't stake him in the middle of a hotel hallway, I was guessing. Roman wasn't used to stepping into the light.

We went back to our rooms long enough to pack and clear out, then checked out of the hotel. We were more than happy to pay for the night we would not be spending there, just for the chance to leave.

* * *

WE HAD to track down the car we'd left parked near Chinatown, which had been towed because that was what happened when you left a car in a pay lot for thirty-plus hours. As problems went, this one was slight and easily mended. Not like battling gods and demons. But when all you wanted to do was go home, every obstacle felt like a great, thick wall with a firmly bolted door. Which was why it seemed to take forever to bail the car out, pile in it, and head east as quickly as possible.

Once we'd left San Francisco, we all breathed easy again.

Dawn arrived while we were somewhere in Nevada. Cormac was the one who broke the thoughtful, tired silence we'd been driving through. "I'm trying to figure out—did we win or not?"

Ben was at the wheel. I'd been dozing off in the front passenger seat. I'd assumed Cormac had been doing the same in back. Apparently, he'd been thinking instead. Funny, I'd been trying to avoid thinking.

"Define *win*," Ben said.

"We're all alive, we won," I said curtly. That was all the argument that mattered—the pack was safe. Right?

"I guess so," Cormac said. "Then why does it feel like we got handed a booby prize?"

Because for all that we'd done what we came to do— help Anastasia protect the Dragon's Pearl, turn back Roman's forces—and learned a few things in the process, the future seemed incredibly hazy. Because I was still thinking that Roman was right and I should stay home. Not get involved.

Not raise an army to fight him, like Anastasia wanted me to do. *That* was the booby prize.

"What do we do about it?" Ben said. We answered with more silence, until he glanced over at me. "You're being quiet."

"So?"

"That's not like you."

I said, "I like how we're talking about this as 'we.' What are 'we' going to do about it. Thanks for that." I smiled at Ben and craned my head to smile at Cormac over the seat. I wasn't surprised that he wouldn't look at me.

"Somebody's got to look after you crazy kids," Cormac said, gazing out the window to the gold-tinged landscape, plains gilded by a brand-new sunrise, scrolling by.

Epilogue

BACK HOME, BEN made me go to the doctor. I didn't want to—my hip was fine now, I could walk, run, shapeshift, no problem. Since becoming a werewolf I hadn't ever bothered with health insurance, because, why? I never got sick, I never got hurt. At least not permanently. But Ben wanted to know. So I went, roughly explained the situation ("I fell and hurt my hip awhile back," I said, using as few details as possible), and the doctor ordered X rays.

The doctor got the films back, and Ben and I waited in the exam room while he studied the image of my pelvis. Before too long, he nodded and made noises of affirmation.

"Right there," he said, pointing to a couple of denser lines of white on the edges of the bone above my right hip joint. I never would have noticed them looking on my own. "The injury was actually to your pelvis rather than the femur, a couple of hairline fractures consistent with the impact from a bad fall. It's completely healed—I'm guessing this happened at least a year ago? And you never went to the hospital for it? I'm amazed you could even function with a break like this. It's usually quite painful."

Ben and I glanced at each other. How much to explain, how much to leave out?

"She's stubborn," Ben said finally. "Likes to tough things out."

"Well," the doctor said, tsking me. "Next time, go to the emergency room. If there'd been any bleeding or infection associated with the break, you could have been in real trouble. We also might want to test for osteoporosis. This may be a symptom of weakened bone structure . . ."

I thanked him for his concern, and we left.

"I've always wanted to know what happens when a werewolf breaks a bone," I said as we walked out to the car. "I ought to send the X rays to Dr. Shumacher for her files, see what she makes of it."

"You were damned lucky," Ben said. "What if it had been more than a hairline fracture? What if it had been a break that needed to be set, and the fast healing made it heal wrong? Then what?"

I shrugged, not really wanting to think about what would have happened if I'd ended up lying on the bottom of that shaft with a snapped femur instead of a cracked pelvis. Ben grabbed my hand, raised it to his mouth, and kissed it. The worried crease on his brow, his pursed lips, suggested he was imagining that same scene.

"Let's not dwell," I said, pulling my hand free so I could wrap that arm around his middle and hold him close.

I MET with Rick in his comfortable office under the art gallery, hoping he could help me make sense of some of what had happened. I told the story, and for him I left in the weird bits. Well, the even weirder bits.

"Anastasia's really gone?" he said when I'd finished. I nodded, grim. "It's hard to imagine. She's always been here."

"She seemed happy, which was pretty amazing to see."

Rick smiled in response. "Well, good for her. And now she's left you to fight the good fight?"

I blushed. I still wasn't entirely prepared to address that part of the story. But I had the coins, a point of access.

"The artifact Anastasia—Li Hua—was protecting, the Dragon's Pearl, has the power to replicate objects. Food, gold, whatever. She thought he was trying to make a supply of these." I placed them on the table for him to examine.

"Isn't that the coin you found in Dodge City?"

"Anastasia recognized it. Roman's followers and people under his power have them. Defacing them seems to neutralize them. We have to assume he used the pearl to make a bunch of them before we took it back."

"He's expanding his army," Rick said. I nodded. Rick turned Anastasia's abandoned coin over in his hand. He murmured, "I had no idea."

"The Dodge City vampires were his, too. Who knows

who else. Anastasia knew about the coins because she escaped him. I don't know if anyone else does. Rick, did Arturo have one of these?"

Rick shook his head. "Arturo wasn't directly Roman's. He was the protégé of a pair of vampires in Philadelphia. But them—they're probably Roman's. Arturo—we might have been able to reach him, with a little more time."

"You mean without interference. Mercedes Cook is Roman's, isn't she?" I thought of all the times I'd seen Mercedes, the Broadway star who came out as a vampire on my show, who'd seemed so ebullient and gracious— who'd manipulated Denver's former vampire Master, hoping to get him to destroy Rick because she recognized the danger he posed. All that time, she'd probably been wearing one of Roman's coins. If only I'd known. But I hadn't even known about Roman then.

Roman was no longer the deep dark secret he once was. Not by a long shot.

"Definitely," he said. His gaze went soft, lost in thought. When he spoke again, his voice was distant, too. "I killed my first Master, the one who made me. He and his clan trapped me, turned me against my will. They didn't belong to Roman—they were destructive and evil all on their own. I killed them all to destroy a plague, so I could choose the way I lived. Make peace with the monster in my own way."

I stayed very still, waiting for him to tell his own story, biting back the millions of questions I could have asked. This was a confession, a private secret, like Li Hua's story.

"I was over a hundred years old before I met another vampire. I think I believed I was the only one in the whole world. Then the Madrid Family sent a branch over to establish its rule in the New World. Can you imagine how astonished they were to find me already here? It turns out the clan that made me was a rebel group, crazy anarchists who'd thought to escape the old Families of Europe by coming to New Spain. We spent some time being very confused by each other." He shook his head, smiling at the memory. "In the meantime, I decided I didn't much like the old Families, either. I spent the next two hundred years or so wandering. Worked in taverns, saloons, smuggled on the California coast when it was still Spanish, helped carve out the Santa Fe Trail. And once again, vampires came west and were surprised to find me already here, running a saloon in Santa Fe.

"I watched new nations come into being. Watched old ones struggle and drown in the face of the onslaught. I've spent my whole life, five hundred years of it, in this part of the world and never been bored." He spoke with love and admiration in his voice, in his smile, in the glow of his eyes.

"Why are you telling me all this, Rick? Why now?" I asked softly.

"A story for a story, like we agreed. And because I think you're right—history is important. Maybe more than ever.

Most of those five hundred years I was cut off from vampire culture. I learned about our nature on my own, for the most part. Learned the rules by trial and error. Learned to blend in, eventually. But I've never really understood, and I don't know the history. I don't know all the stories about Roman—what vampires believe about him, what powers he has, what powers he's thought to have, who knows of him and who doesn't. This is the first time I've ever regretted the way I've lived my life. I wish I knew more."

Smiling, I shook my head. "No. Don't you see it? This is perfect. If you'd been part of a Family that whole time, if you knew everything about him, you'd already be tangled in a web—you'd be one of his servants, or you'd be one of the Families that are terrified of him, like Boss's Family. The way you've lived, the way you are—you're outside it all. Who better to oppose Roman than someone without any cultural baggage about him?" Anastasia had planted a huge weight on my shoulders. To carry it successfully, I couldn't do it on my own. With allies like Rick, how could I fail? "How about it?" I asked. "Would you like to be a general in my opposing army?"

"I thought you'd never ask," he said, and we shook on it.

WHEN I got back from the trip, I found a nine-by-twelve padded envelope in my stack of mail. The return address was a department at the University of Notre Dame. Curious, I tore it open and spilled the contents onto my desk: a one-page letter and a small plastic vial, sealed, that looked like it contained two hairs, dark brown, almost rust color. I held the vial up to the light and stared at the hair for a long, weightless moment.

I had to read the letter a couple of times before it started making any sense. It was from a grad student working at the library archives at the university, which turned out to have a good collection of Sherman correspondence, his family's papers and memorabilia—including a lock of his hair. This grad student listened to the episode from last month about historical figures, heard my offhand remark about Sherman, wanted to help, and asked that I please not tell anyone that she'd smuggled out the strands of his hair sample. But she could verify that this was Sherman's hair, and maybe it would be enough for DNA testing.

Maybe it would. I called Dr. Shumacher at the Center for the Study of Paranatural Biology and asked her if she could run the test for the lycanthropy marker. When she agreed, I overnighted the sample to her. Next, all I had to do was not think about it for the few weeks it took to get back results.

Then Shumacher called. "I've got the test results back on your sample."

"And?" I was hopping a little.

"It's positive for lycanthropy."

Closing my eyes, I let the information tumble around in my head. Positive. I felt like an old grandfather wolf reached across the decades to give me a cuff on the shoulder. A playful knock with a big wolfish paw, as if to say, *ye of little faith.* My ears were ringing from it. Here was a legacy.

"Kitty, who does this sample belong to?" Shumacher asked.

I hadn't told her the source of the hair. And I couldn't tell her. The secret had stayed buried this long, I had to leave it buried. It wasn't out of a sense of right and wrong—intellectually, I ought to tell. Professionally, I ought to be taking credit for making the connection. But I couldn't, and it was because of a sudden sense of loyalty to this long-dead member of a wider pack. I felt some small solidarity with this figure who must have faced incredible struggles, but who never backed away and always told it like he saw it. Sherman did not suffer fools.

General William T. Sherman's life was incredibly well documented. He even wrote a celebrated memoir. But he couldn't talk about being a werewolf. A framework didn't exist for him to talk about it. Who would he tell? Who would believe him? Of course he never mentioned it. But all my new questions—How had he become a werewolf? Did he have a pack? How did he cope with being a werewolf on the battlefield, surrounded by blood and aggression?—would never get answers.

He never talked about being a werewolf. If he'd wanted to reveal the information, he'd have found a way, left clues, given a sign that someone in the know—another werewolf, maybe—could interpret. But he hadn't.

"I'm sorry, Dr. Shumacher. I can't tell you. I promised

I'd keep that information confidential." Who had I promised? Sherman, I decided.

"Does this tell you what you needed to know?" she said.

"Yes. It does. Thank you."

ROMAN SAID werewolves were slaves. Maybe some werewolves thought so, too. But they were wrong. San Francisco's Master vampire had told me that it had been a long time since a werewolf stepped forward to lead. To speak for our kind, to take a stand. But other werewolves had stepped forward and stood up for themselves, once upon a time.

I wondered who those werewolves were, what they had done. What I would have to do. I tried not to be daunted by the task.

War is hell.

Sherman was the one who originally said that. He would lecture students at military academies, assuring them that their dreams of glorious battle were phantoms, destined to die in blood and horror. He'd done what he did—the burning of Atlanta, the March to the Sea— because he saw those tactics as a way to end the Civil War as decisively as possible, so such a war would never have to be fought again. Like a badass alpha wolf would.

He'd been one of those werewolf leaders, I was sure of it. I printed off a copy of his photo, the surly one, and pinned it to the wall next to my desk in my office. I could almost feel him looking at me, looking out for me, saying, "You can do it."

Because you have to.

THE NEXT Friday, I sat in front of my microphone at the start of *The Midnight Hour,* just staring at it. In a minute, I'd have to say something. Speak into it, so it could carry my voice to however many hundreds of thousands of listeners. I imagined them crowding into the studio, demanding.

I couldn't talk about Sherman. In the month since the Chinatown adventure, I hadn't said anything on the air about what had happened. I'd had no interest in raising questions about the existence of God and/or gods and what that meant for religion. I was not keen on igniting that firestorm, so I dodged it. I couldn't say anything about Li Hua, the merchant's daughter who became a slave of Kublai Khan and then a Western vampire. As much fun as I thought it would be, I didn't invite Rick on to tell stories of Coronado, the Santa Fe Trail, and being the only vampire in North America for a hundred years.

The weight of what I wasn't talking about pressed on me, and I didn't know what to say. I knew too much to be able to talk. What did I do? Where did I go from here?

Matt counted down on his fingers, the on-air sign lit, my intro music—CCR's "Bad Moon Rising"—played through my headset. And away we go . . .

"Good evening, this is *The Midnight Hour* and I'm

your host, Kitty Norville. I have to admit I've had a rough couple of weeks, which means the world's feeling a little bigger and scarier than it usually does. It doesn't matter what kind of monster you are, vampire or werewolf or were-badger or something even stranger, and it doesn't matter how tough you are or think you are. One day you're going to face something that throws you for a loop. That's just life, in whatever form your own life happens to take. So let's talk about problems, because we haven't done that in a while. Time to put the big cosmic questions on hold and get back to basics, because when you get right down to it, the big cosmic questions don't mean a whole lot when your own life is out of control. They can wait. Do you have a problem, is your life feeling crazy, do you want some outrageous advice, or are you just looking for a friendly ear to rant at? Give me a call, the lines are open."

The monitor lit up as it always did, but which still surprised me a little when it did. I skimmed the calls and punched one up that looked good—in this case, meaning one that I could actually help.

"Hello, Angela, you're on the air."

"Hi, Kitty? Am I really on?"

"You really are. What have you got for me?"

"Okay. Well. I'm a werewolf—I've been one for a few years now, and I'm doing okay. I'm part of a pack; it's a good group most of the time. But I've been arguing a lot with my alphas. They're a couple, and they've taken good care of me, but it seems like lately they've been coming down really hard on me for every little thing I do wrong. I argue with them about the stupidest things when I should just be rolling over and taking it. I'm talking back, mouthing off, calling them names, and it makes them more furious. I'm thirty years old and I feel like a teenager!"

I smiled. "Would you believe this sounds very familiar to me? I went through something similar."

"Really? How did you handle it?"

Um, I ran away, came back with a posse, killed the alphas, and took over the pack? "It's kind of a long story. The important thing here is that what you're going through is normal growing pains. You're getting more comfortable with being a werewolf, gaining confidence, and you're starting to assert yourself. Your alphas see this and are worried about a challenge to their authority. You may even start moving up in the pecking order, and that kind of disruption is always going to make a pack's alphas twitchy."

"Yeah, yeah, that makes a lot of sense. It explains *a lot,* actually," Angela said, sounding a little amazed. From the outside, the issue seemed obvious. From the inside, she couldn't see it. "What do I do about it?"

"I'm going to suggest you to try and deal with it as a human being instead of a wolf, and ask your alphas to do the same. I know it always sounds cheesy when I say it, but I think the three of you need to lay this out on the table in order to deal with it without anyone getting hurt. Because if they haven't already, they may start getting physical, and that's no fun at all. Maybe you can have lunch or dinner, tell them that you've noticed what's happening, and that you want to work out the problems. Offer compromises—if they stop picking on you, you won't make any challenges. Or maybe you can take on some responsibilities in exchange for higher status in the pack. What would be best of all is if you can somehow make them think this was all their idea."

"Actually, I think they may listen to the show. They may figure out it's me calling. I hope they don't get angry . . ."

"Or what may happen is they'll call you first and start the whole conversation. How about that?"

"That would be such a relief."

"Basically, Angela, you have two choices: work something out, or leave town and go it alone."

"I hope it doesn't come to that. I like it here, I like my pack, I really do. It's just they make me so angry sometimes."

"Then there's a lot of incentive to work something out."

"Yeah. Thank you, Kitty. I feel better."

"I'm glad. And good luck to you."

Sometimes I really could imagine that I was making the world a better place.

BEN PICKED me up after the show, as he sometimes did, and we drove to New Moon, as we often did, to have a couple of beers and decompress. It was a good spot to be. Billie Holiday was playing on the stereo. Shaun was bartending. Between customers he was chatting with Becky and Tom, who were two other werewolves from my pack. Seeing them there, smiling and contented, gave me a warm and happy feeling. The pack was all right. Everything was fine.

Cormac was waiting for us at our usual table in the back. He already had a beer and a basket of buffalo wings, and was leaning back in his chair, surveying the place like he owned it. My alpha Wolf should have bristled at that, seeing his appraising attitude as a challenge. But I didn't, because he was Cormac, and while he may not have been a wolf, he was part of the pack.

Ben and I sat opposite him, and Shaun brought us our usual beers. There we were, perfectly normal, with all the shadows safely outside.

"What's next?" Cormac asked.

"Quiet," Ben said. "That's what's next. Peace and quiet. No vampires, no magic, no nothing."

He glanced at me with a certain amount of trepidation, like he expected me to argue. I had no plans to argue. Well, not exactly. I had plans. I pulled a sheet of paper from my pocket, unfolded it, and held it up.

"What's that?" Ben asked, suspicious. Cormac leaned forward to study it.

It was a flyer I'd printed off from a Web site, announcing the First International Conference on Paranatural Studies to be held in London. We were going mainstream—at least, scientifically mainstream. I grinned at them over the top of the page.

Ben groaned. "No. You're joking."

"They've asked me to be a keynote speaker," I said. "Cool, huh?"

"I suppose you're going to spin this as being good for your career, a great opportunity for publicity and a chance to increase your credibility," Ben said.

I blinked. He had the patter down better than I did. "Yeah. That's exactly what I was going to say. Plus, London! I can go visit London!"

"Are you okay with spending eight hours on an airplane?"

To tell the truth, I hadn't thought that far ahead. I thought I'd be okay on an airplane for eight hours. But Wolf whined—locked in a tiny metal box with all those juicy people for that long . . .

This was going to take some planning.

I said, "This will be a good way to meet people. Find out what's going on in the rest of the world, you know?"

"Another quest," Ben said. "No—you're past quest and into crusade, aren't you?"

I glared. "Is there a problem with that?"

He grabbed my hand, kissing it, melting the argument away. "No problem at all. It's what makes you you."

Cormac was scratching his chin.

"What?" I asked.

"Would being a convicted felon keep me from getting a passport?"

"You want to come along?" I said.

He shrugged and looked at his beer. "Amelia wants to go home."

Ben pursed his lips. "I'll look into it, see what we can do."

"What about you?" I asked him. "Are you okay with this?"

"If you're going, I'm going. You don't have to ask," Ben said.

My heart actually may have skipped a beat at that. He said it so decisively, it really meant *I love you*.

"Besides," Cormac said. "It'll take both of us to keep you out of trouble."

"It's a scientific conference, what could go wrong?" I said. They rolled their eyes at me as if to say, *really*?

Well, we'd just have to find out which of us was right, wouldn't we?

Acknowledgments

I had help from all the usual suspects, and more. Thanks to Daniel Abraham for reading an early draft. To Mandy Douglas for reading an early draft and offering very good advice. To Tor/Forge publicist Cassandra Ammerman for arranging my first book tour and working in the extra time for research in San Francisco, which helped immensely. Thanks as usual to Stacy Hague-Hill, David Hartwell, Ashley and Carolyn Grayson, and friends and family for the sanity checks.